THE LOOKING GLASS WARS™
SEEING REDD

BY

FRANK BEDDOR

SCHOLASTIC INC.

New York Toronto London Auckland Sydney
Mexico City New Delhi Hong Kong Buenos Aires

ISBN-13: 978-0-545-07177-2
ISBN-10: 0-545-07177-1

12 11 10 9 8 7 6 5 4 3 2 1   8 9 10 11 12 13/0

Printed in the U.S.A.   23

First Scholastic printing, March 2008

Logo Design: Christina Craemer
Part 2 & 3 art: Stephen Martiniere
Front, Back cover and part 1 art: Vance Kovacs
Map Design: Cold Open & Nate Barlow
Book Design: Teresa Kietlinski Dikun
Text set in Goudy

For Christina and Luc

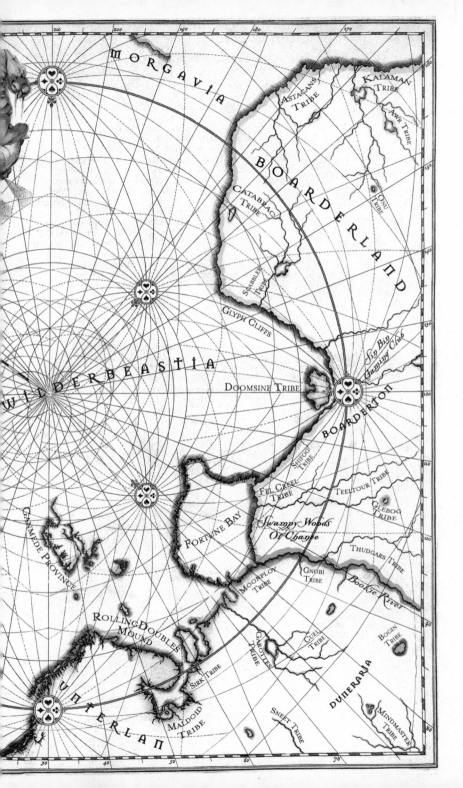

PROLOGUE

She should have been disoriented, her image sneering back at her from the countless dust-filmed looking glasses that surrounded her, but she was too consumed with the quest that had brought her to this maze whose time had passed, its purpose unfulfilled.

"I've come!" she yelled, the words ricocheting off the cloudy looking glasses without cease or loss of volume. The noise pained Redd's ears, but what did she care? She would endure anything. She had made it this far. She would not leave until she had found what she'd come for.

In every direction, mirrored corridors branched off into the dusky reaches of the maze. She tried to locate the scepter in her imagination's eye, but her powers were apparently useless. She would have to find it the old-fashioned way, by systematically walking every corridor, seeking the scepter as might a blind, rudderless fool.

"Not much of a maze, are you?" she muttered, because she discovered that she could pass from one corridor to another merely by walking through the looking glass walls. Hers was a phantom maze, the ghostly residue of what it had once been. A sudden, hissing sound at her back.

She spun, ready for anything. The dust of a looking glass had lifted and formed into the figure of a female: the teenage girl she used to be, before she had allowed corruption to gnarl and ravage her features, before her transformative passage through the Heart Crystal: bratty, intractable and vindictive Rose Heart.

"How dare you show your face, when I'm smarter and more imaginative than you," the dust-figure whispered, then faded into nothing.

Redd continued on, and half-formed images flitted past the periphery of her vision, apparitions pointing and ogling in disbelief that the maze's intended had arrived so long after she'd been expected. Whenever she turned to look directly at them, they shifted and remained at the edge of her sight.

Only one image let itself be seen, and it gave Redd pause: that of her slinking into her mother's bedroom, so soon after being removed from succession to the throne, to place the fatal mushroom on Queen Theodora's tongue. She felt no remorse—her mother had deserved an untimely end—but that night had been the last time she'd employed a lethal mushroom in her nasty doings.

The scepter lay on the floor up ahead as if it were nothing, a useless stick someone had dropped in her hurry to leave. No doubt it had once been vibrant with color, a gleaming, crystalline staff with elaborate, gem-encrusted filigree awaiting the first touch of its intended's hands. But now, the heart at its top was shriveled and gray. What gems still remained had turned black. The filigree was rusted and, in parts, had completely flaked off. But had it been otherwise, had she found a scepter as glorious and pulsating as Alyss Heart's, she would have thought it a trick, a setup. The scepter at her feet, so elaborate in its decay—this was beauty. Yet here it lay, abandoned, discarded, just as she had been by her family.

"And they had the impudence to blame me!" she yelled.

Again, her words reverberated until they became noise.

"It's your own fault, Rose," Theodora had said. "I cannot allow you to become queen. You refuse to listen to anyone's counsel but your own, and you insist on being so undisciplined, disregarding the most basic principles of White Imagination."

"Perhaps I have discipline in other things!" she had spat.

"That's what I'm afraid of. You've already scared a number of important Wonderlanders."

Redd had made it her life's work to scare so-called important Wonderlanders. She had scared a great many of them during her all-too-brief time on the throne. But whatever fears she had instilled, whatever terrors inflicted, were nothing compared to what she would accomplish now that she had navigated her own Looking Glass Maze.

Her fingers closed around the scepter, giving her access

to the full potential of her imaginative powers. She was the strongest Heart alive. She would recapture the Heart Crystal, and no one, not even prissy Alyss Heart, would be able to wrench it away from her. Ever.

PART ONE

CHAPTER 1

WONDERLAND'S FINEST architects had designed it and overseen its fabrication. The most skilled glaziers, carpenters, masons, and gemologists had worked tirelessly to ensure that even its smallest details were built according to plan: Heart Palace, imagined anew on the site of the former palace, which had stood for generations until being cruelly decimated by Redd.

"The artisans labored with such great effort in tribute to you, Alyss," said Bibwit Harte as he escorted the queen and her personal bodyguard, Homburg Molly, through the palace for the first time.

The tips of Bibwit's oversized ears crimped forward. The blue-green veins beneath the translucent skin of his bald head seemed to swell. He was amused by something.

"I need no tribute," Alyss said.

Bibwit's eyebrows leaped up and his eyes widened in pleasure.

So that was it. He had just wanted to hear her say it aloud. Why he never tired of hearing her expressions of selflessness, Alyss couldn't understand. It was as if he thought they proved the kind of queen she was and always would be. *But if he only knew, I am far from selfless.*

"You might not need a tribute, my dear Alyss," Bibwit went on, "but the citizenry does, and those responsible for this magnificent palace—"

"Hmmph!" Molly said, shrugging open her Millinery backpack, its various blades and corkscrews snapping to the ready.

"—have vowed that it should serve as a monument to White Imagination, a declaration of your ascendancy over the—how shall we say?—more sooty machinations of Black Imagination. The palace is an emblem of hope that you will—"

"Yenh!" Molly grunted, retracting the weapons of her backpack with a shrug.

"—return our nation to the peace and contentment of your great-grandmother's reign, when it is supposed the queendom had never heard of dissension. Here we have the ancestral chamber."

Bibwit guided Alyss and her bodyguard into a room whose vaulted, bejeweled ceiling twinkled purple and gold.

In marbled crystal frames around the room hung screens of Alyss' parents, grandparents, and great-grandparents—the generations of Hearts who had ruled in the service of White Imagination.

"Hyah!"

"Molly, please," Alyss said.

"Sorry." Molly shrugged a last time, the knives of her backpack folding shut.

The Millinery, Wonderland's elite security force, had been officially re-established, and the girl had taken to dressing in the uniform of its former leader, Hatter Madigan: the long coat that flared out behind her like a cape when she ran; the deadly belt that, with a punch of its buckle, sprouted a series of sabers along its surface; the bracelets that could snap open and become propeller blades on the outward side of her wrists; the backpack.

"I haven't seen this much optimism since I was a young albino graduating from the Tutor Corps," Bibwit sighed as they left the ancestral chamber and continued down the passage. "But it's best to tell you now, Alyss, that Queen Issa's reign was not as peaceful as Wonderlanders believe. There will always be those who unfavorably compare the present with a past they suppose happier than it was, not having lived through it, as I have."

"I can't imagine you as young, Bibwit," Alyss said.

He was being quite the chatterbox today. She would have thought her tutor had attended too many royal festivities to get excited by them any longer. But didn't she know better? It wasn't the gala itself that had raised his spirits so much as it was her first official function as Wonderland's queen.

"This is one of the libraries," Bibwit said, showing them into a paneled room crowded with books, scrolls, reading crystals.

Only three lunar cycles had passed since Redd's defeat and yet the pressures of Alyss' position were wearing on her. She didn't want to let anyone down, least of all Bibwit. He was the closest thing she had to a father since her aunt Redd had murdered her parents.

"Don't you agree, Alyss?" he asked, interrupting her thoughts.

"About what?"

"I was just telling young Molly—"

"I'm not young," Molly blurted.

The tutor paused. In the short time since Redd's defeat, the girl had grown at least a gwormmy-length and the cute slope of her nose had straightened somewhat, as if in antici-pation of the handsome woman she would soon be. But her unlined face, her pillowy cheeks, and her strong, clear eyes turned defiantly upon him—she was nothing if not a child.

"No," Bibwit said. "After what we've been through, I don't suppose any of us could be called young, although as Alyss has kindly pointed out, it's unlikely anyone would have dared to think me so. My apologies, Molly. But I was saying that although the principles of White Imagination do not concern themselves with the luxuries so plentiful in the new palace, its opulence might be said to represent a time when beauty could exist in Wonderland unmolested by greed or other ill-intent."

Hard to believe this is where I'm to live.

The crystal-shimmering spires and agate-mosaic artworks, floors inlaid with jasper and pearl, walls of quartz and stone and glittering mortar: It was all so unfamiliar and much grander than the former palace.

"Alyss might not care overly much for such things," Bibwit was saying as they again continued down the passage, "but on occasion a queen must follow instead of lead. The wisdom comes in knowing when to do so and, in this instance, Alyss has wisely chosen to follow the will of the people." Bibwit's ears twitched. "We have company."

Alyss soon heard footsteps approaching. General Doppelgänger appeared at the end of the hall, his military boots clicking on the polished floor. He bowed repeatedly and began talking before he reached her.

"My queen, three decks of card soldiers have been dispatched to guard the perimeter of the grounds. The white knight and his chessmen will be stationed inside the palace and its gardens. They have promised to be as inconspicuous as they can, so as not to worry your guests, but—"

Alyss laughed. "They *are* chessmen, General; they will always be a trifle conspicuous."

"That's so, that's so." The general ran a fretful hand

through his hair and split into the twin figures of Doppel and Gänger.

"We urge you to reconsider," said General Doppel.

"It's a risk to have invited so many to the palace all at once," agreed General Gänger.

"We don't wish to cause needless alarm—"

"—but we'll be vulnerable to disruptions from any enemies we still have among the populace."

"To say nothing of the risk to you personally."

"Queen Alyss can take care of herself," said Homburg Molly. "And besides, she has me."

In one swift motion, Molly took the homburg from her head, snapped it into a flat, knife-edged disk, and sent it zinging down the hall and back. She caught it, with a flick of the wrist returned it to its innocent homburg shape, and plunked it on top of her head.

Always wanting to prove her worth even though she's proved it tenfold in battles.

Homburg Molly was still too inexperienced to have mastered the Millinery ethic of keeping her emotions hidden, an ethic Hatter Madigan had epitomized to perfection.

"Your diligence and concern are appreciated, as always," Alyss told the generals, "but the memorial is for all of Wonderland. And to bring out the best in Wonderlanders, I must assume the best *of* them."

"You're starting to sound like Bibwit!" Doppel and Gänger moaned at once, and turned to leave.

"I'll walk with you, Generals," the tutor said. "I must powder my head and poof out my scholarly robes for the party and so will take my leave of the queen."

Once Bibwit and the generals had gone, Molly said, "I don't get it. He's an *albino*. Why does he put white powder on his head?"

Alyss smiled. "When we're as clever and educated as Bibwit, I'm sure we'll know the answer, Molly. But I think it's time we joined the guests."

~

The royal garden, a courtyard at the center of palace grounds, was crowded with happy Wonderlanders, their ticklish eruptions of laughter competing with the singing of the sunflowers planted alongside the war memorial.

Alyss had made only one request of the palace architects: that at the grave site of Sir Justice Anders, former head of the palace guard and Dodge Anders' father, they create a memorial honoring all who had lost their lives during Redd's thirteen-year reign—royals, civilians, card soldiers, chessmen, palace guardsmen, and members of the Millinery. The bodies of Queen Genevieve and King Nolan hadn't been recovered, of course, but Bibwit had surprised Alyss with two of their most intimate keepsakes: a toy spirit-dane invented by her father, and one of her mother's charm bracelets, both of which he'd kept tucked deep within his robes throughout Redd's tyranny. These had been enough for the Hereafter

Seeds to do their work. Just as a bouquet forming the likeness of Sir Justice watched over his grave, bouquets of camellias, gardenias and lilies resembling Wonderland's former king and queen now kept vigil over theirs. On either side of the graves rose a simple stone etched with the names of those known to have lost their lives in battles against Redd. Behind all: an obelisk of emerald green, in recognition of those who had gone missing during Redd's occupation and were now, to their families' grief, presumed dead.

"I've never seen anything like *this*," Molly said, looking around at the variety of people and creatures in the court-yard. "You've got street vendors mingling with suit families as if no one's blood is purer than another's."

Alyss knew this to be a constant theme with Homburg Molly. Half civilian, half Milliner, the girl was particularly sensitive to matters of race and class.

"I don't know, Molly. Judging by the look on Lady Diamond's face, I'd say you overestimated things a bit." Alyss called out to the ranking lady as the walrus-butler passed by with a tray of wondercrumpets: "Have a wondercrumpet, Lady Diamond?"

"Ah. A wondercrumpet. Yes," said the lady, taking one but holding it far from her mouth with no apparent intention of bringing it closer. "You *do* know how to throw a party, Queen Alyss."

"You think so? I wouldn't have supposed you enjoyed brushing against so many Wonderlanders of lesser rank."

"I don't know what you mean," the Lady of Diamonds huffed.

Alyss didn't trust the suit families, but there had been no proof of their conspiring with Redd, either before or after her overthrow of Queen Genevieve. Nor had there been any proof of their engaging in outlawed activities that could have secured a conviction in Wondertropolis' courts. As much as Alyss would have liked the suit families gone, there was politics to consider. Redd had kept them around after her coup for similar reasons: their relationships with business leaders, government officials, and the arbiters who decided the guilt or innocence of the ill-fated brought before them in the name of jurisprudence. Only Jack of Diamonds had been prosecuted, Bibwit's and the walrus-butler's evidence against him too overwhelming to ignore; found guilty of treason and racketeering, he'd been punished accordingly.

But why poison my brain with thoughts of Jack of Diamonds?

Why, indeed, when Dodge Anders had caught her eye from across the courtyard? It was the first time she was seeing him in his uniform as head of the palace guard. She'd almost forgotten how handsome he could be when dressed in formal attire.

As if it were possible to forget.

She had always thought his was a rough-hewn handsomeness, the four parallel scars on his cheek adding to his looks rather than diminishing them. She'd been thrilled when he requested his father's former post, and interpreted it as meaning that he would abide by a guardsman's code instead of avenging Sir Justice's death. She only hoped that he didn't become too much like the Dodge of her youth, who had shown an almost religious devotion to propriety, a guardsman's place in relation to the queen, because now that there was no threat of her having to marry Jack of Diamonds . . .

She glanced away, afraid she would reveal too much of herself in her eyes.

"Molly, there are enough guards and chessmen here to protect a flock of queens. I want you to go off and enjoy yourself."

"But I *am* enjoying myself."

It was Molly's job to shadow her everywhere, Alyss knew. But it could be so bothersome. How was she supposed to have any time alone with Dodge, who was that moment making his way toward her though she pretended not to notice?

"Molly, I order you to enjoy yourself *somewhere else.*"

"Fine," the girl pouted, and stomped off.

Alyss kept her eyes to the ground. She tried to think of something clever to say to Dodge, but her mind filled with the sort of things she might murmur to any old stranger—how are you, lovely weather we're enjoying, at least we have our health. She felt him standing next to her. Her quickened pulse loud in her ears, she looked up and—

It was only Bibwit, with official pardons to sign.

"Must I, Bibwit, even during the party?"

She watched Dodge veer off to confer with one of his guardsmen; he would never interrupt her when engaged in the nation's business.

"I'm sorry you find it inconvenient, Alyss. But these are Wonderlanders who have been punished by Redd's regime for committing no crimes."

He was chastising her, in his gentle way. Why should those who have innocently suffered be made to suffer another moment? Wonderlanders imprisoned during Redd's reign were being interviewed, their cases reviewed to determine if they were legitimate criminals or merely people who had fallen afoul of Redd's temper. For the latter, proper legal channels had to be employed, pardons issued and signed.

"It seems that being a queen involves nothing but paperwork," Alyss sighed, scratching her name first on one pardon, then another.

"Mastering the combat aspects of a warrior queen is the easy part," said Bibwit. "The administrative responsibilities of ruling from day to day, of contending with the bureaucratic procedures that keep Wonderland society functioning—these are more subtle to master and therefore more difficult."

The walrus-butler waddled up as Alyss was signing the last of the pardons. "Queen Alyss, King Arch of Boarderland is here."

Bibwit's ears stood erect in surprise.

"He must have come to wish me well," Alyss said, not quite believing it herself. "Please show him into the garden, walrus."

"Yes, but . . . yes, I tried, Queen Alyss. But he says he prefers to visit with you in a more masculine environment."

"And where would *that* be?"

"In the briefing room."

She saw the king in her imagination's eye, in the company of his intel ministers and bodyguards, a disdainful expression on his face. She flicked a look toward Dodge. He shrugged in good-natured understanding: He would have to wait.

"I'll attend you, Alyss," Bibwit said.

Wonderland's queen shook her head. "No. It's more important that you end the suffering of the falsely imprisoned as soon as possible. Deliver the pardons to the arbiters, as you'd intended. And please arrange for me to inspect the conditions at the mines. The reports I've heard are disturbing."

The tutor appeared uncertain.

"Don't worry, Bibwit. Arch can do nothing to me."

On her way out of the gardens, Alyss passed the Lord and Lady of Diamonds, who were talking with Homburg Molly. The lady suddenly raised her voice as if to make sure Alyss heard what she was saying:

"Jack was forever bending rules to suit his own interest, though we *never* thought he'd go so far as to conspire with Redd. *Of course* we had to disown him, our only son and heir, after his treasonous behavior."

But as inexperienced a sovereign as she was, even Alyss knew: In the garden of state, treason was a weed; just when you thought you'd rooted it out for good, it returned more virulent than before.

CHAPTER 2

THE GUARDS were nearly as unforgiving as the mountain the prisoners labored against every day, their hands cut and swollen from smashing at rock with dull handspikes and blunt pickaxes. They had forgotten what it was like for their muscles not to ache; the day-long monotony of hammering reverberated in their bones even after they slogged back to their dormitories to lie on their bunks and wait for sleep, hoping to dream of open fields and bright light, anything but their lives at the Crystal Mines with its windowless housing bunkers and mining tunnels lit sparingly by fire crystals.

They came from all levels of Wonderland society: once-pampered sons of business leaders and ranking families whom Redd had caught exhibiting goodwill to the less fortunate; law-abiding shopkeepers and restaurateurs who had refused to make monthly donations to Her Imperial Viciousness' accounts; homeless youths Redd had deemed useless, as they had shown no tendency to violence. But among them: one actually deserving of punishment whose backside was, despite his having lost weight since his arrival, still more rotund than the rest of him.

Jack of Diamonds' time at the mines hadn't been as woeful as it might have been, since he was adept at pocketing small fragments of crystal, which he used to bribe guards for an extra bowl of infla-rice or for less strenuous work assignments. Yet physical labor was physical labor and, as Jack often told anyone who would listen, the stuff was beneath him. As for the infla-rice, it was supposed to expand in his stomach and make him feel full, but even two bowls' worth left him hungry, and its blandness caused him to mourn all the more the loss of the savories and feasts he had once enjoyed as a free, high-ranking denizen.

Sitting on the edge of his bunk, grubby and wigless, he bragged to his dorm mates, as he did every night, of his former life.

"I had countless footmen and servants. I wore clothes made of only the most exclusive materials, such as gwynook skin and caterpillar whiskers. And as to wigs, oh ho, I could praise them for an entire lunar cycle and still not relate a tenth of their beauty. I had the finest wigs the queendom has ever known!"

This occasioned much confused murmuring among his

listeners. Jack of Diamonds had plenty of hair. Why would he wear wigs?

"If I had looked down from my privileged seat atop Wonderland society," Jack went on, "I wouldn't have seen any of you, that's how little you would have been. You *criminals* cannot possibly understand how difficult this is for me, having to share a room with you." Then, as he did every night, he suddenly cried, "There's been a mistake! I'm Jack of Diamonds and I don't belong here!"

Tonight, however, hardly had he uttered these words when—

eeeeeEEEEEEEBOOOOOSSSHHHK!

He was knocked to the floor. Chunks of stone flew every which way. The air became heavy with dust.

A glowing orb generator had blasted a craggy hole in the wall.

Jack scurried underneath his bunk, squeezing as far back as he could to keep from sight. Peeking out, he saw guards exchanging fire with a shadowy enemy, the razor-cards of their AD52s (automatic dealers capable of shooting a deck's worth with a single pull of the trigger) zipping past, searing through the night sky.

A figure stepped through the blasted hole into the dorm. "Jack of Diamonds?"

Jack hustled out from under his bunk and approached the figure with open arms, as if welcoming a guest to his drawing room. "What took you so long, my good man?"

"We have to be quick," the figure said.

Jack bowed to his dorm mates, who lay in various degrees of dishevelment and shock from the blast. "Gentlemen, I bid you farewell. My parents' emissary has arrived to take me home!"

And with that, Jack of Diamonds escaped the Crystal Mines.

CHAPTER 3

CHE BRIEFING room hadn't yet been used in its official capacity: thrice-daily meetings during which Bibwit, Dodge, General Doppelgänger, and Alyss' other advisers would apprise the queen of pressing Wonderland business, be it financial, political, or militaristic.

"What's this I hear about you refusing to come to my party?" Alyss teased, forcing a professional smile onto her face as she glided into the room—hexagonal in shape, with holographic viewing screens lining the walls and, at its center, a thick, heavy conference table carved from a single slab of soapstone.

King Arch was not one for teasing. He turned from his intel ministers, with whom he'd been conferring in a lowered voice. "Queen Alyss," he said, "I make no secret of my prejudices. I don't believe the turmoil Wonderland has recently endured would have happened were it a kingdom instead of a queendom. But I have come to pay what respects I can to you, for between you and your aunt Redd, I much prefer having you as a neighbor."

"Thank you, I think," said Alyss. "Shall we sit?"

The holo-screens were displaying real-time scenes from Wondertropolis' major thoroughfares and intersections. Arch lowered himself into a chair before the screen showing the newly-named Genevieve Square. The intel ministers removed themselves to a corner of the room and remained standing while two fellows with faces as inscrutable as masks took up positions on either side of their king.

"I feel safe when I travel with them," Arch said, noticing Alyss' interest in his bodyguards. "Their names are Ripkins and Blister, and their combat skills, I think, would rival those of even the famed Hatter Madigan, though I've been informed that *he* has taken a sabbatical."

Alyss nodded. "He needed some time to attend to personal matters. But he's available to us if we need him."

The truth was, neither she nor anyone else knew where Hatter had gone or when he'd return. On several occasions, she had stood next to the Heart Crystal to maximize her remote viewing ability, searching for him with her imagination's eye. The Everlasting Forest, the Chessboard Desert, the Valley of Mushrooms, Outerwilderbeastia, even the Volcanic Plains: No matter where she looked, she failed to locate him.

He seemed to have vanished from Wonderland altogether.

From out in the passage came a skiffling sound; Homburg Molly ran into the room and took up position at Alyss' right flank.

"King Arch," she said, "I'd like you to meet *my* bodyguard, Homburg Molly."

Homburg Molly bowed, but at the sight of her—what with her coat a trifle too large and the heavy backpack that she wore awkwardly—the king laughed.

"What's so funny?" Molly scowled.

Alyss placed a calming hand on the girl's arm as King Arch struggled to control his laughter. The walrus-butler toddled into the room with a pitcher of flugelberry wine, two goblets, and a platter of tarty tarts. After the wine had been poured and the walrus dismissed, Arch cleared his throat and reluctantly begged the queen's pardon—her bodyguard's too, of course. He did his best to look serious, but his amused glance kept returning to Molly.

"So, where's the Heart Crystal?" he asked. "I was hoping to have a hologram made of me basking in its glow."

"I wouldn't have thought the crystal was of interest to you," Alyss answered. "Possession of it means little to those not gifted in imagination."

Arch waved a hand, dismissive. "Just like a woman not to listen. I didn't say I wanted to possess it, Your Highness. Personally, I find whatever it is you do with your oh-so-powerful imagination to be overrated. Consider me a tourist who has come to see Wondertropolis' main attractions. I'm sure you'll grant that the Heart Crystal, as the source of creative inspiration for the cosmos, is among those?"

"We no longer keep it in the open."

"But I thought Redd had been disposed of. What is the harm in keeping it somewhere for the public to enjoy?"

Disposed of. We can only hope.

Alyss and her advisers had discussed sending a small force into the Heart Crystal in pursuit of Redd and The Cat, which Dodge had volunteered to command. But the risks involved and the unlikelihood of the mission meeting with success had argued against it. No living thing had ever passed through the crystal and there was no guarantee that a physical body survived. Alyss had come up with an alternate plan.

"Bibwit," she had said, "you've claimed that because Redd passed through the Heart Crystal, my aunt in the form we knew her might no longer exist?"

"I *have* claimed that," Bibwit had admitted, "and a great many other things too."

"And whatever passes into the crystal goes out into the universe to inspire imaginations in other worlds—most specifically, Earth, the world that has the most direct link to ours?"

"Sounds familiar."

So she had suggested that Hatters Rohin and Tock, two of the most gifted among the new Millinery class, travel to Earth through the Pool of Tears, to keep watch for signs of Redd, The Cat, or the influence of either.

"Hunh," Arch said when he heard Redd's death had not been assured. He reached for a tarty tart and tossed it to one of his bodyguards.

The guard made a show of flexing his *fingertips*: Glinting sawteeth pushed out of the skin in the exact whorling patterns of his fingerprints. Without a wince of emotion, with hands moving as fast as the spinning blades of Hatter Madigan's top hat, he reduced the tarty tart to a pile of crumbs, then nodded to Arch: The food was safe to eat. The sawteeth sunk back into the skin of his fingers, and Arch helped himself to a tarty tart and finished it off in one and a half manly bites.

"I see that Mr. Ripkins deserves his name," Alyss said, for as she used her imagination to fuse the tarty tart crumbs back together, she noted that they weren't crumbs at all, but shreds. He had *ripped* the treat apart.

The king pretended not to notice the tart settling on the platter, again in one piece and ready to be properly consumed. "My guards are prodigies when it comes to more traditional modes of combat," he said, looking at Homburg Molly. "Blades, orbs, crystal shooters, what have you. But why should I limit them to traditional modes when they can do so much more?"

He snapped his fingers. One of his intel ministers stepped forward and pushed up his sleeve. Blister lowered an index finger toward the minister's forearm.

"Ah, ah," Arch said, and waggled a pinkie. "We don't want him permanently scarred, do we?"

Blister pressed the tip of his pinkie against the minister's exposed skin. The minister clenched and began to sweat. His entire forearm blistered.

"It's best to have it drained as soon as possible," Arch explained, "otherwise complications arise."

As the blistered fellow was taken into the fold of the other ministers, Molly reached for her hat, which was vibrating in anticipation of action. She would show Ripkins, Blister, and their smug king who the prodigy was.

"Molly!" Alyss warned.

It required all the discipline the girl had to restrain herself. Did the queen doubt that her bodyguard's abilities would impress these men?

"It's been brought to my attention, Arch," Alyss said, troubled by the groans coming from the intel ministers' huddle, "that you're developing a weapon capable of destroying not only all of Wonderland but Boarderland as well."

"How do you know that?"

Alyss shrugged. "My people hear things."

"Bibwit Harte hears things, you mean," said Arch, impressed. "But so what if I'm building such a weapon? Surely you believe in scientific progress?"

"I see no 'progress' in creating a weapon capable of producing massive devastation."

"Don't you? I'm sure a *man* would."

Alyss sighed. On the viewing screen behind him, Genevieve Square was the picture of activity. Merchants who'd chosen to keep their shops open instead of attending the gala stood outside their groceries, gemstone ateliers, bakeries, and clothing stores, greeting passersby. Not long ago, as Redd Square, the area would have been nearly deserted, a slum of abandoned apartment buildings and boarded-up storefronts that even her card soldiers had been reluctant to patrol.

"You don't think the overriding need for our citizens is peace and security?" Alyss asked. "And perhaps for a—"

"The threat of total annihilation faced by those who'd attack us is a deterrent that provides Boarderland with all the security it needs. But I wonder, Miss Majesty, how aware you can be of Morgavia's military stockpiling if you question the need for such potent weapons."

"Aware enough," she said, though it was the first she had heard of it.

"Then perhaps you don't have the latest intelligence regarding the failed negotiations between Unterlan and its breakaway province, Ganmede, because if you did, surely you wouldn't doubt the need for whatever weaponry our scientists can devise."

Failed negotiations? "I have been briefed on the latest intelligence," Alyss lied. "But I wonder if there isn't a way to secure Boarderland without the threat of severe destruction or the loss of innocent lives or—"

"*Innocent lives?!* Oh, wise queen, is anyone really as 'innocent' as you suppose? If I weren't dealing with threats from *outside* Boarderland, I would yet be forever stamping out the ones from *within*. After your battles with Redd, I can hardly believe it, but you seem to retain a touch of naiveté. Citizens are not innocent, Your Highness. If the reins of government are not manfully applied, their aggressive, self-seeking nature will always upset peace and security. True peace is only possible through the absolute power of a single sovereign."

"And what if this absolute ruler were as self-seeking and aggressive as the most restless citizen, out for his own glory instead of the common good?"

"And what if women devoted themselves to domestic chores as they should?"

She would not allow herself to get angry, especially in front of Molly, whom she could feel bristling beside her. The difference between Redd and King Arch might only be one of degree. She would have to be more circumspect around him.

"I apologize," said Arch. "You are my host as Wonderland's queen and I should behave accordingly."

Alyss stood. "It's time I returned to my party, Arch. You're welcome to join the festivities or not, as you choose, but I thank you for offering your respects."

Alyss and Homburg Molly started for the door.

"You know that I was one of the last people to see your father alive?" Arch asked.

Alyss paused, not turning to face him.

"I've never met a finer king than Nolan," Arch went on. "He was a brilliant politician and a brave soldier. The loss of such a king is itself cause to mourn. But when I consider that he and I were on the verge of securing greater cooperation between our nations, to create a united front against the unknown threats of the future, ah well . . . "

Even if Alyss had been looking directly at Arch, she couldn't have known that he was lying, that he had in fact thought Nolan a weak and ineffective king who was forever at his wife's skirts, and that he'd sooner have had his head lopped off than ever entangle his government with Wonderland's. She swept out of the room, Molly following, careful not to step on the train of her dress.

A minister approached the Boarderland ruler. "Will we be joining the celebrations, my liege?"

Arch bent down, picked up a cracked button that had fallen unnoticed off Molly's coat. "I think not," he said. "I've found what I needed."

CHAPTER 4

CHE GROUND became increasingly less fertile as the Everlasting Forest approached the gorge that separated it from the Volcanic Plains—the full heat and lava streams of which were visible to the card soldiers patrolling Wonderland's most isolated military outpost.

"How am I supposed to prove myself in battle if we never get into one?" the Two Card complained.

"If you *had* been in a battle," answered the Four Card, "you wouldn't wish for one."

The Four Card knew what he was talking about, having been shuffled here after most of his former deck had been annihilated in skirmishes with Redd's forces. He had spent the lunar cycles of Alyss' exile deep within the Everlasting Forest, guarding the camp that had once served as headquarters for the Alyssian rebellion.

The Two Card glanced toward the parched, scanty trees that made up this part of the forest—which, from this vantage point, didn't seem so everlasting. He looked off toward the plains with its shimmers of heat, its bright, slow-moving lava flows, and its occasional burst of the stuff from underground, as if the planet were nauseous and coughing up what it couldn't digest.

"Who would ever attack us from here? It makes no strategic sense. We're near nothing of vital importance to the queendom. Our enemies would have to use most of their strength just getting through the plains to reach us. Plus, they wouldn't exactly be leaving themselves an easy route of retreat. There's only one way to go, and that's back into the Volcanic Plains."

The Four Card had to admit this was all true. After Alyss' ascension to the throne, General Doppelgänger had established these far-flung military bases throughout Wonderland to serve as an early warning system: The first sign of anything unusual was to be immediately relayed to the bases closest to the trouble, as well as to Central Command. It was not possible to be too vigilant, the general preached. Decks of card soldiers had thus been deployed to the distant jungles of Outerwilderbeastia, with its brambles and wildlife, and to the outermost quadrants of the Chessboard Desert, with its alternating squares of ice and black rock. Only the Valley of Mushrooms and the Volcanic Plains had been spared an influx of military personnel. General Doppelgänger had ordered bases to be erected *around* the valley, on various peaks of the Snark Mountains, so that the caterpillar-oracles' habitat could enter a period of new growth after being cleared of the mushrooms hacked to virtual mush by Redd's forces. As for the Volcanic Plains, the belching heat of the place was so inhospitable to all life save jabberwocky that General Doppelgänger considered it a buffer zone or no-man's-land between the queendom and any opposing force.

But, thought the Four Card, even supposing that enemies did attack *this* outpost and somehow managed to fight their way into the thick of the Everlasting Forest, they would still be confronted with the Wall of Deflection—a series of looking glasses unconnected to the Crystal Continuum that spanned the entire breadth of the forest. Just as the glasses around the rebel Alyssian headquarters used to overlap one another at countless angles, these were aligned in such a way that, as you approached them, you saw not your reflection but what looked like dense, impassable arborage and so were deflected away from Wondertropolis.

"To attack the queendom from here would be suicide," muttered the Two Card.

Funny, but what the Two Card most despised about life on this post was precisely what the Four Card appreciated. It was the least likely ever to be attacked. He had seen enough of battle and death.

"I wish you'd stop that humming," said the Two Card.

The Four Card was about to explain that he wasn't humming when all at once the forest trees began to whisper—

troubled, hoarse whispering. Then he heard it too, a steady hum, approaching fast and growing into a great swell of—

"Incoming!"

He dove to the ground as a cannonball spider smashed into the wall behind him.

The Two Card fumbled with his weapon, unable to get off a single shot before the giant arachnid pricked him with its pincers and he crumpled to the ground, dead.

Not about to become food for some artificial spider, the Four Card scrabbled to his feet and ran, spraying razor-cards from his AD52 in the direction of incoming fire. Whoever his attackers were, they had begun to launch whipsnake grenades; electric coils crackled, hissed, slithered all around him. In the frenzy of the eye-burning explosions and ear-stabbing squeaks of cannonball spiders, he saw the enemy rise up out of the gorge with amazing agility—ordinary-looking Wonderlanders except for the colorless crystal embedded in their eye sockets.

"How's it possible?"

The Glass Eyes, a breed of fighters manufactured by the maliciously inventive Redd Heart, were supposed to have been destroyed. Their return could mean only one thing: Redd had survived the Heart Crystal and was back in Wonderland.

"I fought her armies once and survived. I'll do it again," the Four Card vowed.

He emptied his AD52 at the Glass Eyes. *Thwip thwip thwip, thwip thwip thwip thwip.* Razor-cards shot out into the fireworks of battle, slicing through the enemy, dealing death. He dropped behind a bulwark to reload, was slamming home his last projectile deck into the AD52's ammo bay, about to take aim, his finger on the trigger, when—

The Glass Eyes swarmed him.

CHAPTER 5

HEART PALACE'S inaugural gala had drawn to a close and the verdict was unanimous: The event had been a success, a sparkling gemstone in the crown of a queen still new to the complexities of party planning. Alyss herself, however, was not pleased, too prickled by her meeting with King Arch to have enjoyed the festivities as thoroughly as her guests.

Why did he have to mention my father?

Indeed, she had never heard her father mention *him*. But then, why would Nolan have troubled a seven-year-old with matters of state involving an unlikable neighbor-king?

The sudden loss of her father was like living with a wound that would never heal, yet her memories of him were fading more and more every day. She'd been so young when she last saw him—in person, that is, because she had seen him twice since his death: once in the Looking Glass Maze, and once in a glass at Mount Isolation's Observation Dome shortly after Redd's defeat. But it wasn't only on Nolan's account that she was agitated. She had recently realized that any mention of a father caused her to think not only of him, but also of her *other* father, the one from her thirteen years on Earth—Reverend Liddell of Christ Church College, Oxford University. Her memories of the Liddells were so much more vivid than anything she remembered of Nolan and Genevieve. But then, she had spent more time with the Liddells than she had with the king and queen whose blood throbbed in her veins.

More than half my life.

Alone in one of the palace's seven state rooms, Alyss tried to recollect times spent with her beloved parents. But she was unable to concentrate. In her imagination's eye she watched the walrus-butler supervise the sweeping and hosing of garden paths, the spritzing of sunflowers that had sung their voices ragged, the distribution of leftover wondercrumpets, tarty tarts, and other treats throughout the capital city. She gazed at these things, thinking not of her mother or father, nor of the Liddells, her loving adoptive parents; she thought of Bibwit.

Why didn't he tell me Morgavia is stockpiling weapons? Or of Unterlan's troubles with the Ganmede province?

She had felt like an idiot lying to King Arch and feared her ignorance of these matters had showed on her face. Bibwit's keeping intelligence from her—he wasn't up to anything diabolical, she knew; only trying to prevent her from being overwhelmed by the responsibilities that fell to her as queen. The politicking within the queendom *was* enough to deal with without being burdened by inter-realm squabbles, but . . .

From now on Bibwit must inform me of everything, every scrap of intelligence, no matter how small or apparently meaningless.

Her imagination's eye fell on what had once been the Five Spires of Redd construction site. The monstrous edifice had been torn down before its completion, its mottled crystal recycled in the urban renewal projects of the neighborhoods most blighted by Redd's tyranny. The grime and soot of Wondertropolis had been scraped off a layer at a time until the once radiant surfaces emerged and could be buffed to a sheen. Spangles of luminescent blues again mingled with vibrant reds and dusky golds on office towers; spires of sunburst hues rose gleaming and incandescent above the rooftops of various government buildings and hotels. The city's landscape designers had removed all weeds and dead vegetation from the curbside gardens, replanting the same assortment of amaryllis, daisies, and aromatic, blossoming shrubs that had thrived before Redd had sprayed them with Naturcide.

What if Arch is right? What if the entire world should be under the command of a single, absolute ruler and the only way to establish a lasting peace among nations is to make them one nation?

Because there were limits to what she could accomplish with her gift, though who had set these limits even Bibwit couldn't say. Imaginationwise, she was still learning what she could and couldn't do.

And probably will be forever.

Alyss' imaginative eye focused on the new urban resort, Wondronia Grounds, formerly known as Redd's Hotel & Casino. Wondronia offered families a vacation destination without their having to leave the city. For adults there were spa treatments, massages, elegant restaurants, nature hikes through indoor parks so vast and lush you never would've known you were indoors. For children there were smooth quartz water slides, treasure hunts, and Total ImmEX gameplay, where boys and girls could inhabit the persona of Hatter Madigan and perform an impressive repertoire of his acrobatic, blade-spinning maneuvers.

Think of mother and father . . .

But her imagination's eye, as if independent of her, skipped over Wondertropolis' holographic billboards, which in Redd's time had announced nothing but crackdowns on suspected Alyssians and White Imagination practitioners, punishments of avowed dissenters, and incentives for turning in a neighbor or relative as a traitor to government. These same billboards now streamed the latest traffic reports, aired advertisements for White Imagination starter kits and safaris in Outerwilderbeastia. Gone from the streets were the Reddisms that had emanated from overhead speakers. *In Redd we trust. The Redd way is the right way. Better Redd than dead.* Gone were the speakers themselves. Gone from street corners were the gwormmy-kabob carts and crystal smugglers hawking contraband. Gone were most of the pawn shops and money lenders.

Think of mother. And father. Mother and father . . .

"Have I really found you alone," asked a voice behind her, "without faithful Molly attached at your hip?"

It was Dodge. He stepped up beside her.

Alyss smiled. "I made her take the rest of the night off."

"Nice view."

She hadn't noticed. She was standing before a window of telescopic glass that looked out over the lights of the capital city. "Yes, it is."

"All I've got for a view is the back of the royal kitchen. The treatment of a palace guardsman these days, I tell you."

A joke. He only told jokes when he was feeling awkward.

This is the part where he puts his arm around me, pulls me close, and says that no matter how many Looking Glass Mazes I pass through, no matter how many crowns I wear, I'll always be his Alyss, the same little girl who used to run through the palace halls with him when we were younger . . .

"What good is my imagination if it can't bring happiness to every Wonderlander?" she asked, biting her lip to stop herself from adding "myself included."

"I wouldn't think I'd have to answer that. We're *here*, aren't we? Redd and The Cat are not."

"That's not what I mean."

Redd's more public works might have been dismantled or renovated into oblivion, but her influence on Wonderland's culture was still noticeable. Redd had rewarded the worst in them. Their narrow-mindedness, selfishness, and pessimism had flourished at the expense of kindness, generosity, and goodwill toward others—the fundamental principles of White Imagination. General Doppelgänger insisted on retaining peace-keeping contingents throughout the city, and at least once between every rising of the world's twin suns, a Wonderlander would approach one of these to report a parent or neighbor for treason.

Arch was right about one thing. Never mind contending with forces outside one's borders, there will always be enough trouble dealing with disruptive elements from within.

"It's just . . . peace really isn't so peaceful," Alyss sighed.

Whether Dodge was annoyed by her conversation or the plea for sympathy in her tone, she didn't know; he changed the subject.

"How's Molly working out?"

"Fine."

He twisted his features into a doubtful expression.

"What? She's better than fine. Great, really. We all know how skilled and courageous—"

"It's not her skills and courage I'm worried about," he said. "It's her maturity."

Alyss almost laughed. Here she was, twenty years old, having passed through the Looking Glass Maze and defeated her evil aunt so as to govern the queendom in the name of White Imagination, yet she hardly felt more mature than when she used to play harmless pranks on Bibwit—turning his food into a plate of gwormmies or imagining a thick bushel of hair on his powdered head. Sure, she was more powerful than she used to be. Her strength came easily and she could feel it tingling every nerve. But maturity? What was *that*?

"It gives Molly confidence to hold the position," she said. "Besides, I know what it's like to exist in two worlds as a halfer does, being neither wholly one thing nor another. And most of the time, I like to have her around."

Dodge bowed. "Then I must trust Molly to keep the most beautiful of queens safe."

Alyss looked at him. He'd never been so direct with his affections before. "You think I'm beautiful?"

"So-so," he joked. "I know of this other queen a few nations over . . . "

She slapped him playfully on the arm. *Tell him you love him, that his being the son of a palace guardsman doesn't matter if he still loves you as you hope.* But when Alyss found her voice, she was surprised at what came out.

"Do you think Hatter might have gone to Earth?"

The moment for confessions of the heart had passed. Wonderland's queen and the leader of her palace guard stared out over Wondertropolis, their feelings for each other too big for utterance, neither of them knowing that wherever Hatter had gone, they would need him soon.

CHAPTER 6

BOARDERLAND: WHERE women could be given away by their husbands to pay debts, and young, rowdy gallants from Wonderland, fresh from the rigors of formal education, came to indulge themselves in roving pleasure tents; where maps were useless because the nation consisted wholly of nomadic camps, settlements, towns and cities, and a visitor might find the country's capital, Boarderton, situated in the cool shadows of the Glyph Cliffs one day but spread out along Fortune Bay the next.

King Arch's domain was a sprawling place with large tracts of unpopulated land to traverse between nomadic settlements. Often, it happened that after an evening of revelry a visiting Wonderlander would fall into a heavy, wine-induced sleep and fail to be roused by the packing up of tents and equipages, the folding up of street signs and storefront displays, the snorting of laden spirit-danes. When he woke, he'd find himself alone and unsheltered in the middle of nowhere. Sometimes the tents of the settlement in which he'd caroused the previous night would be visible on the horizon, but no matter how quickly he traveled toward them, they would remain forever on the horizon, an oasis. For further Boarderland companionship, he could only hope that another settlement would cross his path in its ceaseless wandering.

It was a tribal land, and except for clashes, every tribe kept to itself—self-contained and, as King Arch would inform certain of his guests, to a *small* extent, self-governing.

"I let them do what they wish in trivial matters such as healing rituals and marriage ceremonies," he would explain. "I even let them choose their own leaders. But only so long as they acknowledge me as their king. And only so long as they abide by my edicts in several other important matters."

To prevent the Astacans, Awr, and other Boarderland tribes from forgetting these edicts, Arch had had them carved, blasted, scorched, chiseled, and branded into the landscape.

Carved in a great slab of rock alongside the Bookie River: *Boarderland men do not cry when watching sentimental crystal-vision programs with their wives. Boarderland men do not watch sentimental crystal-vision programs with their wives.*

Blasted into the otherwise smooth face of a Glyph Cliff:

47

Boarderland men can take as many wives as they're pleased to enjoy, being more intelligent than women of every nation, country, world, and universe known or unknown.

Chiseled into the jetty in Fortune Bay: *Boarderland men do not talk about their feelings. Boarderland men do not whine or complain. Boarderland men never show weakness or vulnerability, nor admit to having either.*

Branded on sun-bleached rocks amid the undulant sands of Duneraria: *Boarderland men are fixed in their convictions, from which no feminine argument can sway them. If a Boarderland man changes his convictions, he does so at his whim, not by the consideration of a wife's views.*

With row after row of military tent-barracks, open-air markets and restaurants, promenades of dry-goods stalls, avenues of housing for intel ministers and other officials, countless servant canopies and its own pleasure-tent district, Arch's royal entourage was a city unto itself. His palace, always positioned at the center of his encampment, consisted of fifteen interconnected, pastel-colored tents whose billowy walls were made of materials more plush and smooth than any velvet, silk, or velour found on Earth. Having snaked its way across the wind-sculpted dunes of Duneraria toward the Bookie River, then through the Swampy Woods of Chance, Arch's convoy had made camp within sight of RollingDoubles Mound. And if not for the edict he'd ordered scorched into the side of the mound in letters twice his own height, and which was visible to him now—*Boarderland men eat their food with passion and with an urgency that signifies their virility*—Arch would have doubted that one of his present guests was a man.

"Delicious," Jack of Diamonds said through a mouthful of crunchy gryphon wing.

Freshly bathed and dressed, emitting a scent too flowery to be called manly, the scion of the Diamond clan sat between his parents, shoveling food into his mouth with the eagerness of two men.

A servant girl entered carrying a platter of conical-shaped treats, with what looked like tiny antennas poking out of them, their pointed ends charred.

"Try a dormouse snout," Arch offered. "I think you'll find them equal to any delicacy you've ever tasted."

Jack bit into one. "Mmm, more than equal."

"My chef will be so pleased," Arch said, a hint of disdain in his voice. He turned his attention to the Lord of Diamonds. "Do you think I'm lacking in intelligence, Lord Diamond? Or that I don't know enough about manipulating people to get what I want?"

"By no means, my liege. But—"

"At this moment, a gang of warriors from the Onu tribe are being entertained in one of my pleasure tents. By the time they leave this encampment, I'll have them fully convinced that the Maldoids, with whom they have an unstable peace, are planning to attack them. I fail to see how I can lack the intelligence necessary to my position and yet be clever enough to maintain my dominance over *all* Boarderland tribes by keeping them fighting one another."

"'Cause as long as they're fighting one another," Jack interrupted, popping a dormouse snout into his mouth, "they can't band together to defeat you."

Arch leaned menacingly toward the Lord of Diamonds. "Stop insulting my intelligence with your excuses, *milord*. Your son is returned to you. I have fulfilled my half of our agreement. It's time you fulfilled yours."

"Yes, um . . . there's a maid of Queen Alyss' who, I believe, is ripe for manipulation . . . possibly."

King Arch smirked at his bodyguards, Ripkins and Blister, who were standing off to one side. "A maid, eh? And you 'believe' she might 'possibly' be ripe? What helpful information. I almost prefer your excuses."

"We could better identify a target for you, Your Majesty, if we knew what you wanted the person for," said the Lady of Diamonds.

Arch looked curiously at this upstart woman, who sat fidgeting in increasingly uncomfortable silence until the king at length addressed her husband: "Expecting your inability, I myself made a reconnaissance mission to Wonderland and have found my quarry—Queen Alyss' bodyguard, Homburg Molly."

"But Molly is devoted to Alyss," said the Lord of Diamonds.

"Her desire to prove her devotion and worth is what

I will depend on. Alyss spent a great deal of her strength and resources against Redd. The more time that passes, the stronger she will become. Therefore, I have decided—very selflessly and courageously—that to ensure a proper future for our world, I must take control of Wonderland as soon as possible. And the Heart Crystal."

"The Heart Crystal?"

It was no secret that the Lady of Diamonds, as well as Wonderland's other ladies of foremost rank—the Lady of Clubs and the Lady of Spades—wanted to possess the crystal, each believing herself more gifted in imagination than she truly was.

"While I don't claim to gain any strength of body or mind from the crystal," Arch explained, "its influence over Earth will prove helpful in my charitable endeavors. It's a burden to care for others more than they care for themselves. But as my intel ministers have informed me, the only way I can prevent Earth from devolving into utter ruination is to take control of it too."

Jack had by now finished off the platters of gryphon wing and dormice snout and was indulging in a heap of sliced dingy-pear to cleanse his palate. Anyone watching him would have thought him too intent on filling his belly to pay attention to the conversation going on around him. But Jack was a talented listener, ever sifting through what he heard for information that, at some time or other, in some way, he might exploit to his own advantage. Swallowing down the last of the dingy-pear, he eyed Blister. Was this the fellow who'd freed him from the Crystal Mines?

"You there," he said. "Instead of standing around being useless, how about you fill my glass with wine?"

Blister's expression revealed nothing. "Certainly."

The bodyguard made his slow, deliberate way to Jack, reached out to put his hand over Jack's with the apparent intention of helping to steady the glass as he poured, but—

"Leave him, Blister." To Jack, Arch said, "Believe me, you don't want *his* help." He snapped his fingers and a servant girl hurried in on silent feet to fill Jack's glass. "I have already unleashed several regiments of fighters that Alyss and her people should find familiar. It's merely a diversionary tactic, a ploy to focus their military attentions off into the distance so that the bulk of my forces can enter relatively unopposed into Wondertropolis itself. I can forgive your failure, Lord Diamond, only if you do something else for me."

Ripkins stepped forward and set an exquisitely carved chest the size of a bread loaf before the Lord of Diamonds.

"I want you to present this little item to Homburg Molly."

"It's beautiful," whispered the Lady of Diamonds.

"Its exterior is nothing compared to what it contains. It's a small prototype of a weapon I'm developing. A fraction of the strength of what it will ultimately be, but enough to serve my present purposes. Though I warn you all, if you value your lives—"

"Only in so much as they give us power, wealth, and influence," Jack declared.

"—if you value them for *any* reason, you will not open that chest. You will leave that privilege to Homburg Molly." Arch leaned back in his chair, letting himself relax, the end of this pertinent business near. "Tell me, Lord Diamond, what do you think of kings?"

"I think they make the best sovereigns. Much better than queens."

Arch laughed. "You're wiser than you look. As a reward for your wisdom, and assuming you don't prove inept at delivering my weapon into Homburg Molly's girlish hands, once Wonderland is in my care, I intend to grant you back your ancestral lands to govern as you please."

"The Diamond Hectariat?"

The king nodded. "The borders of which will be exactly as they used to be before your ancestors and those of the Club, Spade, and Heart clans formed the coalition that eventually became Wonderland. Who knows? Perhaps I'll even throw in a bit of the Clubs' former hectariat for you to govern?"

Well, well. That was something the Diamonds hadn't expected. The hectariat theirs again? They could always scheme to get control of the Heart Crystal later.

Bloated with family pride, Jack emptied onto the table a pocketful of rhyolite crystals he'd filched from the mines. "Is there a wig merchant in this settlement you can recommend, Arch?"

"In Boarderland, men do not wear wigs," said the king, thinking he'd have this carved somewhere on his nation's landscape at the next opportunity. "Now listen well, all of you. Here's my plan . . . "

~

After the Diamonds had been escorted out of the tent, Arch dismissed everyone save Ripkins and Blister.

"You know what you're to do?"

The bodyguards nodded.

"She'll be unconscious from the blast, but she shouldn't be too injured. Do *not* make her more so."

Their disappointment was obvious—they who usually held themselves so taut had slackened somehow.

"Scent the seekers with this." Arch handed Ripkins the button that had dropped off Molly's coat during his interview with Alyss. "You should have no trouble once the Crystal Continuum is out of commission, as Wonderland's military will be too preoccupied. Remember: Alyss and her forces do not know that I'm the aggressor, so don't let yourselves be seen. But as I won't begrudge you having *some* fun on your outing . . . should anybody see you, you're not to let them live."

The bodyguards shrugged off their disappointment, their usual spirits returned.

"Blister thanks you," said Blister.

"Ripkins too," said Ripkins.

Showing proper deference to their king, these rivals to Hatter Madigan's military prowess took their leave, and before Arch had retired for the night, they crossed the border into Alyss' realm with nowhere near the cunning they might have, hoping to be seen by as many Wonderlanders as possible.

CHAPTER 7

DODGE HAD left to perform his guardsman duties. Not wanting to be alone, Alyss donned a cloak against the night's chill and ventured out onto the palace grounds. She probably should have gone to sleep. In his teasing, avuncular manner, Bibwit was always reminding her that, for a queen to be at her best, she should get at least eight lunar hours of sleep a night in order to avoid making an unwise decision due to fatigue. There would be reasons enough for unwise decisions in this life, he explained. Yet here she was, scepter in hand, following a path between the palace and the outer wall that separated the grounds from the rest of Wondertropolis. Geraniums of yellow, lavender, and red bowed as she passed. The branches of hollizalea shrubs unique to Wonderland dipped in respect. The night air carried the melody of "The Queen's March" softly hummed by sunflowers.

Alyss approached a hedge indistinguishable from those around it, paused to make sure she wasn't being watched, then stepped into the hedge and—

Vanished.

The roots of the hedge had unlocked a large hatchway camouflaged with furry groundcover. Alyss descended through the opening into a subterranean chamber, the location of which was known only to her most trusted advisers and the select few Bibwit had recruited to secretly move the Heart Crystal here one moonless night.

Ridiculous that I have to act the thief whenever I want to visit it.

There it was, the creative source for the universe, its glow—as always—causing the crystal to seem on the verge of swelling beyond its confines.

Depressing to see it stowed in this underground prison. How can I reinstate the Inventors' Parade if the crystal must remain hidden away, as it does in order to be kept out of the hands of those who'd misuse its power?

But being in possession of the crystal as well as the scepter from her Looking Glass Maze, wasn't she powerful enough to defeat any foe? Presumably. But why risk it? She and Bibwit had decided: Better to keep the crystal hidden.

Alyss knew that reviving the annual Inventors' Parade didn't rank high in the hierarchy of what was important to

Wonderland's security and improvement. But whenever she remembered the parades of her earliest youth—the Heart Crystal out in the open for all to enjoy, the public lining the streets to see the latest contraptions dreamed up by fellow citizens, the inventors doing their best to show off so that Queen Genevieve might pass their inventions into the crystal, upon which, in some other world, a version of them would come to be—whenever she remembered all of this, Alyss longed to bring back the Inventors' Parade, hoping it might signify a small return to . . . well, if not a better time (as Bibwit would surely deny it), then a *different* time, one in which her parents had been alive.

The hatchway slid closed and Alyss took up her usual position on a viewing platform halfway to the chamber floor, as close to the crystal as possible. Her scepter in one hand, she reached out toward the crystal with her other, to maximize her remote viewing ability. Her imagination's eye immediately filled with the bright wash of the crystal's light, which faded by degrees to reveal an old-fashioned dining room with mahogany wainscoting, floral-patterned wallpaper, a heavy wooden sideboard: the dining room at the deanery of Christ Church College, Oxford. Among those enjoying a dinner of roasted hens at the table, she saw herself—rather, she saw her double, whom, by twining her powers with those of the Heart Crystal, she'd created and sent to Earth to take her place in the Liddell family.

Miss Alice Liddell: adopted daughter of the reverend

and his wife, former friend of Charles Dodgson, near-wife to Queen Victoria's youngest son, Prince Leopold, but now enamored of Reginald Hargreaves, who was sitting across the table from her.

Reginald was a student at Christ Church, a country squire who enjoyed tramping about the fields of his Hampshire estate, Cuffnells, much more than being holed up in a room with books and theories. Although he sat between two of Alice's sisters, Edith and Lorina, his attention was markedly fixed on Alice—which the reverend and Mrs. Liddell, presiding happily over all, did not fail to notice.

How cozy and simple things seem.

Alyss knew better. She had eaten in that room many times, and when in the thick of whatever traumas a day in Oxford had offered up, nothing had seemed simple. But she couldn't help thinking it—things were simpler there.

She watched, feeling like one of the company even though the scene was silent and she could only guess at the amusing anecdote Reginald had related that set everyone laughing. Alice was laughing the hardest to show how much she liked him. He grinned, not taking his eyes off her even when Lorina asked for his attention, apparently reciting some humorous tidbit of her own.

The easy way they show their affection ...

She thought of Dodge, of herself and Dodge, how theirs was a stuttering kind of love, a tentative, timid thing, a—

Tzzzz.

Something's wrong. The hatchway had opened. The march of pressing business was descending toward her.

"What is it?" she asked as Dodge, Bibwit, and General Doppelgänger came into view.

"The queendom is under attack," said the general. "By whom we don't yet know."

"We know," Dodge said, a vengeful, dissatisfied look about him, a look that Alyss knew had everything to do with Redd, The Cat, and Sir Justice's murder.

"Several of our outposts have been routed," the general continued, "and several more are engaged with the enemy as I speak. I have ordered the deployment of reinforcement decks to prevent any attacks from penetrating farther into the queendom."

Under attack? Outposts routed? They were waiting for her to say something.

"There are reports," Dodge said.

"Of?"

"We have reason to believe that those attacking us are Glass Eyes," Bibwit informed her. "We're in the process of verifying the intelligence."

"Glass Eyes?" Alyss echoed in disbelief. After Redd's downfall, attempts had been made to reprogram them, but this proved a more difficult task than Wonderland's engineers and programmers had originally supposed. Only a small number of them had been successfully reconfigured when she and her advisers realized that the populace was too used to being terrorized by them to ever view them as a safeguarding element.

Dodge spoke in a tense whisper, as if to raise his voice was to unleash unappeasable fury: "Redd must have survived. You should have let me go into the crystal after her."

"We don't know that it's Redd," insisted the general.

"How else could the Glass Eyes be attacking us?"

It was a good question. Alyss looked to Bibwit. He shrugged. His ears swiveled sideways, as if abashed. "Learned albino that I am, I hate to admit ignorance, but in this instance it's all I have."

Alyss closed her eyes and cast the gaze of her imagination around Wonderland's borders, glimpsing one military outpost after another . . .

In a shady jungle of Outerwilderbeastia, a Seven Card was battling a couple of Glass Eyes with his crystal shooter, getting the better of them until an orb generator exploded against the cache of munitions he was guarding and he lost his life.

In a quadrant of black rock in the Chessboard Desert, pair after pair of card soldiers stumbled choking out of a half-destroyed bunker, managing to escape death by fire or asphyxiation only to be skewered by waiting Glass Eyes.

And at one particularly distant outpost, situated between a scrubby edge of the Everlasting Forest and the lava geysers of the Volcanic Plains, Alyss saw the aftermath of a battle the Glass Eyes had clearly won; wherever she directed her imagination's eye, card soldiers were splayed in various attitudes of death, among them a Two Card whose hand was on his still-holstered crystal shooter, and a Four Card who, if she was to judge by the bodies surrounding his, had taken out a respectable number of the enemy before giving up his life.

"It is the Glass Eyes," she said finally. "But I don't see Redd."

"She's not going to show herself with the front line," Dodge said, impatient. "She'll wait for a better opportunity."

General Doppelgänger nudged Bibwit and jutted his head forward, urging: *Tell her.*

"Is there something else?" Alyss asked.

"Jack of Diamonds has escaped the mines," said the tutor.

Just what she needed: on top of everything, to worry about a renegade brat of high birth and large buttocks who believed that the world owed him . . . the world. "Are his escape and these attacks related?"

"There's no intelligence to prove it," said the general, "nor rule it out."

She trained her imagination's eye on an outpost in an icy quadrant of the Chessboard Desert, where an entire platoon of card soldiers was about to be annihilated by a cascade of AD52 razor-cards. In the Heart Crystal's chamber, she swung her scepter. Dodge, Bibwit, and the general jumped, startled. But the motion of Alyss' arm rippled across great distances and the razor-cards suddenly changed direction, as if bouncing off an invisible force field. The Glass Eyes responsible for the attack stood in momentary shock, but the card soldiers, finding themselves still alive, shot round after round of their own razor-cards at the enemy and ran for cover behind the charred remnants of a bunker, surviving for the moment.

"Send as many reinforcement decks as you need," Alyss told General Doppelgänger. "Ready the chessmen, if you haven't already. Use every means necessary to keep the violence out of Wondertropolis. Bibwit, issue a warning to citizens: There is scattered fighting on the distant edges of the land, with little threat of harm to any of them. But to be safe, they should remain indoors whenever possible."

She would again test the limits of her imagination, use her powers to aid each and every outpost. Too bad she couldn't kill the Glass Eyes simply by imagining them dead, but such a thing wasn't possible. Glass Eyes were, in their limited way, willful. Imagination by itself, no matter how powerful, could not kill those who possessed the will to live.

"I'll do what I can from here," she said. "That is all."

Bibwit and General Doppelgänger turned to leave.

"And me?" Dodge asked.

"A guardsman's duty is to guard the palace," she answered, knowing he wouldn't like it. "However ..." Something in her tone made Bibwit and the general stop and turn. The queen stared only at Dodge. " . . . as for Redd, we should expect the worst."

CHAPTER 8

"TO BE embarrassed of me 'cause I'm a halfer!" Homburg Molly complained as a pair of imagination-stimulant dealers came at her, each wielding a Hand of Tyman—five short blades rising from the handle grip. She had never fought against Hands of Tyman before, but what did that matter? She could deal with them. She could deal with anything.

"Not to let me show them what I can do!"

Somersaulting over her attackers, she shrugged open her knapsack of blades and corkscrews, landed on her feet and jumped backward, felt the momentary resistance of Wonderland steel entering flesh.

She would lose points for that.

She had noticed too late: Her so-called assailants were

only two hungry men hoping for charity; what she'd mistaken for Hands of Tyman were alms cups. She pulled away quickly, before her blades could do much damage. The men stood with stricken faces, their hands pressed to their wounds.

"Sorry," she said, backing away from them. "I'm . . . sorry."

She continued down the street, had hardly gone the length of a jabberwock's tail when her homburg started to vibrate. She ducked left and—

A rock whizzed past, barely missing her.

She turned, assuming one of the homeless men had thrown it, but they had vanished. Her hat vibrated again. She ducked right and—

Weesh, weesh, weesh, weesh.

A rusted garbage can lid hurtled by, nearly taking her head off. That's when she spotted them: indistinct figures in the dark at the left edge of the street, taking cover behind a half-tumbled wall and the rotted hulks of what she guessed were transports of some kind. (Where *was* she anyway? This street was like none she'd ever seen in Wonderland.) She flicked her homburg flat and held it over her head, shielding herself from the hunks of masonry, weather-rotted window-panes, and other junk scavenged from the surrounding buildings being thrown at her.

"Probably Black Imagination enthusiasts," she mumbled. They always seemed to be the least gifted in imagination.

Clang! Bongk! Dink! A sleet of debris pelted her homburg shield.

But what if she was wrong? What if those bombarding her were simply innocent civilians who were afraid of her, a stranger with a curious arsenal at her disposal? The question was, should she use the full force of her skills to combat them or was she just supposed to warn them, to hint at what they'd endure if she gave free rein to her abilities?

Clangk! Thonk th-thonk thonk thonk!

More street-waste was raining down around her than before, as if the number of her antagonists had grown. Yet they weren't closing in on her; they stayed hidden, under cover.

It was probably another test of her self-control.

She would abide by the Millinery code of resorting to lethal violence only after every other option had failed. She'd already been wrong once this mission. She couldn't afford to be wrong again.

With an underhanded twist of the wrist, she sent her homburg shield whirling toward the oncoming projectiles. Almost in the same instant, she snapped open her wrist-blades. The homburg ricocheted from one makeshift missile to another, deflecting them back upon those who'd thrown them. With the spinning blades attached to her wrists, she easily knocked away the odd chunks of mortar that made it past the homburg, which now boomeranged back to her like an eager pet. As she listened to the fading footfalls of her assailants, she snapped the weapon back into its traditional homburg shape and flipped it onto her head.

Something was glowing in the half-ruined wall. She

approached for a better look: a luminescent top hat emblem embedded in the brick.

"That was too easy," she said, reaching out to touch the emblem, when—

Eeeeeech! Eeeeeech! Eeeeeech!

A flock of seekers came soaring out of the sky, dive-bombing toward her. No need to debate with herself this time. Seekers were part vulture, part fly, all nastiness.

Molly punched her belt buckle. The long, crescent-shaped sabers of her belt flicked open and, with both sets of wrist-blades activated, she at last exercised her abilities to their fullest, twisting and tumbling through the air, slashing at the shrieking creatures, sending them headlong to the ground with a blood-wet splat until—

They were gone, the street deserted.

She snapped shut her weapons, touched the glowing symbol in the wall and the scene vanished. She was standing in a vast armory, two city blocks square, the ceiling four stories above her head: the Holographic and Transmutative Base of Xtremecombat training, or HATBOX, at the Millinery.

"Definitely too easy, even for someone as embarrassing as me," Molly huffed.

She marched back to the control booth at the opposite end of the room. Sure, Alyss and Bibwit and everyone else said it didn't matter that she was a halfer. Sure, she had been made the queen's personal bodyguard. But it wasn't as if the position came with any serious responsibilities. Alyss was too powerful to need a bodyguard. And when Hatter had held the post, she knew, he'd been more involved in policy making and missions vital to Wonderland's security. She'd probably never be treated like a full-fledged Milliner, never be considered good enough. Why else would Rohin and Tock have been sent to Earth to keep a lookout for Redd and The Cat? She was at least as talented in combat as they were.

"More so!" she exclaimed aloud.

At the control booth, she turned the dial to Z, the most advanced skill level. No one in her class had ever gotten past W before, including Rohin and Tock.

She planted herself firmly at the starting position—the top hat symbol inked on the floor. "Begin!" she said loudly, and though she remained stationary, it was as if the walls of the room had been set spinning.

The HATBOX, which never presented the same scenario twice, was scanning its infinity of locations, enemies, and weapons for a suitable trial. The scanning was meant to disorient her, upset her mental balance. Whatever. As a hall in Mount Isolation solidified around her, she took a single step forward, felt the tickle of something like a whisker against her cheek and—

Ooomph!

She was knocked to the ground, her coat shredded near the right shoulder. She looked up and saw The Cat, Redd's top former assassin, laughing at her. A muscular humanoid who could morph into a cute kitten at will, he stood erect on two legs, his thighs each as thick as her waist. He had powerful, sinewy arms tapering to paws, claws as sharp and long and wide as butcher knives, and a feline face with flat pink nose, whiskers, and a slobbery mouthful of fangs. Bits of Molly's coat hung from one of his claws. She didn't even have time to get to her feet before the scene dissolved.

"Again!" she yelled.

This time she activated her wrist-blades while the room was still scanning, its walls flickering with possible scenes and enemies. At the briefest sighting of The Cat or anything feline, she lunged forward, determined not to be caught off guard again. Yet when a new environment took on form and substance around her, The Cat was nowhere to be seen. She stood backed up against one end of a long, narrow canyon of volcanic rock, trapped by three jabberwocky.

"Nice jabberwocky," Molly said. "Molly jabberwocky's friend."

Jabberwocky didn't need friends. One of them exhaled a jet of fire at her and—

She dropped and rolled, tapped her belt buckle, and the belt's sabers sprung open and sliced into the beast's underbelly.

Bad move.

A jabberwock's skin was nearly as hard as fossilized lava. Far from fatal, the saber wound only provoked the beast into a rage. It stomped and spat fire in all directions, Molly rolling first one way, then another, deftly maneuvering to get out from under the thing without being crushed. Problem was, she came out exactly where she'd been before: trapped against the canyon wall by three jabberwocky.

She shrugged open her backpack—*flink!*—and from among the variety of blades and corkscrews it offered took hold of two crowbar-shaped weapons, their pointed ends veering off at right angles from the long handles. With one of these in each hand, she leaped toward the canyon wall, knife points driving into the rock and holding her momentarily aloft over the jabberwocky. She pushed off from the wall with her feet and landed on the back of the nearest jabberwock. The beast went insane, bucking and twisting its head around on its long neck, snapping its jaws at her. It required all of Molly's strength not to fall off, just to keep her grip on the bony protuberance near the top of the beast's spine—a lucky vertebra, not unlike the pommel of a spirit-dane's saddle on the otherwise cratered moonscape of jabberwock skin.

Something hot flashed against Molly's leg.

One of the jabberwocky had spit a fireball. It grazed her—worse, it grazed her mount, and now her jabberwock and the other were fighting, burning each other alive with their furnace breath even as they reared up on their hind legs, raking and clawing at each other with their forelegs.

Thwap!

A tail came around and laid Molly flat on the ground. She had time enough to see a jabberwock approach, its mouth opening wider and wider in the yawn-like motion that inevitably preceded a fire-shot from its throat before—

The scene dissolved and the lights came on.

"Again!" she yelled.

She had to set aside her anger and resentment. She had to relax. If her time at the Millinery had taught her anything, it was that adrenaline made you impulsive, overanxious. It could trick you into doing something stupid. If she was to complete level Z, she had to stay calm.

The HATBOX began its dizzying scan of possible locations and enemies. Molly took deep, even breaths and closed her eyes, opening them only when she heard the steady murmur of strangely accented voices, the clop-clop of hoofs on cement, the trundling of squeaky carriages.

She was in a city—an ancient one, judging by the looks of things. Carriages like the ones rumbling past hadn't been seen in Wonderland for generations. And as for horses, those beasts of burden were straight out of the history programs Molly was forced to study as part of the Millinery's classroom curriculum.

Amid the crush of pedestrians coming toward her: a man wearing greatcoat and bowler. She instinctively reached for the brim of her homburg, but he only dipped his head in greeting and continued past. The pedestrians, those in the carriages—they all seemed intent on their errands. But she wouldn't be fooled. An attack was imminent. From what quarter, instigated by whom, she couldn't say. But under no circumstances would she lessen her vigilance or—

A voice rose above the street's general clamor: "Read

about the carnage in Piccadilly! Death and destruction in Piccadilly! Only a tuppence to read the latest reports!"

A boy was selling newspapers on the corner. Molly walked up to him and he shoved a paper into her hand. *The London Times?* She'd heard Alyss talk of London. It was a city the Queen had visited during her exile from Wonderland.

"Two pence," the boy said.

She didn't have the leisure to find out what he wanted, snapped open a set of wrist-blades to spook him and—

Seeing that a trivial flick of the wrist produced such a blur of deadly copter blades, he sprinted off. But Molly didn't want to draw too much attention to herself. Not yet. She quickly flicked shut the blades.

The newspaper's description of the carnage and destruction in Piccadilly read familiar. In the cheese shop hollowed out by an explosion, Molly recognized the aftermath of an orb generator. In witnesses' clumsy attempts to describe a rifle that coughed bolts of light, she recognized Wonderland's crystal shooter and its ammo of bright NRG rods produced by the frizzling together of certain gemstones. And as for the carcasses that looked like pin cushions with legs tucked underneath them, those were easy to identify—cannonball spiders in the death pose, their brief life spans having run their course, though not, according to the reporter, before the outsized creatures had taken scores of Londoners with them.

A sound like scissor blades rapidly opening and closing.

Molly's hand jumped to the brim of her homburg. She scouted the scene.

Nothing. Just Londoners going about their business the same as before. But as she turned her attention back to the newspaper—

There it was again. Unmistakable: the sound of card soldiers being dealt in preparation for battle. She didn't sight them until Londoners were screaming and running for shelter. They'd already unfolded themselves: a flush of soldiers from one of Redd's decks. Unengaged, they resembled ordinary playing cards, albeit life-sized ones. But engaged for battle as they were now, unfolded to twice their usual height, with limbs of Wonderland steel and a forward lilt to their every movement as if perpetually stalking prey, they presented an undeniably menacing aspect.

"Stay calm," Molly whispered to herself. "Stay cool."

The only way to "kill" one of Redd's late-model infantry was to stab it hard in the medallion-sized area above its breastplate, at the base of its steel-tendoned neck. The knife blade would cut through its vital circuitry and send sparks spurting like fiery blood. Thing was, in the harassment of battle, this kill spot seemed to shrink to the size of a gwormmy's eye, to a—

Bolts of NRG shot toward her—*thip thip! thip thip!*—from the muzzle of a Five Card's crystal shooter. Molly whipped the homburg from her head, used it as a trap, hands moving at the speed of a thousand hurrying caterpillar feet as she caught each of the bolts in the hat's underside. *Fwiss!*

She sidestepped the swing of a Six Card's lance, but only to leap twistingly into the air, barely avoiding an orb generator shot by a Seven Card. She slammed her homburg flat and spun it around and around over her head as if she were a cowgirl from the American West working her lasso. The NRG bolts she'd caught streaked out from its edges, shooting into a Four Card's kill spot.

The soldier folded up, inanimate.

Her next victim didn't present himself so readily. It would have been difficult enough fighting so many card soldiers even if they hadn't been well armed. But armed as they were, with whipsnake grenade and orb generator . . .

Time and again she unleashed her homburg, which rattled and jarred and dented the soldiers without inflicting serious harm. Her wrist-blades in perpetual motion, her belt sabers whistling through the air, whining to make contact with the enemy, she at last pierced the Six Card's kill spot with a sword from her backpack's never-diminishing supply of blades.

Three more to go.

The Five and Seven Cards fired their AD52s. One hundred and four razor-edged cards ripped through the air, clanged against her centrifugal-spewing wrist-blades and skittered away from her. An Eight Card took aim at her with an orb cannon. The blades of one bracelet activated to deflect the incoming razor-cards, Molly used her free hand to whip her homburg at the Eight Card and then cartwheeled toward him.

The homburg knocked the cannon from the soldier's grip and—

Still cartwheeling, she caught it before it hit the ground, fired.

The orb generator's explosion engulfed all three rogue soldiers. In the blast's aftermath, they lay twitching in the street, outer steel scorched, inner circuitry in need of rebooting. Working her way from the Eight Card to the Five, Homburg Molly—halfer, orphan, supposedly untrustworthy bodyguard to a queen who didn't need one—thrust a blade into their kill spots, quieting them for all time.

She stood for a moment, catching her breath, not quite believing what she'd accomplished. Level Z. She had completed what no one else . . .

But then she saw what she should've seen sooner: a puddle where no puddle should have been, surrounded as it was by dry pavement on a sunny day. Concentric ripples expanded outward from the puddle's roiling center, and in a sudden froth of water—

A Glass Eye launched into the air.

Several more Glass Eyes leaped from nearby puddles. In the whorl of action, it was hard to tell exactly how many there were—more than Molly could defeat with just her Millinery weapons, that was for sure. So she ran. The Glass Eyes fired their weapons, cannonballs searing toward her, hatching open to become giant spiders.

She ran straight for the brick outer wall of the nearest

building—the Hotel Burberry. She looked as if she were going to slam right into it, but at the last possible moment she dived to her right. Too late for the spiders to change course. They latched on to the hotel and began to crawl up floor after floor, on the hunt for prey. Food was food to a cannonball spider, whether Alyssian, Londoner or tourist.

Dink! With her homburg shield, Molly swatted away a spikejack tumbler, that nightmare missile consisting of six flesh-grating spikes that stabbed out in all directions from a common center.

She had to take a risk. The unnatural puddles dotting the street, maybe she could . . .

Another spikejack was tumbling toward her. No choice. She gripped her homburg firmly in her hand and took a running jump into the nearest puddle, plunged under the surface, pulled ever deeper by the portal's gravity until she slowed, reversed directions and was pushed up, up and—

Whoosh!

She came twisting out in a spray of water, her belt sabers slicing into a Glass Eye that had the misfortune to be standing nearby. Time had seemed to slow down while she was underwater, but her disappearance and reappearance above the surface were nearly simultaneous. She again dove into the puddle, came leaping out of another, plucked a dagger from her backpack, and speared a Glass Eye that was still facing the spot she'd occupied half a moment before.

If she had truly been in London, these puddles would

have served as return portals to Wonderland's Pool of Tears, once thought to be a watery black hole for Wonderlanders unlucky enough to have fallen in, a vortex that carried them to another world. For generations, nobody who'd fallen into the pool had ever returned to report of this other world, and so their loved ones had been left to gather at an overhanging cliff, letting their tears fall into the water and thus giving the pool its name. Not until Hatter Madigan and Princess Alyss Heart had returned through it—thirteen years after jumping in, feared dead—was the truth discovered.

But the universes created by the HATBOX had their limits. Puddle portals that would have carried Homburg Molly back to Wonderland in the real world here only connected to other portals. And she made the most of it—jumping into one, splashing out of another, using them to serially ambush the Glass Eyes until she emerged from an inkblot-shaped splotch of dirty water, on the verge of adding to her body count, flicking her homburg at whoever would be her next casualty, but—

The unmoving bodies of her enemies littered the street. She had killed them all.

"You forgot this."

Shwink! Every weapon activated, Molly saw an ordinary-looking woman approach with something cupped in her palm. She retracted her weapons when she realized what it was: a luminous paperweight in the shape of a top hat. She touched it and the London scene dissolved into darkness, all black as pitch save a life-sized hologram of Hatter Madigan, who smiled approvingly at her.

"Today you've shown the courage, skill, and intellect required to be a first-rate Milliner," he said. "Let's see how you fare tomorrow."

For two blinks of a spirit-dane's eye she thought it was really Hatter, that he'd returned. But the image faded and the lights came on.

"Impressive," a voice echoed.

Molly turned to see the Lady of Diamonds emerge from the control booth. No one but Milliners were allowed in the BOX. "You're not supposed to be here," she said. "How'd you get in?"

"When will you learn, child, that as a member of a ranking family, I can find a means to do whatever I wish?"

"When will people stop calling me a child?" Molly shouted.

The Lady of Diamonds looked quizzically at the girl. "I didn't realize you were so sensitive. Don't you want to dry off? You could catch cold."

"I'm fine."

"You should at least have those tended to."

What was the Lady of Diamonds talking about? Have *those* tended to? Have *what*—

"You're bleeding." The lady gestured at Molly's torso, right shoulder, and left thigh.

She had a few cuts, scrapes. Who cared? They were just

superficial wounds. "I'm all right," Molly said.

The Lady of Diamonds sighed like one used to having her advice go unheeded. She held up the ornately carved chest King Arch had entrusted to her husband. "I came to give this to Queen Alyss. I've been told she's here with you."

"She's not."

"No?" Worried wrinkles crowded the Lady of Diamond's brow. "That's odd. I could've sworn . . . I guess I'll have to leave it with Bibwit Harte or Dodge Anders then. It's too important to leave with anyone else." She turned to go.

"I can take it," Molly said.

"You?"

Molly nodded. "I *am* the queen's bodyguard."

The Lady of Diamonds pretended to consider it. "Well, I suppose if she trusts you with her life, I can trust you with this. Be sure to tell her that it was given to me by her mother, Queen Genevieve, just before her death, and that, as her mother requested, I have faithfully kept it safe from Redd."

"Uh-huh," Molly said, suspicious, "and why're you only giving it to Queen Alyss now? I mean, why'd you wait?"

The Lady of Diamonds adopted a sweet, kindly expression. "Because, clever girl, Genevieve left strict instructions that if Alyss ever returned to rule the queendom, it should be given to her after the sixth lunar cycle of her reign had passed. Obviously it contains something of great value to the queendom that requires Alyss to have occupied the throne for a time—intelligence or instructions, I assume. I've been curious about what's inside, but . . . " the Lady of Diamonds grew sheepish, " . . . I haven't been able to open it."

"I'll present it to the queen with all possible speed," Molly said, bowing, acting every bit the professional Milliner and bodyguard that she was.

With a great show of reverence, the Lady of Diamonds surrendered the chest to the girl's care. "Will you be returning to the palace through the Crystal Continuum?" she asked.

"It's the fastest way."

"That it is," agreed the lady, "although I can't be seen taking public transportation myself, being of high rank as I am. I'm sure you understand."

Molly didn't understand but kept her mouth shut, not wanting to spend any more time with this snob than was necessary.

"Tell the queen I said hello," the Lady of Diamonds cooed, and before Molly could respond, she was alone in the massive open space of the BOX, the pneumatic hiss of the door lingering after the exit of Wonderland's most self-important lady.

She gazed around at the empty room, its blank walls and faraway ceiling, all void of evidence from her recent battles against jabberwocky, card soldiers, Glass Eyes. It was just a big impersonal room. What had felt like a tremendous accomplishment only a short time before—her completion of level Z—now felt small.

Without bothering to dry herself off or bandage her wounds, Molly hurried out of the Millinery to the looking glass portal located outside a sandwich shop on Bandersnatch Avenue. She entered the glass and zoomed headfirst through the kaleidoscopic, tubular-shaped passage until it linked up with another, larger one—the Crystal Continuum's main conduit. She was adept enough at continuum travel to focus on her destination while mulling over her interview with the Lady of Diamonds. Queen Genevieve had trusted *her*? No way. From everything Molly knew, the Hearts and Diamonds had never been on great terms. The whole story sounded like a lie. The pretty little chest she was carrying to Alyss could be part of a trap. The Lady of Diamonds might be trying to ensnare the queen in a scheme designed to cost her the respect of government officials and the general population. It was easy to believe: the Lady of Diamonds conniving to gain advantage over Alyss in political dealings that a needless bodyguard was not allowed to know anything about.

And if it *were* a trap? Well then, she might be able to prevent it, because what was so hard about opening the chest as the Lady of Diamonds had claimed? It had a single clasp and . . . there, she unlocked it. Now all she had to do was lift the lid. If she could protect Alyss from the Lady of Diamonds' intrigue, whatever it was, she would thus ensure the still fragile stability of the queendom. Then Alyss would *have* to let her take a more active part in military and other important meetings. She would have proven beyond all doubt that, halfer or not, she deserved the most the queen could grant in the way of responsibility and honor.

Impatient, careening past commuters toward Heart Palace, the continuum's prismatic surfaces a smear of twinkling colors, she lifted the lid of King Arch's weapon no more than a vein's breadth and—

Whoomp!

CHAPTER 9

ATOP THE second-highest peak in the Snark Mountains, at a military base overlooking the Valley of Mushrooms, card soldiers armed themselves with AD52 projectile-decks, fortified the grounds with orb cannons and whipsnake grenade launchers. The latest communication from Doppelgänger's headquarters had informed them that there was no discernible pattern to the attacks on other outposts, no strategic principle by which the general could deduce which base would next come under siege.

Seven other outposts had already been destroyed; the card soldiers had no intention of becoming the eighth. They cautiously walked patrols, stood their lines. Yet there was no sign of Glass Eyes or anyone else, no sign of life whatsoever unless they counted the wind, the scudding clouds. They were remote enough from civilization that, if not for the shadow cast over them by Talon's Point to remind them where they were, they might have supposed themselves the lone community in the world, isolate in the vast, unpopulated upper reaches of the sky.

Talon's Point was the highest peak in the queendom and thought to be unreachable by ordinary means, the winds too fierce even for the two-person crafts operated by Wondertropolis sightseeing firms. But unbeknownst to the nearby card soldiers, it was here, on the only upsurge of land closer to the heavens than they, that an extraordinary Wonderlander had taken up residence, one who had wanted to utterly remove himself from his responsibilities, to wallow in the fact that he was not first and foremost a Milliner, but a man. He had fought against this for so long, struggled to subordinate every impulse, every desire, to the dictates of Millinery duty. It had been futile to try. He knew that now.

He had helped Princess Alyss ascend to her rightful place on Wonderland's throne and been granted leave. Packing only enough provisions to last the journey, planning to forage for food on the lower parts of the mountain as needed, he came to Talon's Point, wanting time and space and solitude to mourn the loss of Weaver, a woman he loved more than he had realized. Completely severed from his responsibilities for the first time in his life, he unburdened himself of his Millinery backpack, took off the long, battle-scarred coat that had been his uniform for as long as he could remember.

He unhooked his Millinery belt and unlocked the cuffs that held his wrist-blades in place. He removed his top hat last, sensing its reluctance in the suction-like hold that made it slightly more difficult to lift from his head. He arranged all of his Millinery gear in a neat pile and set it aside, doubtful he would use any of it again.

Far from the bustlings of Heart Palace yet within easy sight of Alyss' imaginative powers if she but knew where to direct them, the legendary Hatter Madigan—unflinching in combat, role model of the duty-bound stoic for all those born to the Millinery, was allowing himself to *feel*.

~

Long before, he had chosen Talon's Point for his intermittent rendezvous with Weaver *because* it was presumed to be unreachable. Untrodden by Wonderlander and Boarderlander alike, it would be safe from trespassers.

He'd made the first visit alone—by means of blades pulled from his backpack, scaled the sheer cliff that towered up to the summit of Talon's Point, where he discovered a ridge wide enough to support a smail-transport and, in an outcropping of ice-glazed rock, a cave that could comfortably accommodate two. Weaver, the Millinery's sole civilian employee, would never be able to scale the cliff, he knew, so over the course of several following visits, he'd used his wrist-blades to bore an upsloping tunnel from the cliff's base to the cave at the summit, pressing his whirring blades into the mountain, his entire body vibrating with the friction as they churned bedrock to pebbles and flinty dust.

He had brought Weaver after the tunnel was complete, showed her by what flora to recognize its entrance and where he stowed the fire crystals she could use to light her way up to the cave. They had never been able to spend as much time at their refuge as they might have liked, Hatter being too busy with his duties to Queen Genevieve, and Weaver with her lab work. But what days they had carved out for themselves on Talon's Point were all the more treasured for being infrequent: welcome hours of respite from the daily tussle and wear of living; rare moments of relaxation for Hatter, the only time another living being had seen him slough off the cloak of stoicism his position forced him to wear.

But now Weaver was dead, murdered by Redd's assassins, as had been every member of the former Millinery. What better place to indulge his mournful reminiscences than at the hideaway that most reminded him of her? Because in a way, the pain of her absence, the loss of her, was a living thing. It had a life inside him that he wanted to coddle, to nurture. Weaver's dying was her final physical act, the last thing she'd ever do that would impact him; he wanted to make it last as long as possible.

In the farthest recess of the cave he found a leather satchel blanketed with dust, half buried in drifts of dirt formed by the wind. Weaver's satchel. Had she brought it on one of their earlier visits or left it for him, a clue to how she had spent her last days? But if she'd left it for him, troubling questions came to mind. Why would she have abandoned Talon's Point, since it was where she'd had the best chance of avoiding Redd's assassins? Or what if she *hadn't* abandoned the Point, but instead had been ambushed by Redd's assassins while gathering food lower down on the mountain and—

He couldn't tolerate thinking about it. To mourn the loss of Weaver was one thing; to envision the actual event that had forever wrenched her from his life was another. Plus, the satchel might only contain clothes and other provisions she had needed to survive. It might not have been left for him at all.

He spent entire afternoons staring at the bag or avoiding it altogether. He who feared no enemy was afraid to open it. But enough time had finally passed. He thought himself ready. He took the satchel in hand, brushed it clean of dust and dirt. He removed one item at a time, letting each conjure what memories it would . . .

A trio of old notebooks tied together with flugelberry vine. Weaver had carried them everywhere. They contained the esoteric formulas of her art. Hatter untied the vine and opened one of them, wondering if the indecipherable symbols on the page in front of him were responsible for the scarf she had once give him . . . or at least the timing of the gift. "For your birthday, whenever it might be," she had said, because Milliners were not supposed to know or celebrate their birthdays, such personal trifles falling outside their duty to protect the queendom. Hatter's birthday wasn't listed in his official file, but he had always suspected that Weaver, by means of some concoction or other, might have discovered it and this had been her way of telling him.

He took a carton of jollyjellies from the satchel. Even in his grief, he had to smile. Weaver had been addicted to sweets: frosted cakes with lollipop sprinkles, chocolate biscuits with swirls of vanilla batter at their center. It was just like her, so lovably willful, to accommodate her cravings while hiding out from Redd and her minions, on the run for her life.

Next out of the satchel came a first-aid kit, complete with cauterizer, skin grafter and the U-shaped sleeve of interconnected NRG nodes that a surgeon had once used to fuse Hatter's shattered shoulder back together. But also inside the kit, smashed as if with a rock or other blunt object: Weaver's Millinery ID chip. She must have removed it from under the skin of her forearm to aid in her survival, destroyed it to prevent Redd from tracking her. It was a tiny thing, roughly the same size as the mole Weaver had had on the nape of her neck, but one of the chip's circuits wasn't adequately destroyed. It had probably been enough to betray her location to Redd's assassins.

He should have trusted his instincts. Originally against the idea, put forward by the Millinery's board, of hiring a carefully vetted civilian to handle the facility's alchemistic needs, he had changed his mind only after he considered: better to have every Milliner out in the field than in a lab.

Besides, none had Weaver's gift, her ability to discover and exploit the hidden properties of things; she could take some secret mixture of liquid metals, combine it with a beaker full of who knew what, and produce the strongest, most responsive of Millinery blades. Weaver was no ordinary civilian. But he should *not* have let her work there. He might never have known her, never have fallen in love with her or even known that he was capable of such love—he'd have lost these things, but she'd still be alive, filling her civilian days with civilian concerns.

He thoroughly crushed the ID chip against a rock, returned it to the first-aid kit. He upended the satchel and let the lone item it still contained drop into his palm. As slim and compact as a playing card, it resembled a typical book from Earth in every detail except size: Weaver's diary. What he'd hoped and feared to find.

Mustering his courage, Hatter pressed the sides of the diminutive book, the covers sprang open and—

More than three lunar cycles after arriving here, the man who had fought too many battles to remember, who had faced a thousand different deaths and come away from all of them more or less intact, suffered the blow of his life when the 3-D image of Weaver materialized and he heard the sound of her voice.

"Hatter, my love, we never got a chance to say good-bye."

CHAPTER 10

U HOOMP!

Most continuum travelers had to concentrate on their destinations to keep from being projected out of a looking glass portal at some undesired location. Portals were stationed throughout Wonderland; the interlinked channels they created could prove slow going for inexperienced travelers who might enter a portal with the intention of visiting the Unnatural History Museum across town only to find themselves projected out of one at the end of their block. Navigating the continuum took time and practice. But on this particular day, at this particular hour, even the most skilled travelers were helpless. Commuters streaming home after a long day at work, families returning from visits with friends or relatives: One moment they were traveling along the continuum's network of crystalline byways, the next they were shot out of the nearest looking glass like cannon fodder, their limbs flailing desperately for purchase on something, anything.

Wondertropolis descended into tumult: the cries of the injured; the breathless reassurances and urgent calls of those rendering first aid; the bawling of frightened children; the moans and prayers of the superstitious who thought a sky raining Wonderlanders signified the end of the world. All was shock, confusion, pain, in the midst of which lay the girl who had caused it, unconscious, untended to, and unnoticed by everyone save two Boarderlanders on an illicit errand for their King.

~

Whoomp!

A bright hot force knocked Molly unconscious as what few splinters remained of the once beautiful chest fell from her hands. Catapulted out of a looking glass on Theodora Avenue, she landed hard on the quartz-and-pyrite-mottled pavement, in front of a pet store full of squawking tuttle-birds and screeching lizards. Even before her homburg came tumbling out of the continuum after her, four seekers began to circle in the sky above, signaling her location.

Deaf to the injured Wonderlanders strewn about the desperate streets, blind to everything save the seekers, Ripkins and Blister stepped onto Theodora Avenue and sighted their quarry. As they approached, Ripkins shook his head, dismissive of the young bodyguard.

"What could Arch want with *her*?"

Blister said nothing, not one to try and guess Arch's motives the way Ripkins did. What did he care of motives so long as he got to use his gift of touch to hurt people? He noticed Molly's homburg on the pavement and picked it up. He had never seen a Milliner's hat in operation before, but with the instinct of one given to all things military, he flicked it and—

Fwap!

It flattened into a razor-edged shield.

Ripkins scanned the scene: no one was watching. Lucky them.

"Are we supposed to be impressed?" Blister scorned, returning the homburg to its original shape.

Ripkins took Molly's limp body in his arms, laid her over his shoulder, and Blister led the way through the alleys of the city. Not until the assassins had crossed back into Boarderland did they make contact with their king, who was in his palace with his ministers when the alert came and Blister's face hovered before him.

"We have her," the assassin said.

CHAPTER 11

ALYSS WALKED purposefully through the palace's night-dimmed halls, through three state rooms and as many parlors, trying to convince herself that her sole aim was to become more familiar with her new home, but . . .

Can't I even admit it to myself?

She was looking for Dodge. To seek him with her imagination's eye had felt like spying. Now, if and when she found him, she would feign surprise and say that she was simply exploring the palace, familiarizing herself with its well-appointed rooms, glittering floors, tumbled stone staircases that resembled frozen waterfalls, hand-hewn balustrades, and spacious landings.

She stepped out into the courtyard. The sunflowers and poppies slept under blankets of dew. Moonlight glinted off the war memorial's obelisk for the anonymous dead. The Hereafter Plants, whose pistils resembled the faces of Genevieve, Nolan and Sir Justice Anders, cast wistful shadows across the walk.

Something sniffed, moved. Just as Alyss realized who it was, standing with bowed head at Sir Justice's grave—

Dodge.

—he whirled around, the point of his sword aimed at her throat.

"Not the warmest way to greet your . . . " She was about to say "queen" but changed her mind. " . . . friend."

He immediately sheathed his weapon and fell to one knee. "I apologize, Your Highness. You surprised me."

"*You* surprised *me*," she said. *He expects an attack even here? He is too ready to fight.* "I wish you'd get up, Dodge. You don't belong at my feet."

He looked as if he wanted to argue the matter, but he stood, saying only, "I thought you were with the Heart Crystal, helping the military bases defend themselves."

For better or worse, she'd stopped aiding the outposts when the reinforcement decks had arrived. She had needed to find *him*.

Dodge nodded toward her parents' graves. "I'll let you have some time alone."

"No, stay," she said quickly. "I was only . . . walking around." She flapped a hand to take in the whole of the palace. "I'm trying to get used to this place."

"Really?" He tugged at the lapels of his guardsman's coat, adjusted the weight of his sword. "Then if Her Majesty will allow me the honor, I would be pleased to accompany her on a guided tour."

She would tell him nothing of the tour Bibwit had already provided. "Her Majesty will be pleased to have your company," she said, "if you give over your formalities and call her by her given name."

"Alyss," he said, and offered his arm.

They entered the palace and walked for a time in silence.

Nice to have the warmth of him so close. Try not to feel guilty, the both of us strolling along as if card soldiers aren't battling for their lives on the queendom's outskirts.

"I was worried, Dodge," she said. "Back at the crystal chamber. The look on your face at the possibility of Redd's return. No one wants to lose you again to an all-consuming vengeance."

"No one?"

Say it. Tell him. "Me."

She felt blood rush to her face, hoped that he couldn't see her blush in the half light. For an interminable moment his only response was the click-click of his heels on the marble floor, then—

"When you first returned to Wonderland, Alyss, I didn't understand why you weren't angry. I thought you should've been twice as vengeful as I was, since Redd murdered your mother and father. It bothered me that you weren't, and I couldn't help thinking that, in some way, you were dishonoring their memory."

"I don't honor my parents through vengeance," Alyss said. "I honor them by watching over the queendom to the best of my ability, for the continued glory of White Imagination. As they tried to do."

"I know, I know," he sighed. "Did I take unnecessary risks as an Alyssian? Did I put myself in harm's way because I cared less about my own life after Redd's coup? Probably. What did my life matter in a universe that allowed Black Imagination to *win*?"

"It mattered," she whispered.

Dodge shook his head, uncertain. "That's what's funny— as in, not funny at all: I was unnecessarily risking my life but I had vowed to live in order to kill *him*."

They had come to a series of rooms whose familiarity struck Alyss mute. Bibwit had not shown her these rooms, which were a re-creation of her mother's private quarters in the former Heart Palace.

"I'm told the architects meant for these rooms to serve as a sort of shrine," Dodge explained, "a place where you could commune with your mother, if you ever desired her guidance."

A noble intention, and yet, the last time she was in these rooms . . .

I never saw my mother alive again.

"If it *is* Redd," Dodge said quietly, "if she *has* returned . . . I don't know how much control I'll have over myself."

Alyss tried to sound reasonable, as if whatever Dodge chose to do wasn't of the greatest importance to her. "You could let me deal with them and not get involved. I can protect you—from them, from your own worst impulses. Whatever power I have is nothing if I can't use it to keep safe those who . . . mean the most to me."

"*You* protect *me?*" he laughed. "Alyss, your responsibilities as queen make it necessary for you to keep yourself out of harm's way whenever possible."

She started to protest.

"Yes, yes, you're a warrior queen, absolutely," he said. "But I think even Bibwit would agree when I say, just because you personally can defeat an enemy doesn't mean that you always *should*. The queendom can't afford to see you injured or worse. Besides, you have card soldiers and chessmen more than willing to engage in battle for you. And if card soldiers and chessmen aren't enough . . . " his voice sounded choked, like something was stuck in his throat, " . . . my life might not have mattered to me, Alyss, but yours always has."

Did he just say that? Did he . . . ?

"A lot of men would be intimidated by a warrior queen, never mind one as intelligent and powerful as you are," Dodge went on. "But I know that you wish you didn't always have to be strong. You wish you could let someone else be the strong one for a change, someone who could support and comfort you. I might not have your powers of imagination, Alyss, but let that person be me. Let *me* protect *you*, always and forever, no matter who attacks the queendom—Redd or anyone else."

"Dodge," Alyss said, putting a hand to the parallel scars on his cheek, that brand left so long ago by The Cat. She pressed her lips against each of them—four delicate kisses. When she pulled away, he was smiling.

"I have to check in on a couple of guards," he said. "Wait for me?"

She nodded, watched him stride in among the plush couches and oversized pillows that furnished the first of her mother's replicated rooms, a room heavy with the past but now the site of an overwhelming present. With a last happy look at her, Dodge slipped through a door in the far wall.

~

His ears stiff with alarm, the veins in his skull pulsing faster than usual, Bibwit let his hearing guide him. He followed the sound of their voices through half the palace, at last rounded the corner and saw them—Alyss at the threshold of her mother's quarters, Dodge stepping rather proudly toward the guardsman's balcony that overlooked the courtyard. He hurried up to the queen and spoke with breathless urgency.

"Alyss, Glass Eyes have entered the city. They're on our streets."

"On our . . . ?"

"And there's something else. The Crystal Continuum—"

She didn't give him time to say more, turning her imagination's gaze on Genevieve Square, where Wonderlanders were being launched out of looking glasses with such speed that they smashed through shop windows, upset tarty tart carts, knocked unsuspecting shoppers to the ground, and sent skittish spirit-danes galloping off uncontrollably with their riders. On the corner of Tyman Street and Wondertropolis Way, Alyss watched as a smail-transport in the midst of boarding its passengers was slammed on its side by a knot of Wonderlanders jettisoned from the continuum. And even Wondronia Grounds—normally the site of so much pleasure—was not exempt from the hailstorm of Wonderlanders; Alyss witnessed dinners and cocktail parties thrown into disarray as continuum travelers crashed onto tables, bars, dessert carts.

She had to defend her realm with all the imagination she possessed. The sooner Redd and her Glass Eyes were put down, the less opportunity Dodge would have of succumbing to revenge, of risking his life for the sake of *killing*.

"Don't tell Dodge," she said, and sprinted down the hall.

Bibwit stared after her for several moments, worried that she might not yet be ready to again battle her aunt, when—

"She was supposed to wait for me."

Dodge. Surprisingly, and not a little ashamed of it, Bibwit

had been too absorbed with thoughts of Glass Eyes to hear the guardsman emerge from the balcony. "Who was?" he managed.

"Alyss."

"Oh, was she here? I've been looking for her myself." From the folds of his robe, Bibwit retrieved the menu of the Lobster Quadrille, his favorite restaurant in the city. "I have a pardon that needs her signature."

Dodge squinted, suspicious. "Is that right? With your acute hearing, Bibwit, you can usually find anyone you like."

Bibwit considered running off. He had never been a good liar. The only way to keep news of the Glass Eyes' invasion from Dodge would be to avoid the young fellow's company, for surely the guardsman would pry it out of him otherwise, but—

"Mr. Bibwit, sir! Mr. Bibwit!"

The walrus-butler came waddling toward him from one of the ballrooms.

"I hope you've had better luck than I," said the creature, "because I've had none! Not the tiniest bit! No, indeed, I cannot find the queen anywhere!"

"I was just with her," Dodge said. "I'm sure I can find her for you."

Behind Dodge's back, Bibwit shook his head at the walrus—*No, shhhh, say nothing*—but the poor animal was carried away with worry and woe.

"Then you must tell her, Mr. Dodge—oh, it's bad news,

very unfortunate!—you must inform Queen Alyss that the Glass Eyes have invaded Wondertropolis!"

Before Bibwit could stop him, Dodge was halfway down the hall with his sword drawn.

"Tell Alyss to stay in the palace!" he shouted, and kept running.

CHAPTER 12

THE FIRE crystals in the shallow pit cast a modest heat as Hatter sat staring at Weaver's stilled image. He had paused the diary, wondering if something were wrong with its inner workings, because his beloved appeared blurry, as if seen through a veil of water. But then he felt the wet on his cheeks. It wasn't the diary; he was crying.

She was dressed in the Alyssian uniform: rough-fibered and nondescript except for the emblem of a white heart on the cuff of the right shirtsleeve.

His hand twitched. The diary began to play.

"If you're viewing this," Weaver said, "then you have proved wrong all those who currently believe you and the princess are dead . . . although it also means that *I'm* most likely dead."

She smiled sadly at the space between them. Hatter nearly slammed the diary shut. He'd been wrong; he wasn't ready for this. But to relegate Weaver's image back inside the book . . . No, he couldn't do that either. It would be too much like shutting her away in a tomb. And so he sat there, watching her recorded image, listening to her every word.

"This diary is for me as much as it is you, Hatter. I hope I'll be able to tell you what I have to say in person, but circumstances here are dangerous. Just because I'm alive today is no guarantee that I'll be so tomorrow. You probably already know that Redd has destroyed the Millinery. Her goal is genocide, to wipe the Milliner breed from existence. It's believed that she salvaged the ID tracking system from the Millinery and is using it for this purpose, after which she'll destroy it. You often told me that one born a Milliner still needs the proper training to make the most of his or her natural gifts, but Redd puts more credence in the birth than in the training. As soon as the first Milliner was ambushed by Redd, I hid out here, not sure if I'd be targeted too. There *are* rumors that a few Milliners have so far managed to escape their assassins and are hiding undercover somewhere. If the rumors are true, I hope they will continue to evade their would-be murderers so that once the rebellion succeeds—and I believe it must—they will come out of hiding and you can lead them in a new Millinery."

Hatter felt a twinge; reestablishing the Millinery was the last thing he felt like doing.

"I understand that our relationship was difficult for you, Hatter," Weaver went on. "I know that despite how thoughtful and loving you always were to me, a part of you was angry with yourself for succumbing to your feelings for anyone, let alone a civilian. A master of self-control as all of Wonderland believes you to be, you shouldn't have been consorting with me. You thought your feelings a mark against you, an indication of weakness."

"I no longer think so," he said aloud.

"I always knew your duties could call you away," Weaver continued. "It was wrong of me not to tell you when I first found out, but . . . Hatter, my love . . . I'm sorry." She wiped her eyes. "I should've told you before you left . . . I was pregnant."

Hatter remained perfectly still. Pregnant? With *his* child? So long did he remain unmoving that, when he again became conscious of his surroundings, he thought he had paused the diary. But then he saw Weaver's chest rise and fall, rise and fall; she was breathing, struggling with her own emotions.

"I know how you feel about halfers," she said at last, "and I was never sure how you'd react to hearing that you had fathered one. Every time I thought to tell you of my joy—of *our* joy—I found an excuse not to. I *did* plan to tell you the next time we'd be on Talon's Point together. But as you know, there was no next time."

Too preoccupied with the vision before him, Hatter didn't hear the pop that sounded—either the bursting of an air bubble in one of the fire crystals or an explosion from outside the cave.

"I couldn't give birth alone, so I risked an overland journey to the Alyssian camp in the Everlasting Forest. Doctors there delivered me of a beautiful baby girl." With the saddest smile Hatter had ever seen, the smile of one who had long ago resigned herself to a life incomplete and unsatisfactory, Weaver said, "It's time you knew your daughter's name, Hatter."

But just then, as if surprised by an intruder, she looked off at someone or something not recorded by the diary, and the pop that Hatter had failed to hear a moment before proved to be the opening salvo in a battle raging on the nearby mountain, which Hatter now heard without hearing, his whole being fixed on Weaver's image, already fizzling to nothing as she whispered, "Molly."

CHAPTER 13

"WHAT DO you mean you can't locate an enemy to fight?" the general cried, indicating the havoc surrounding them in Genevieve Square, then splitting into the twin figures of Doppel and Gänger so as to worry twice as much, both of the generals pacing and rubbing their brows.

The white knight and rook exchanged an uneasy glance.

"My chessmen have canvassed the vicinity and found no one," explained the knight. "We have a great many injured among the civilian population, but no casualties as of yet."

"Let's keep it that way," said Doppel.

"Yes, let's," said Gänger. "But someone caused this!"

"Or some*thing*," offered the rook. "Whoever or whatever it was, it's made the continuum impenetrable."

As if to prove the point, a panicked Wonderlander with blood-matted hair sprinted past. "Must get home to my family," he was saying. "Must make sure they're safe."

The chessmen and generals watched as the traumatized fellow ran straight for the nearest looking glass portal and was knocked back, repelled, when he tried to enter it. The generals called for a nurse, who led the victim off to a triage center located in a tailor's shop on the corner.

"That's what happens whenever anyone tries to enter the continuum from any portal whatsoever," the rook said. "It's impossible to gain access and we've no idea if the condition is temporary or permanent."

"Not good," fretted Doppel.

"Not good at all," agreed Gänger.

"Sir!" A young pawn approached, accompanied by a pair of Wonderlanders. "These men were in the continuum when that, uh . . . thing happened. I thought their experiences might be able to give us some insight into what we're dealing with."

"Let's hope so," said the knight.

At a nod from the pawn, one of the men offered what he could: "I don't know exactly how to describe it, really. It was like a feeling, like I was a piece of junk being carried along on a tidal wave or—"

"Not for me, it wasn't," said the other. "I'm not sure if this will make any sense, but a bright nothingness came up and knocked the breath out of me. I don't remember anything after that, except that once I could see and breathe again, I wasn't in the continuum. I was stranded high in the branches of an unappreciative tree, and my wife—we'd been returning home from a barbecue at her cousin Laura's, she makes the best barbecued dormouse you'll ever taste in your lives, so tender that the meat slips off the bone, and she seasons it with a scrumptious glaze just the right amount of sweet and tart and spicy, oh and her corn relish!"

The knight cleared his throat.

"Right. So anyway, I landed in a tree and my wife was half a block away, sprawled on top of a citizen who—the nerve of him—complained that she'd landed on him purposely."

The pawn waited, eager to learn how helpful his civilians had been. The generals resumed their pacing and the rook blinked at the men with something like disbelief. Only the knight remembered himself.

"You've done the queendom a great service, providing such a smorgasbord of helpful information," he said. And to the pawn: "See that these gentlemen are examined by a physician before you release them."

"Yessir."

The pawn saluted and led the Wonderlanders off.

"We'll have to station guards at all the portals," said Doppel.

"And see if we can't analyze whatever's contaminated the continuum," said Gänger. "What is that bleeping?"

It was coming from the rook's ammo belt, which looped

108

over his battlements and crossed in an X on his chest. "It's the latest model crystal communicator, Generals," he said. "I press this button here . . . " the chessman pressed a button on the miniature keypad strapped to his forearm, " . . . the incoming message alert stops sounding, and then this little hole here . . . " he pointed to a nozzle-like opening on his ammo belt, " . . . shoots out a visual of the transmission that all of us can view equally well."

A screen formed in the air before him, on which appeared a frantic pawn patrolling Wondertropolis' Obsidian Park neighborhood.

"Glass Eyes are in the city!" the pawn shouted. "Repeat: Glass Eyes have infiltrated Wondertropolis! A *lot* of them!"

Behind the pawn, fleet-footed Glass Eyes could be seen rampaging through the streets, overpowering one chessman and card soldier after another.

"Unable to locate their point of entry!" the pawn shouted. "They seem to be coming from *everywhere!*"

A Glass Eye was rocketing up fast behind him, getting closer and closer—

"Look out!" the rook cried.

The transmission went dead.

The generals were already barking commands into their flip-screen, older model crystal communicators:

"All available decks deploy to Obsidian Park!"

"For White Imagination's sake, get civilians off the streets!"

But neither the generals nor the chessmen voiced what all knew to be true: They were not equipped to counter a major attack on the capital city, not with the continuum rendered useless, and the numerous decks that had been dispatched to military outposts stranded along the edges of the queendom.

"The queen must be informed," the knight said.

"There's no need."

They all turned to see Alyss Heart, gifted with the most powerful imagination ever to legally occupy Wonderland's throne, walking toward the middle of the square with scepter in hand. The sight of her, so matter-of-factly confident, might have been enough to give even the walrus-butler courage, but the chessmen and generals weren't the walrus-butler. Their courage didn't need bolstering. They would not whine about the Glass Eyes' superior numbers. They would not disappoint their queen. The rook unholstered his AD52, checked the supply of projectile decks in its ammo bay. The knight unsheathed his sword and stood at the ready. Generals Doppel and Gänger each split in two, and the four generals each divided again, forming eight generals in all—four Doppels and four Gängers. The more bodies to aid in Wonderland's defense, the better.

"There!" the knight said.

Alyss had already seen them: a contingent of Glass Eyes bearing down from Slithy Avenue, keeping close to the buildings, darting from vestibule to vestibule. The rook started forward, not one to wait for trouble if he could help it.

"No," Alyss said. "Let them come."

"It'll be the last thing they ever do."

Alyss spun to her left and—

There stood Dodge, sword in one hand, crystal shooter in the other. They held each other's gaze. *What's he doing here? I told Bibwit—*

"Shouldn't you be guarding the palace?" the rook asked with a knowing smirk.

Dodge shrugged, didn't take his eyes off Alyss. "First they're in Wondertropolis, next thing you know they're marching through the palace halls." He looked at the rook and winked. "Besides, I have to make sure you do the job right, don't I?"

The Glass Eyes were letting civilians climb out of ground-floor windows, burst from doorways, and escape into the distance. Unconcerned with ordinary Wonderlanders now that they'd located the queen, they holed up in the suddenly abandoned shops and office towers, took aim with their AD52s, crystal shooters, spikejack tumblers, and orb cannons.

Ch-ch-ch-ch-ch-ch-ch-ch-ch-ch!

They strafed the square, orb generators burning a path through the air toward Wonderland's queen. Even before Dodge, the knight, the rook, and eight generals could dive for cover—

Alyss used the power of her imagination to hurl the missiles back upon the enemy. At the slightest dip of her scepter, the orb generators reversed directions and broke into smaller orbs, each of them homing in on a Glass Eye.

Bloosh! Kabloosh! Bloosh-bloosh! Bloosh!

A rapid series of blasts as Glass Eyes exploded into millions of Glass Eye bits. Not one of the enemy was left functioning, alive.

"A second wave," Alyss breathed, because more Glass Eyes were streaking in from Slithy Avenue's horizon.

"They're on Whiffling Heights," called the rook.

"And Gimble Lane," said Dodge.

"And Brillig," said the knight and generals.

Not the most life-affirming news: Glass Eyes storming Genevieve Square from every available street. Alyss and Dodge, the chessmen and generals—they were surrounded.

CHAPTER 14

IF THE ever-wise Bibwit Harte had been with Hatter on Talon's Point, he would have bent his ears in sympathy, sensitive to the news divulged by Weaver's image.

"The diary has left you with more questions than it has answered, Hatter," he might have said, "but you shouldn't be surprised. The most important questions are always answered with yet more questions."

Which wisdom would have comforted the Milliner not at all.

If Weaver had given birth at the Alyssian camp within the Everlasting Forest, why had she left the safety of the camp? Why had she abandoned her daughter? Merely to place the diary at Talon's Point in case he returned? It hardly seemed worth it. There must have been another reason, but . . . Here

Hatter was overcome with a peculiar feeling. He'd been having peculiar feelings for a while now, but this one was *really* peculiar. He was feeling *paternal*. How old had Molly been when Weaver left? What did she remember of her mother? Had she been told anything of *him*? Hatter thought back to the time he had spent with the girl—the battles they had fought against Redd and her forces. He'd been impressed with her fidelity to Alyss, her courage and fortitude in helping the princess recover Wonderland's throne, and he hoped he had said as much when he recommended her to be Alyss' bodyguard. But he could recall nothing that definitively told him she knew who he was. Her sass and occasional disregard for his opinions could have been either the lashing out of a bitter daughter or the antagonism of a teen determined to elbow a space for herself in the adult world.

He repeated the fact to convince himself of its reality: *Homburg Molly is my daughter, Homburg Molly is my daughter.* How could he act the recluse, pining away on a mountaintop for a woman who would never return, while her daughter— their daughter—lived? *Because it's in Molly that Weaver most lives.* Yes, and for Weaver's sake, for his and Molly's sake, he had to return to Wondertropolis. He got to his feet, would prepare immediately.

Blooooachchch! Kablooooomshkkrkkkrk!

He'd been hearing explosions outside the cave for some time, he realized. He stepped out onto the ridge and saw, on the nearby mountain below, the comet streaks of orb generators, the fiery blossoms of exploded barracks and munitions caches; a Wonderland military post was under attack.

In an instant, he returned to the depths of the cave. From the dust-covered pile of Millinery gear, and with the skill of a footballer chipping the ball into the goal, he kicked up his top hat, sent it flipping onto his head.

~

Shoulder to shoulder and ankle to ankle, the card soldiers locked themselves together to form a shield around the communications bunker. How many of their deck were still alive they had no way of knowing. Perhaps only the pair of Ten Cards inside the bunker. And themselves. It had been a while since they'd sighted anyone else. Yet they would defend the bunker so long as they had breath left in them. Not a single soldier harbored any illusions: The attack had caught the base unprepared; they were outnumbered; they would not survive.

Too much smoke in the air to see the enemy, but suddenly—

A series of whishing sounds like something repeatedly cutting the air, then a lull, the quiet that inevitably precedes the wind-shriek of an incoming orb generator. The card soldiers braced themselves for impact, but instead of the expected explosion—

Thump. Thump thump. Thump thump thump.

"What the . . . ?" one of the soldiers said.

The limbs of Glass Eyes clomped down around them. Arms chopped off at the shoulder joint, legs ending at the top of the thigh, hands and feet and torsos, all with a spaghetti of wires and lab-grown veins spilling from holes where no holes should have been.

From the direction the card soldiers had expected their death to come, the silhouette of a Wonderlander appeared out of the smoke—a Wonderlander they would have recognized anywhere. The hat, the dramatic swing of the coat, the spinning blades on his wrists: Hatter Madigan.

CHAPTER 15

FOR A manufactured species with questionable brain power, the Glass Eyes were fighting with surprising intelligence. Rather than face Wonderland forces in the open of wide avenues, squares and parks, they used the cityscape to their advantage, as defensive cover. They moved purposefully from building to building, sheltered position to sheltered position, battling card soldiers as they converged on Genevieve Square.

The moment Alyss had been located, the knowledge of it spread to every Glass Eye in the city—or so it seemed to Bibwit Harte, who, with the walrus-butler, was watching the invasion on the holographic viewing screens in the palace's briefing room. Wonderland's queen had been sighted, there followed the slightest hesitation in the Glass Eyes' movements, and they all began to fight their way toward her.

"Oh, oh, I can't watch," grieved the walrus. He tried to cover his eyes, but his flippers were too short to reach and he waddled around the room in even greater consternation. "I'm not watching, I'm not watching!" He turned his eyes anywhere but at the holo-screens. "What's happening, Mr. Bibwit? No, don't tell me! Oh, why can't Queen Alyss simply defeat those horrid things with the strength of her imagination? Please tell me that something good is—"

Clicketyclacketyclicketyclicket! Clacketyclicketyclack!

"What. Are. Thooooooose?" the walrus moaned.

On the holo-screen airing the happenings in Genevieve Square, a swarm of scorpspitters released by the Glass Eyes was scuttling toward Alyss and the others. Never before had a Wonderlander seen these scorpion-like contraptions that could shoot bullets of deadly poison from their "tails"—not even Bibwit, who assumed they were the latest in a long line of armaments invented by Redd. But before a single scorpspitter curled its tail into a C to take aim at the queen, she imagined into existence a horde of disembodied boots with steel-plated soles, which hovered momentarily in the air, then—

With a slight nod, she brought them down hard, stomping the scorpspitters flat, squishing their armor-carapaces and making abstract art of their wiry guts.

"Ooh, now why can't Queen Alyss do *that* to the Glass Eyes?" the walrus-butler cried.

"Because Alyss cannot, even in her imagination, be in all places at once," Bibwit explained, "not with the intensity required to defeat a scattered enemy. Whether she produces a construct with enough reality to deceive the eyes or she brings into existence an actual weapon or boot, imaginings require tremendous precision of thought and attention to detail. She could perhaps mount a successful defense in two locations simultaneously; she has the strength for that. But to imagine herself in every Wondertropolis neighborhood, battling all the invading packs of Glass Eyes simultaneously, would spread her gift too thin and she would fail."

Waddling laps around the room, alternately looking at the ceiling and the floor—anywhere but at the holo-screens—the walrus-butler heard none of this. Bibwit himself was hardly aware of what he'd said. In times of great stress, the pale scholar became more verbose than usual.

"At least the palace has been locked down," he observed, hoping to calm the walrus as, on the walls around them, the uncontrollable nightmare of battle raged in Wondertropolis' streets. "So we are safe."

But even the walrus-butler wasn't naïve enough to believe this. They were safe only so long as Queen Alyss Heart remained so, and right now—the animal cast a fretful eye at the nearest holo-screen—things looked very bad indeed.

~

They were surrounded. Directly ahead, cannonball spiders rocketed closer and closer while, on their left, a cannonade of orb generators eclipsed all but death. On their right, umpteen decks of razor-cards cut through the distance toward them and, at their backs, spikejack tumblers churned air in prelude to churning their flesh.

The Glass Eyes were trying to overwhelm the queen, to catch her imagination off guard.

I won't let it happen.

Alyss flicked out her fingers and a cannonball spider shot out from each of them, hatched in midair, and clashed with those shot by the enemy. Halfway between Wonderland's queen and the Glass Eyes, the mechanical spiders fought, dismembering one another as heartily as they would have dismembered any Wonderlander, while—

Thrusting her scepter skyward, Alyss veered the incoming orb generators away from her and the others, imagined them streaming out high over Wondertropolis to land in the Volcanic Plains, home of the jabberwocky.

Can't let it happen.

Dodge, the chessmen, and generals were standing with swords raised in the futile hope that they might deflect enough razor-cards away from themselves to survive. The missiles were nearly close enough to shave the hair off their arms when—

Fith, fith, fith! Fith, fith, fith, fith, fith, fith, fith!

—Alyss imagined them into neatly stacked decks,

grounded and harmless. Immediately, she whirled around to face the spikejack tumblers and sent them crashing into one another. Their spikes latched, holding the tumblers together to form a sort of worrisome jungle gym that hit the ground and skidded toward them, scraping and gouging the pavement.

"When I give the go ahead, go ahead," Alyss said, the spikes of a jungle gym having come to a stop less than a gwormmy-length from her face.

"What?" the four General Doppels cried at once.

"Run when I say so."

Dodge frowned.

"We have to get out of this square," she said. "Find a better vantage from which to fight."

"Wondronia's just up Brillig Way," the knight offered. "We'll have the most number of options there."

"To Wondronia Grounds then," Alyss said. "But first, you'd all better duck."

They barely had time to drop to the pavement before she spun, her scepter held horizontally above her head with both hands, sparks of imagination spewing from its ends, shooting out in all directions and—*peewthungk! peewthungk!*—laying low the surrounding Glass Eyes with heat-seeking accuracy.

"Now!"

The chessmen and generals took off, razor-cards ripping from their AD52s, cover fire issuing from their crystal shooters. Running behind them, Dodge kept close to Alyss.

"You should get back to the palace," he urged.

She guffawed. "I understand. You were preoccupied and didn't notice that I just saved your life?"

"The queendom needs you safe," he said. "*I* need you safe."

"But I'm the only one who can defeat Redd."

"For Issa's sake, Alyss!"

Ahead of them, the chessmen and generals were battling their way into the elaborate complex of buildings that made up Wondronia Grounds.

"You want me to return to the palace," Alyss said, "then you have to come with me. The Cat nearly killed you once, Dodge. If you insist on fighting him again, I won't let you do it alone."

A few more strides and Wonderland's queen and the leader of her palace guard would have caught up with the chessmen, just a few more steps and—

A Glass Eye leaped out from behind a parked smail-transport, blocked their way. "Did you drop something?" Dodge asked the assassin. "'Cause I think I see your . . . " he unsheathed his sword and swung, decapitating the Glass Eye in one blow, " . . . head over there."

Hand in hand, Dodge and Alyss ran, their feet a blur on the pavement, explosions all around them, and then—

Relative quiet. They were in Wondronia Grounds, stood catching their breath with the chessmen and generals in the enormous promenade.

"Spooky," the rook said.

It was: to see a place dedicated to entertaining thousands of Wonderlanders at any given time empty of the usual families, strolling couples, retirees, and cliques of teenagers. All vacationers had been evacuated, all amusements abandoned; unfinished meals sat on restaurant tables; the massaging cloaks and hairstyle helmets of the salons buzzed and clicked as if clients were still relaxing beneath them. Nothing but water coursed down the quartz water slides at the far end of the lobby while, closer to Alyss, carnival rides such as the Whipsnake Coaster and the Spinning T-Cups were completely still.

Chkkchchkkchchchrshshshkkkk!

A dozen Glass Eyes burst through Wondronia's locked front doors. The knight, rook, four Doppels, and four Gängers surged forward to engage them. Dodge grabbed Alyss' hand and pulled her into the closest shelter—the Total ImmEx unit, where, as Hatter Madigan, visitors could do battle against various enemies. By the time a trio of Glass Eyes chased after them, the Total ImmEx unit was in operation—Dodge, with Hatter's coat and weaponry superimposed on him, twisting and leaping in his fight against the Glass Eyes it manufactured, the real Glass Eyes momentarily confused by the sight of their false selves until—

Simultaneously, they turned their heads, quick and jerky as tuttle-birds sensing prey, and sighted Alyss Heart on their right flank. But she was on their left flank too. There were three Alysses in total. Only one of them could be Wonderland's real queen. The Glass Eyes would do away with them all.

"Hagh!"

Dodge somersaulted over two of them—sword in one hand, Hand of Tyman in the other—and sent them to the nothingness of their afterlife. The remaining assassin, ducking and swiveling to avoid the crystal shot of its unreal brethren, was about to spray the place with its AD52 when Dodge snatched a circular blade from his Millinery backpack and threw it. The Glass Eye, not knowing that weapons produced by Total ImmEx couldn't cause harm, moved to knock it away with the muzzle of the AD52. The opening was all Dodge needed. He lurched forward, his sword extended out in front him, and he thrust it into the assassin as far as its hilt.

Dodge and Alyss—the real Alyss, the decoys she'd imagined gone now—found each other, safe amid the scything and eager trigger-pulls of the Total ImmEx Glass Eyes.

"All right?" Alyss was breathless.

"No problem."

They ran out to the lobby, where the white knight and generals were surrounded by an ever-growing number of Glass Eyes. And the rook, where was . . . ? There, on the Spinning T-Cup ride, in a replica single-seater fighter craft shaped like a capital T, its guns parallel to the cockpit and located at the end of each wing. The rook was slashing at the assassins trying to climb up and put an end to him.

With blades swinging, Dodge offered what support he

could to the generals and knight, but Alyss remained where she was, a pillar of calm amid the turmoil of battle as she employed the weapon of her imagination. The Spinning T-Cups kicked into operation. The ride's fighter craft began to rotate, increasing in speed until the Glass Eyes climbing up to challenge the rook blade to blade were flung off like so many—

Crack!

The rook's fighter craft was free of the ride altogether, independent, flying under the distant ceiling of Wondronia's lobby.

"Yeeeeah!" the chessman shouted, piloting in low over Dodge, the knight and generals, and firing his craft's guns into the Glass Eyes, annihilating half of them. A second flyby finished off the enemy and, with no small skill, he landed the fighter so that it blockaded Wondronia's exposed front door.

"If you imagine every entrance and exit blocked, we'll have time to defeat whatever Glass Eyes are still inside," the four General Gängers said to Alyss.

"No. I want as many of them as possible to come in."

"You want what?!"

She didn't need Bibwit to tell her that, being unable to imagine herself at every skirmish simultaneously, she couldn't annihilate every Glass Eye in the city with a single strike of her imagination. She knew her limits all too well.

I have to kill off as many as can be brought together in one place.

"What's the largest room here?" she asked.

"Penniken Fields on the second floor."

"Take us there."

Clicketclacketclacketyclick!

Scorpspitters, released by the Glass Eyes outside, skittered through small gaps not blocked by the rook's fighter. Out the forked ends of their curled tails shot bullets of black liquid. Dodge, the chessmen, and generals tried to shield themselves with their weapons, but—

Splat! Sploink! Splish!

The liquid bullets imploded in midair, hung in their splattered state as against the windshield of a smail-transport. Alyss had, by the power of her imagination, cocooned herself and the others in a protective NRG shield and the bullets had smacked against it. A good thing too, because the few that had zipped past them hit the trunk of a guppy tree planted in the lobby, the poison causing its fish-faced leaves to audibly suffocate and its bark to fall off in colorless strips.

"Penniken Fields," Alyss said again.

They stayed close together, the better to remain within the protection of the NRG shield. The Glass Eyes were now entering Wondronia by the smail-loads, having gotten the better of the rook's T-Cup, and they fired orb generators, crystal shot, and razor-cards at the Alyssians while the scorpspitters let fly with round after round of their poison bullets. The bullets splatted against the NRG shield; the crystal shot and razor-cards bounced off of it, visiting damage upon the lobby's restaurants and theaters and shops.

"Couldn't we at least *run?*" the rook asked.

"No," said Alyss.

Penniken Fields: the largest indoor park in Wonderland; a masterpiece of landscape architecture that might have made Nature jealous if it hadn't paid such beautiful homage to Her with its arrangements of flower beds and shade trees, meandering paths, picturesque ponds, streams, and gently sloping vistas. At the Fields, the architect had managed to hide the ceiling behind the deep blue of an artificially produced atmosphere complete with clouds. With Glass Eyes and scorpspitters trailing them, Alyss led the others to a meadow bordered on one side by a hedge three Wonderlanders tall.

"Now we wait until there are more of them," she said. "Keep me informed."

"Keep you—?"

Mentally, she was already deep within herself. She had to focus, to concentrate on imagining a weapon that could explode with ten times the force of an orb generator. She thought of the munitions factory in the flatlands between Outerwilderbeastia and the suburbs of Wondertropolis that she'd once toured.

"How many Glass Eyes are there?" she asked.

"About a hundred," answered Dodge.

Not enough. She remembered the production line where orb generators were assembled. She visualized the round, lightweight casings that might have been balls in a children's game if not for the arrangement of molecules and atoms they contained.

"How many now?"

"Somewhere between three and four hundred maybe."

In her imagination's eye, she gazed into the hot center of an orb generator—the chambers that would open into one another on impact, allowing the nuclei they held to fuse in a chain reaction that gave the weapon its deadly force.

"And now?" She was tired. The protective cocoon, the outsized orb generator—all this imagining required stamina, physical strength.

"I have no idea," Dodge said. "A lot."

She opened her eyes and saw nearly a thousand of them. This had better work. She wouldn't be able to maintain the NRG shield for much longer.

With the sound of a straining girder—*eeeeeeeeeeeeeeehh*—the largest orb generator ever seen by Wonderlanders dropped from the artificial sky: armageddon for the Glass Eyes in Penniken Fields.

WaboooooooooooooOOOOOOOOOOOOOOOOOMMMB!

The force of the explosion knocked Alyss and the others through the hedge that bordered the meadow and served a double function—as decorative planting and as camouflage for the wall behind it. Alyss and Dodge, the chessmen and generals went crashing through the wall and out to the street below. Alyss lost her imaginative focus; the protective cocoon was dissolving as they hit the pavement, making their landing not as pain-free as it might have been.

Stunned, they were still picking themselves up when—

Thew, thew, thew, thew!

A whir of S-shaped blades, spinning fast around a common axis, coptered over their heads and sliced through an unnoticed Glass Eye that, from a fourth-story window of the Wondronia Hotel across the street, had been taking aim at them with an orb cannon.

Thew, thew, thew!

The weapon boomeranged back to the gloved hand of its owner, Hatter Madigan. With a flick of the wrist, he returned it to its innocuous incarnation as a top hat and set it on his head.

"I'm ready to return to service, if my queen will allow it," he said, bowing to Alyss.

"Hatter!" She would have hugged him if she hadn't thought he'd be bothered by the display of affection.

"Pretty good timing." Dodge smiled. "A little sooner and you would've been perfect."

The eight generals surrounded the Milliner, each insisting on shaking his hand and offering a hearty welcome.

"Your return is a boon to the confidence of our military," said one General Gänger.

"The queendom simply isn't the same without you," enthused another.

"Welcome, welcome!" cried a pair of General Doppels.

Bleep bleep. Bleep bleep.

"Incoming transmission." The rook pressed a button on the keypad strapped to his forearm. A projector-like light beamed out of the nozzle on his ammo belt. A screen formed in the air, visible to all, on which Bibwit appeared, still in the palace's briefing room.

"Were we not in the midst of a crisis, Queen Alyss," gushed the royal tutor, "I would tell you that I am as proud as I've ever been of any of my students! Such a clever strategy you employed! Such victorious ways! Such wisdom in so young and inexperienced a sovereign!"

"Bibwit?" the queen said.

"Quite right, yes. I shall embarrass you with praise some other time. There *are* still troops of Glass Eyes in Wondertropolis, but few enough now to be handled by our card soldiers and chessmen. You must return to the relative safety of the palace so that we can discuss what's to be done about the woman who is to remain nameless—by whom, I think you know, I mean your aunt Redd."

"Bibwit . . . have you seen Homburg Molly? It's unlike her not to throw herself into a fight where she can show off her skills."

"It is not at all like her," the tutor agreed, "but I haven't seen the girl."

While Hatter tried to act as if Molly's whereabouts didn't mean everything to him, Alyss quickly scanned the palace with her imagination. She didn't glimpse her bodyguard anywhere.

Probably still sulking because I sent her off. She'll have to learn not to take things so personally.

"Expect us momentarily, Bibwit," she said.

The tutor's ears dipped in acknowledgment. The screen faded, the transmission ended.

"My queen," said the knight, "with your permission, as long as a single one of my chessmen risks death against the Glass Eyes, so must I."

"I should stay and fight," agreed the rook.

One glance at Dodge and Alyss could tell that he wanted to stay and fight too. *Till every living vestige of The Cat is rent from the world for all time.* It was ironic that to keep him from further risking his life and sanity for revenge, she had to tempt him with a greater opportunity to accomplish its end.

"Dodge," she said, "the Glass Eyes are only foot soldiers, as you've said yourself. Redd and The Cat won't be so easily coaxed into the open. Come with me. Together we'll devise a plan to flush them out of wherever they are. Return to the palace with me and we can confront them together."

She held out her hand. The Wonderlanders were silent, and Dodge's jaw looked diamond-hard as he stared off into the distance. But at last he turned to the woman who was both Wonderland's queen and his love. He would follow her.

PART TWO

CHAPTER 16

Montmartre, Paris. June, 1873.

THE PAINTER awoke from a fitful sleep, his nightmares cut short by the cries of his newborn son, who seemed to be suffering unquiet dreams of his own. Outside, rain thrashed the streets and lightning split the sky. The painter's wife complainingly went to check on the baby, and the painter himself stared out the window at the few pedestrians making their way through the downpour; with their shoulders hunched and their heads bowed, they looked—to his trained eye—furtive and morose, people bent on illicit errands.

"What are you gawking at?"

His wife was standing at the door of their room with the whimpering baby in her arms. If he'd had any doubt before, he had none now: Her mood was as foul as the weather. What did he propose to do about the landscape he'd been commissioned to paint with a storm raging the way it was, she wanted to know. How was she supposed to pay for the milk and butter they needed? No wonder the child was bawling all the time with such a useless thing for a father!

To get away from her, the painter locked himself in his studio, where he sat sulking and blinking at his blank canvas. But after what felt like an endless morning, the weather broke: The sky was overcast, the sodden streets blanched by a flat, pallid light.

"It will have to do."

He packed up his box of paints and brushes and, with a folded easel under his arm, escaped into the streets. The gutters were choked with mud and litter. The rumble of carriages attacked his ears like the roaring of giant beasts, and the faces of those he passed, peering out sullenly from between lowered hat brims and upturned collars, seemed marred by unfriendliness if not outright hostility.

In the Jardin des Tuileries, he placed his easel next to an oval pond, with a view across its surface to a stand of chestnut trees. Normally a quick painter who finished canvases in a matter of hours, this one gave him trouble for some reason. He tried to empty his mind, to forget the morning's fret and lose himself in the ecstasy of creation. But when he put away his brushes at the end of the afternoon, his canvas boasted little more than the clouds of color that comprised his background tones, in the middle of which he was surprised to see daubs of black paint.

"Let's have a look at what you've done," his wife commanded when he returned to the apartment. She reached for the canvas. Her lips pursed in perplexity, her brow collapsed. The baby, whom she held absently in one arm, began to cry. "What are *these*?" She pointed to the spots of black paint.

"I will correct them tomorrow," he said.

"You'd better or you won't get paid, and then where will we be?"

The next day's painting went much like the first. He struggled to tap the vein of inspiration, to let himself become hypnotized by the wonder of nature, the rhythmic dipping of his brush in oils and the feel of its bristles on canvas. When he packed up his supplies in the late afternoon, he was stunned to see, amid the rough contours of pond and trees he had produced with hours of effort, that not only were the daubs of black paint still there, they were larger and more detailed—not daubs at all but the crude beginnings of human figures walking over the pond's surface toward . . . him. Nor were they strictly black in color. One of the figures had taken on a decisively reddish hue.

He covered the painting with his jacket to avoid looking at it and, full of a foreboding he couldn't explain, started the walk home, passing squalid brasseries and dingy apartment houses he had never noticed before. His usual route was blocked off, clogged with onlookers of some police activity—the crowd so greedy for a glimpse of others' misfortune that he became frightened and turned off into the nearest lane. He took an unfamiliar course home and was hiding in his studio when his wife burst in.

"I want to see it," she said.

"I don't . . . It's not . . . " he stammered.

She noticed his jacket hanging over the easel. "Is that it?"

"No."

She stepped to the easel before he could stop her, yanked the jacket off and—

"You said you were going to fix them!" she protested when she saw the strange figures. "Do you want your son to starve? Are you trying to kill us through hardship?"

After three full days in the Tuileries, there was hardly any landscape to speak of; the pond, the chestnut trees—the painter had buried all beneath streaks and daubs of paint that formed the two figures who had so hijacked his imagination. The palette he had used to render them was more primary than usual—consisting of heavy reds, blacks, and browns—but, as in all his paintings, the hard lines of the figures were blurred to suggest the constant movement of things. One of the figures wasn't human but a broad-chested creature with overmuscled arms and legs and, where its hands should have been, thick paws with claws as glittering and long as polished carving knives. What's more, it had the face of a cat, complete with whiskers and a menacing set of fangs. The other figure was probably a woman, though nothing about the thick bramble of red hair or the sneerful face with its wrinkles of disgust and eyes steeled with condescension suggested femininity. No, it was the couture that made the painter think the figure was a woman—a dress made entirely of thorny roses and their long, twisting vines. The blooms on several of the roses faced him, their innermost petals baring teeth like eager mouths hungry for a bite of . . . he didn't like to guess.

In his studio, hiding from his wife, he threw the painting on the fire. The haunting figures were gone, cinders and ash; burning them had been for the best. But by noon the following day, among the background tones that had been all he'd managed to set on canvas, were two black splotches of paint he didn't remember making. He painted over them immediately. *Paint a landscape, any landscape.* But they were already back by the time he was packing up to go home: the humanoid feline and the cruel woman in her dress of roses, taking up his entire canvas.

His next attempt turned out exactly like the others. As did the one after that. He could paint nothing but the cat-beast and the snarling woman. Bitter and depressed, he welcomed his wife's scoldings. He deserved them; he was a failure. He carried his failings to a nameless alley. He entered a nameless establishment where neither beauty nor virtue were to be found—just cheap wine, which he slung down his throat until he could see nothing clearly, until everything inside and outside his head was a tilting carousel, spinning around in a blear of colors and textures. He had to dull his senses, had to keep himself from envisioning the cat-beast and its female companion.

Somehow, in the early dawn, and despite lampposts frequently darting into his path, he made it back to his apartment. In the unlit studio, he couldn't see his latest attempt at a landscape, but he sensed it—a large canvas as tall as himself covered with a bedsheet and leaning against a wall in the corner.

"What's that?" he said aloud because he thought he'd heard . . . was that the sheet rustling? Did he hear breathing? Purring?

"Ngah!"

He gasped awake, still in his suit. He lit the lamp and gazed around, trying to focus his thoughts, to understand what had—

"My God!"

The studio door was in splinters. The sheet that had been covering his painting lay on the floor. He started to lift his glance. He didn't want to look; he was afraid. But he had to: Slowly, he raised his eyes to what was left of the canvas, too horrified to cry out at what he saw. Where the cat-beast and woman had been there was nothing, just a hole exactly the shape of their outlines, as if someone had cut them out of the picture or—

"Impossible," the painter breathed.

Because things like that didn't happen. A pair of painted

figures escaping their canvas? It was a joke. Inanimate figures did not come to life as in some fairy tale. It was one thing for his paintings to suggest vitality and life, but to have actually created them? With nothing more than brushes and oils?

"It's impossible! Impossible!" he kept repeating.

But if it was impossible, why did he have a dream-fuzzed memory of the ferocious woman and cat-beast standing over him as he curled in his cot, sleeping off his drunk, a memory in which he was both participant and observer?

"The only reason I don't kill him," he remembered the woman saying, her voice sounding like the scrape of iron against iron, a corrosion of vocal cords, "is because he's not important enough."

CHAPTER 17

MOLLY'S HEAD felt like it had been cracked open and poorly fit back together. Her shoulders ached. Her forearms tingled raw, as if skinned. Her swollen hands were so sensitive that it hurt to make a fist. It hurt to do most things—including blink, so she lay with her eyes closed, remembering what had happened: the Lady of Diamonds; the carved wooden chest that was supposed to have gone to Queen Alyss; her suspicion of a plot to upset Alyss' reign (which, judging by her present pains, had not been ill-placed). But an attempt on the queen's life? The Lady of Diamonds was bolder than she had supposed. Alyss had to be informed.

Molly forced herself to sit up and open her eyes. What the—? King Arch was sitting in a chair next to her mattress. What was Arch doing in Wonderland?

"She lives," he said.

A minister scurried in on silent feet and whispered in the king's ear, which was when she realized: Arch wasn't in Wonderland; she was in Boarderland. But how had she ended up in Boarderland? Where was her gear? And *what* was she wearing that encased her like a second skin? Instead of her usual pants and belt, she had on a formfitting one-piece made of some unfamiliar pink material, and there were no visible buttons or clasps by which to remove it. The collar fit tightly about her neck, the leggings tightly around her ankles, and the cuffs of the long sleeves came close to choking off the blood supply to her hands. She hated tight-fitting clothes. Worse, she hated pink.

"Send her in with the dumplings," Arch told the minister, who left as quietly as a curl of smoke. The king smiled down at Molly. "And how are we feeling after our much-needed nap?"

"Where are my things?"

"Right there."

He pointed to a table across the room, on which her homburg, Millinery coat, backpack, belt, and wrist-blades were neatly arrayed. Standing on either side of the table were two creatures from a species she had never seen before.

"You underestimate me," she said, and lunged for her gear.

Her legs gave way as if they'd been shorn of all muscle. Her arms were useless and she was unable to steady her vision, as if her eyes were swirling in their sockets independently of each other. She fell to the floor. Far, far away she felt someone pick her up and set her back down. Her head began to settle and she found herself on the mattress.

"It seems, Molly, it is you who underestimates me," Arch said. "I should've perhaps told you the item you're wearing is a drug-delivery system. When you make any sudden move, it will secrete through your skin a certain something that . . . Well, I hope you'll never succumb to the illusory charms of artificial crystal, but let's just say that this certain something produces an effect similar to a night of overindulgence with such unhealthy ingestives."

"What do you want with me?" she asked.

"You had an unpleasant tumble." He nodded toward the unfamiliar creatures. "My Ganmede friends and I are nursing you back to health, that's all."

"By drugging me?"

Molly tried to intimidate him with her most vicious glare, but not getting much of a response, she fell to pulling at her collar and the cuffs at her wrists.

"You might as well try to remove your own skin," Arch said. "Please understand, Molly. I have no intention of harming you. The Lady of Diamonds has caused you enough inconvenience, I think. Your flattering outfit is simply a precaution in case you overreact at finding yourself here. I hope that soon you'll choose to stay here as my personal guest."

Molly rose to her feet—slowly, steadily. "I have a duty to

my queen, who will be missing me. I would like to go home now."

"I wouldn't be so hasty. The queen you left might not be the one you return to."

He was trying to trick her into something. She would be smart. She would keep her mouth shut, learn as much as possible, and report back to Alyss.

"I want you to know that I find it appalling how the Lady of Diamonds attempted to deceive you," the king said. "You're to be commended for protecting the queen from opening the Lady of Diamonds' 'gift,' however much your doing so has jeopardized the queendom itself." Seeing Molly's questioning expression, he explained: "Yes, it seems your little adventure in the Crystal Continuum has limited the mobility of Queen Alyss' army, a circumstance the Diamond clan has taken advantage of to try and gain the crown."

Molly didn't believe him, *refused* to believe him. Besides, the Lady of Diamonds could never defeat Alyss Heart.

Arch rose from his chair and paced about the tent. "The Diamonds came to me for support, but as you can see, my loyalty lies with Queen Alyss rather than with a scheming lady of rank in her queendom." He was at the table, picking over her wrist-blades and coat and backpack as if they were a merchant's untidy wares. "I should never have been so dismissive of you when we first met at Heart Palace. I should have realized that you possessed formidable skills, since it's not anyone who can take Hatter Madigan's place."

Molly said nothing.

"Your parents must be extremely proud of you." He turned abruptly to face her. "Oh, I'm sorry. I forgot that you don't have parents."

King or not, he was lucky she didn't have access to her homburg.

Arch sat back down in his chair and, with practiced nonchalance, asked, "Do you know much about the people who brought you into this world?"

"I know enough."

"Really? Is that why you don't seem very curious about them?"

"There's nothing to be curious about," she said.

"Nothing to be . . . ? But don't you want to know why they gave you up?"

"They didn't give me up!"

She flung herself at him, but her legs refused to obey her, her arms belonged to somebody else, and her head filled with kaleidoscopic jelly. When her wits were again hers, she was back on the mattress.

"I apologize," Arch said. "I should have taken into account how the trials of life can break a family apart for reasons that have nothing to do with ill will or a lack of love in any of its members. With Redd in control of Wonderland as she was, the actions of your parents might have only appeared uncaring, when in fact they were just the opposite—necessary to your survival."

"Uh-huh," Molly said, hating him.

"Do you, by chance, remember how old you were when you last saw your mother?"

She wasn't going to answer. She would tell this man nothing, especially not that she'd been just three lunar years old when Weaver left the Alyssian camp in the Everlasting Forest and that, if not for the holographic crystal of her mother posing in front of the Unnatural History Museum shortly before Redd's coup, she wouldn't even know what the woman looked like.

"Her name was Weaver, wasn't it?"

Molly was startled. "How'd you know that?"

He waved off the question. "I've hardly begun to astound you, Molly. Not only do I know your mother's name, I know who your father is. And what's more, so do you. You've already met him."

Molly was so taken aback by all of this that she didn't hear Arch call for his bodyguards. Shadows fell over her as Ripkins and Blister entered the tent.

"Molly wants to know her father's name," Arch said to them. "Why don't we give her a hint?"

"His first name rhymes with 'splatter,'" said Ripkins.

"And 'matter,'" put in Blister.

"Also 'fatter,'" said Ripkins.

"Likewise 'chatter,'" added Blister.

"And his surname?" Arch asked.

"It rhymes with 'that again,'" said Ripkins.

"And 'Flanagan,'" put in Blister.

"Also, um . . . 'pad a fin'?" offered Ripkins. "Or 'pan a tin'?"

Arch and Blister looked at him.

"'Pannikin'!" he said proudly.

"Shut up, shut up, shut up!" Molly screamed. "You don't know what you're talking about!"

"Perhaps not," Arch said. "But I can think of at least one person whose knowledge you'll trust." He got to his feet as a strange aroma wafted into the tent. "Here she comes now with a plate of DoDo dumplings, one of my favorite Boarderland delicacies, to help you regain your strength."

Ready to deny all, to denounce Boarderland as a nation of liars, Molly turned and saw the last person in the world she had ever expected to see alive.

"M-Mom?"

CHAPTER 18

REDD FOUND her usual bitterness amplified by her passage through the Heart Crystal. The roses of her dress gnawed the air, their petal-mouths mutely opening and closing in echo of her black melancholy as she stalked the predawn streets of this alien city and lashed herself with gloomy thoughts.

"If anyone tells you it's painless to be turned into pure NRG and formed again from the muck of some Earth person's imagination," Redd hissed, "don't believe them."

"I won't, Your Imperial Viciousness." The Cat glanced sidelong at his mistress, licked a paw and rubbed it over his eyes.

"If I'm not powerful enough to defeat Alyss . . . " Redd murmured, and dropped into a depressed silence.

The otherworldly pair walked the length and breadth of

Montmartre, not knowing what else to do. Few people were out and about, and none had passed within twenty yards of them when Redd stopped as if slapped.

"I *am* more powerful than that disgustingly well-intentioned niece of mine!"

But what if her journey through the crystal had weakened her power, diluted it to a laughable remnant of what it used to be? *What if what if what if.* She would test it, flex the muscle of her imagination, and it would tell her all. She reached a hand out to nothing. A stick as long as one of The Cat's claws formed in her palm, extended lengthwise until it resembled the twisty, knobby thing she'd used as a scepter in Wonderland.

"You try," she said to The Cat, who morphed from humanoid to kitten and back again, testing his own powers.

"Good."

But Her Imperial Viciousness wasn't done. She banged the end of her makeshift scepter on the pavement and, from the point of impact, cracks branched out in all directions, widening enough to let vines of flesh-eating roses slither out of them. Growing at a rate never before seen in nature, the vines methodically covered the entire block—buildings, lampposts, street, and sidewalk. It was then that an unfortunate butcher, hurrying to his shop at this early hour as was his custom, emerged from his apartment. He saw the roses and the menacing figures of Redd and The Cat and he tried to run, but the thorn-laden vines wrapped around his ankles and held him rooted. Thorns dug into him as the vines wound up and around his legs, torso, and arms. He opened his mouth to scream and a vine stuffed itself down his throat.

"It's like watching an enjoyable narrative on an entertainment crystal back on Mount Isolation," Redd said as the roses finished with the butcher. She motioned with her stick—a conductor leading her orchestra—and the roses retracted into the pavement's cracks. "You've been to this world before, Cat. Take me to where I can sulk and complain in peace. Someplace suitable to my delicate temperament."

"Yes, Your Imperial Viciousness."

The Cat preferred not to admit his ignorance. True, he had recently plunged through the Pool of Tears and traveled to Earth in his hunt for the exiled Alyss Heart, but nothing looked familiar to him and he was certain that he had never been in this city. He led Redd through a series of turns and along countless blocks. They rounded a corner and came upon the dead butcher. They had traveled in a circle.

"You don't know where we are?" Redd asked.

Her voice was so quiet that it made the fur between The Cat's ears stand on end. He hadn't risked a leap into the Heart Crystal only to die now.

"When I was last on Earth," he said cautiously, "I must not have come to this city."

"Tell it to the steel," Redd snarled, conjuring the end of her stick into a blade, with which she was about to pierce him, when—

"I have only one life left," he reminded her.

She held the spear aloft, ready to strike. With a grunt of vexation, she lowered it, imagined the blade-end back into a nonlethal nub, and jabbed it against his chest with every other word. "Then you'll have to be more helpful in the future, won't you? Because I might not be so lenient a second time."

The Cat licked his paw and rubbed his eyes.

"Why do you keep doing that?" she asked, annoyed.

"What?"

Redd pretended to lick her hand and rub her eye.

"Don't take this the wrong way, Your Imperial Viciousness, but I look around and everything is clear and hard. Except you. You're . . . blurry."

"You're not so clear yourself," Redd snapped. "It's probably just the lingering effects of the Heart Crystal."

She had noticed it too: The Cat out of focus while everything around him was clear and distinct. It was the same whenever she looked at any part of her body. She seemed to exist within a soft fuzz, the edges of herself dissolving into the surrounding air. Not until she and The Cat passed a furniture shop on the Avenue de Clichy and she glimpsed her reflection in an oval looking glass did she understand the cause.

"That hack of a painter! His style was too soft! His coloring too gentle!" She exploded the mirror into thousands of fragments with the force of her anger. "I'll kill him!"

The Cat was all for it, but neither he nor Redd could remember the way to the painter's studio. Her Imperial

Viciousness focused her thoughts, searched for him with her imagination's eye. But she wasn't sure where to look; no vision of the painter or his studio appeared. Instead, the eye of her imagination alighted on a crumbling stone staircase half hidden by garbage in an alley behind a charcuterie. The bottommost steps were lost in darkness as unremitting as the grave, a darkness that, for generations, had attracted lesser beings given to Black Imagination—occultists, drug addicts, outcasts seeking a shelter devoid of society's judgment, thieves and murderers seeking refuge from the police.

"Come," Redd said. "I've found a place for us."

Descending the crumbling stairs, enveloped by the darkness, Redd and The Cat entered a dank catacomb whose size was belied by the echo of their footfalls. Redd conjured a throne for herself, its seat and backrest resembling a splayed-open rose blossom, its legs and armrests thick, petrified rose vines. Her Imperial Viciousness flopped down into the throne like a woman falling into her favorite chair after a hard day's work.

"You best remember how to return to Wonderland," she warned The Cat.

"I remember, Your Imperial Viciousness. The portals look like ordinary puddles. I'll know them when I see them."

"Let's hope for your health that you will. But it'd be no use returning to Wonderland now, when my army is at best scattered and at worst imprisoned en masse."

Her assassin began to clean himself. "With your strength

and power, you could rule as much of this world as you wanted."

Redd's nostrils flared with impatience. "I know it's difficult for you, Cat, but try to use your brain, as small as it is. Why would I want to lord myself over this world when it's nothing but a weak reflection of my birthplace? Wonderland belongs to *me*. I intend to get what's mine."

"Won-der-land!" echoed a voice in the dark. "How long it's been since I've set foot on her soil!"

A flickering glow bobbed toward them from the distance of a tunnel: a torch, carried by what appeared to be a dead man, as emaciated as he was and having the complexion of a week-old cadaver. He was dressed entirely in black and wore black gloves. In addition to the torch, he carried a violin case. With him was a tall, bald albino with elongated ears sprouting from his head and a map of veins visible beneath semi-transparent skin: a near twin to Bibwit Harte, identical in every feature except that his nose was more pointed and his cheeks pitted with acne scars. Neither he nor his cadaverous companion showed signs of alarm at the sight of creatures as extraordinary as Redd and The Cat.

"Are you from Wonderland?" the albino asked.

Redd knew a member of the tutor species when she saw one. She also knew that the tutor before her must be a criminal—someone who had leaped into the Pool of Tears to avoid prosecution in Wonderland courts and make what life he could for himself in this antiquated world. She might have considered such ex-Wonderlanders sooner. She could put them to nasty purpose.

"What business is it of yours where we're from?"

"It's none of my business whatsoever," the stranger answered. "It's just that I used to have a few friends in Wonderland. The one I'm most curious about, however, I can no longer with justice call my friend."

"Justice is overrated," Redd brooded.

"Quite," the stranger agreed. "But perhaps you know this former friend of mine? He's a tutor, as am I, and he likely holds a position of eminence in the queendom. His name is Harte."

"Everyone knows Bibwit Harte," The Cat said. "He's tutored three queens."

With growing interest, Redd asked, "Who are *you* that you've made an enemy of him?"

"My name is Vollrath. Mr. Harte and I were in the Tutor Corps together many, many moons ago, when Queen Issa was still a newborn princess. We were, the top two students in our class, but for as long as we were in the Corps, Mr. Harte remained first-in-class while I was supposed to be content with second. I am incapable of being satisfied with second place in anything, so . . . " the tutor's ears angled back, stiff, as if buffeted by a strong wind, " . . . not wanting to be forever at Mr. Harte's heels in the propagation of White Imagination, I began to devote my knowledge and intellect to the service of Black Imagination. And with as much truthfulness as I allow myself—for too much makes one dull, dull, dull—I may say that I became its premier scholar. I offered my services to any Black Imagination practitioners willing to pay me the outlandish sums I demanded, and I lived a life of glorious decadence. But about the time of Issa's coronation, I became entangled with an overambitious smuggler and it became necessary for me to throw myself into the Pool of Tears. I haven't been back to Wonderland since."

A graduate of the Tutor Corps in the service of Black Imagination? A scholar of malice and foe of Bibwit Harte? It was time for Redd to announce herself:

"I am Redd Heart, granddaughter of Queen Issa and eldest daughter of Queen Theodora and King Tyman, both of whom are dead."

Vollrath immediately dropped to one knee, his head bowed. "I didn't realize I was conversing with royalty," he said. "I apologize for my lack of proper respect, Princess."

Princess. Redd bridled at the word. "You might ask why Wonderland's heir apparent is in this foul and slummy place. The answer: because my birthright has twice been denied me, once by a traitorous mother who connived with my younger sister (both dead by my hand), and again by an upstart niece who this moment wears the crown that looks so much better on my head than it does on hers. Now get up. And call me 'Your Imperial Viciousness.'"

Vollrath rose to his feet and put a thoughtful finger to his bloodless lips, about to speak, when—

"Monsieur Vollrath," the skinny torch-bearer said, "unless you want to be late . . . "

"Yes, yes, Marcel. Your Imperial Viciousness, if you will deign to tell me, I'd like to hear more about your niece—and of course, what you intend to do to her—but I'm presently on my way to an engagement in a catacomb not far from here. I'd be honored if you and your feline friend would join me as my special guests. The entertainment is to be provided by a pupil of mine—one who, although not from Wonderland, has talents I think you'll appreciate. Afterward, we may discuss your niece at our leisure, and if I can be of any service to you whatsoever, I shall not hesitate."

So Redd and The Cat followed Vollrath and Marcel along a zigzag of cobwebbed tunnels until they emerged into a catacomb well lit by torches. Though large, the crypt was crammed with tables. At one end, opposite a bar made of coffins, a pile of human bones took up most of an elevated stage. In the center of the room, a heavy-set man with an ink-dark mustache was urging on what appeared to be waiters readying the room for an influx of customers.

"Chop chop!" the man was booming. "Chop chop! Sacrenoir's performance will begin on time or not at all! Marcel, where have you been?"

"Forgive my delay, Master Sacrenoir," Marcel said.

"I'm to blame for our tardiness," interrupted Vollrath. "But I've just made what I hope will be a profitable association for all of us. This is Her Imperial Viciousness, Redd Heart, and her feline companion, who have just arrived from my former home." Addressing the Wonderlanders, he said: "This robust gentleman is Master Sacrenoir, a former apothecary from Lyons gifted in a particularly unsavory practice of black magic."

"A 'master,' is he?" Redd said, amused.

Sacrenoir eyed the visitors. "I hope the lack of focus so evident in their persons doesn't represent what's within their heads. I need to check on my bones." The magician hulked over to the stage, where he made a great clatter rearranging femurs and pelvic bones and skulls.

"Master Sacrenoir has never shown much talent for courtesy," Vollrath said, "especially before a performance. Come, we shall sit at the best table in the house."

The tutor led Redd and The Cat to an alcove at the left of the stage, separated from the main room by a curtain of heavy black velvet. Within the alcove was a single table.

"We should be comfortable here," said Vollrath. "We have an unobstructed view of the stage, but if I pull the curtain partway closed, like so, we have complete privacy, as we're out of sight from the audience. Any refreshments you desire are of course compliments of moi."

Guests were starting to arrive, and Marcel had hurried over to the catacomb's entrance to greet them. "Good evening, my pretty friends! Good evening! And how fortunate you are to be at the master's one and only Paris performance! The event is shortly to begin! You risk the master's wrath if you don't immediately take your seats! Also, let's not forget, there's a two-drink minimum."

The guests consisted solely of the wealthy and aristocratic, the women decked out in pearls and embroidered lace, smoking cigarettes through long ebony holders, while the men looked sophisticated in their tuxedos, tapping canes of polished rosewood against polished shoes as they sipped absinthe from narrow glasses. Within minutes, the catacomb filled to capacity. Touched by no human hand, an iron gate clanked shut across the entrance, unnoticed by the illustrious guests packed in at their tables, who were chatting loudly and laughing the hearty laughter of the privileged until—

Ffftsssst!

The room fell dark, the torches miraculously snuffed out as one. A woman screamed. A ripple of titillated laughter passed among the tables. A violin began to play a melody at once languid and stern, the work of no known composer. With the sudden crack of breaking wood—

Voila! A single cone of light illuminated Sacrenoir standing center stage before his pile of bones. In the light's dusky reaches, black-gloved Marcel could be seen playing his violin.

"Hurrah!" the audience cried. "Sacrenoir, magician extraordinaire!"

They rose to their feet, whistling and applauding and calling out in approval. Sacrenoir put a finger to his lips—*Ssshh!*—and waited until they had resumed their seats, quiet with expectation.

"It is said that when a person dies," he began in a voice that seemed to address not those before him, but a numberless multitude as yet unseen, "whichever of his animal appetites are left unsated at the time of his death do not die but live on in the ether, in the very air we breathe, waiting to take up residence in another. I say, let the dead have their appetites back!"

"Give the dead their appetites!" the audience shouted.

Sacrenoir closed his eyes and his lips moved in an incantation impossible to hear over the strains of Marcel's violin. The bones piled behind him began to shift and creak.

"Oooooh!" someone moaned, in imitation of a ghost, and everyone laughed.

Neither Sacrenoir nor Marcel seemed aware of the audience, the one mesmerized by his own incantation while Marcel's melody rose to a crescendo, his bow streaking faster and faster on the strings of his violin. The bones skittered and scraped across the stage, arranging themselves into complete skeletons and, as if sprung from their very marrow, rotted burial clothes formed, hanging loose from hips and shoulders. The audience sat rapt and horrified.

The resurrected dead turned empty eye sockets on the crowd, fleshless jaws moving up and down in a grotesque imitation of speech. But the sounds coming from those empty throats and tongueless mouths, and which passed through clicking teeth, were no imitations.

"Hungry," the skeletons chanted, stepping off the stage and moving among the tables. "Hungry, hungry, hungry."

One gentleman who'd been gulping absinthe with abandon mumbled that magic was only harmless illusion. He got to his feet and began to dance with the nearest skeleton, reached out to twirl his skeleton-partner and—

"Gaaaaaahghg!"

The skeleton's jaws clamped down hard on his hand. With a relentless turn of the skull, it tore off three of the man's fingers and swallowed them and they clattered through its rib cage and fell to the floor. Shouts erupted. In an instant, tables were being overturned, glasses broken, drinks flung into the air, torches knocked from the walls, setting fire to the puddles of spilled alcohol. The iron gate remained locked, the audience trapped. Again and again, the skeletons lurched at them with hungry jaws. Yet the dead were unable to fill their bellies. Every swallow of living flesh passed down through their empty rib cages and splatted on the floor.

"Hungry," they chanted. "Hungry, hungry."

Sacrenoir gazed upon the carnage with pride. Marcel continued to play his violin, though his melody was now drowned out by screams and moans. Redd and The Cat remained with Vollrath in their alcove, its curtain pushed completely open so that they could get a better view of things. The last guest collapsed to the floor. Marcel set down his violin and for a time there was only the sound of the skeletons chomping desperately on the wealth of fresh kill, then—

"Bravo," Redd called out, bored, with a single clap of her hands.

Alerted to her presence, the skeletons turned, started jigging toward her, the snap and clack of their jaws answered by the eagerly chomping roses of her dress. "Hungry, hun—"

The Cat sprung from his seat. With a single swing of his arm, he shattered four skeletons into so many pieces that all of Sacrenoir's powers could not have put them together again.

"Don't waste your strength," Redd yawned.

The Cat stepped aside and watched as, motioning with a finger from where she sat, his mistress sent one skeleton careening into another. She again gestured with her finger and two skeletons slammed together and fractured to crumbs. But Redd was not known for her patience, so she sucked air deep into her lungs, imagined the heat of jabberwocky breath as her own and exhaled, her breath hot enough to disintegrate every bone of every skeleton to dust. And even before she pressed forefinger against thumb to douse the numerous fires burning around the catacomb, Sacrenoir was bowing before her.

"Forgive my former rudeness, Your Imperial Viciousness. I didn't realize the extent of your powers, to which mine compare as a candle flame to the great fire of London. If you'll accept of it from such an undeserving wretch as here kneels before you, I offer you my eternal allegiance."

As Redd considered, she turned to Vollrath. The tutor inclined his head and smiled, having expected his pupil to grant her proper respect all along.

"You were right not to subordinate yourself too readily,

Master Sacrenoir," Redd said at length. "I would find no value in the allegiance of a fool ready to give himself up to any old hag of Black Imagination who presented herself. I will accept your allegiance. For now. But if I ever decide you're useless, you are a dead man."

"To be killed by you is to be desired more than a life excluded from your service."

"Bravo," Her Imperial Viciousness laughed with genuine feeling. "Bra-vo!"

Hardly ten hours removed from the crystal, Redd Heart had found her first two recruits. And if Vollrath and Sacrenoir were any indication, the army of ex-Wonderlanders and talented earthlings she was determined to amass would be a stronger military than the one she'd used to wrench the crown from Genevieve. With the discipline and single-minded purpose she would instill in troops so gifted in Black Imagination, she would not, could not, fail to overthrow her nauseatingly well-intentioned niece.

CHAPTER 19

Doomsine Encampment, Boarderland.
Six lunar cycles earlier.

W HEN KING Arch learned that the newly crowned
Alyss Heart had ordered the annihilation of all Glass Eyes
in her realm, his scheming brain went into hyperdrive. He
had occupied Boarderland's throne for more than half his life
by remaining several ruthless steps ahead of his enemies. To
what particular use he might put an army of Glass Eyes, he
wasn't yet sure. But to have access to such a military force
without anyone knowing he had it was an advantage he
could not let pass.

Lounging in his palace tent with wives numbered eleven,
six, seventeen and twenty-eight, all of whom were trying not

to look or act depressed, he called Ripkins and Blister to his side.

"My ministers have informed me that Alyss is ridding her land of Glass Eyes."

"Her people can't control them," confirmed Blister.

"Overriding the imperative that Redd embedded in them is harder than she thought," added Ripkins.

"In other words, they're designed to kill and nothing more."

The bodyguards bowed that this was so.

"Perhaps the trick is not to override their imperative," Arch mused, "but to reprogram them to acknowledge a different master. Everyone in Wonderland—even the otherwise rebellious Redd Heart—is, was, or always has been occupied with inventing *things*. But what good are things if there are no clever schemes in which to use them? I put *things* to unexpected and imaginative use."

The man wasn't named *Arch* for nothing. Arch politician. Arch tactician. Arch strategist. By the age of seventeen, he had risen through the ranks of his birth tribe, the Onu, to become Boarderland's first sovereign. Before his ascension, the country's nomadic tribes had been completely independent, with nothing in common other than the landscape over which they traveled. He had forced them into having something else in common: the honor, respect, and obedience they showed to him. This, he often reminded his ministers, was what *united* the tribes of Boarderland. His subjugation of them gave the nation its identity, its focus and culture.

"I'm a uniter, not a divider," he would laugh.

By the time he crowned himself, he had amassed his own tribe, the Doomsines, having siphoned off from the Onu and others the most skilled fighters, the smartest intel ministers, the most beautiful females to become his wives and servants. He had also recruited numerous wayward souls and misfits from Boarderton, Boarderland's de facto capital city. Among the Boarderton recruits: Ripkins and Blister.

"Leave us," he ordered, shooing his wives toward the exit.

Promptly, and with a tinkling of jewelry, the women removed themselves from the tent.

"You are to enter Wonderland and capture a Glass Eye," he commanded Ripkins and Blister. "I want it fully intact or it will be useless to me. That means every pore of its engineered skin, every swath of its manufactured muscle and tissue, every nanochip and filament in its brain: all undamaged so as to be properly dissected and understood. You must bring back a live one."

Ripkins nodded, but Blister stared coldly at nothing. Impossible to know what he was thinking.

"Do you understand what I'm saying, Blister?"

"I understand."

It had been an annoyingly peaceful time in Boarderland, Blister cranky and depressed because he hadn't filled anyone with pus for nearly an entire lunar cycle. Only the previous day, Arch had found him in a spirit-dane corral, blistering the creatures to the point of death, such was his need to touch and destroy.

"No one can know of your mission," Arch said. "You must remain absolutely invisible. It's necessary for Alyss and her people to believe they will have cleansed the realm of Glass Eyes. I intend to manufacture my own army of them, using the one you bring me as the model from which the rest will be cloned."

Following Ripkins out of the tent, Blister sulkily pinched the blade of a silver-leafed palm between finger and thumb. The blade bubbled, swelled. Then another and another. The longer he held on to the plant, the more it suffered until—

Swollen to bursting, it leaked yellow liquid from every blade, and died, a wilted husk of a thing.

"Intact, Blister," Arch warned.

Blister bowed, was gone.

~

Crossing into Wonderland was, for the average citizen, a tedious way to spend several hours. One had to wait in long lines, undergo elaborate security searches, sit through mild or not-so-mild interrogations conducted by overworked officials. *What is the purpose of your visit? The expected length of your stay?* But Ripkins and Blister had a difficult time blending in with average citizens and so they chose to cross into Alyss' territory, not at one of the official checkpoints, but at an unpopulated spot between a silty edge of Boarderland's Duneraria and a particularly dense patch of Wonderland's Outerwilderbeastia.

To be invisible meant that whatever death and injury the bodyguards caused would have to be done by conventional methods—no ripping or shredding for Ripkins, no blistering for Blister, lest their victims' bodies serve as evidence of their mission. Accordingly, Blister wore elbow-length gloves, and he and Ripkins carried a wealth of traditional Boarderland weapons hidden in their clothes, munitions that might be used by a variety of the nation's tribes: mind riders, remote eyes, kill-quills, gossamer shots. They were likewise armed with the whipsnake grenades and crystal shooters so prevalent in Alyss' armies. But to be invisible also meant that members of their own tribe could not witness their doings; unwanted chatter, possibly compromising intel, could come from any quarter.

The guards patrolling the Boarderland side of the demarcation barrier were members of the Doomsines—two youths born into the Astacan tribe who had found life among their own kind uninspiring. Like all Astacans, their long, spindly legs and foreshortened torsos, which had evolved from generations of Astacans making camp in mountainous regions, rendered them particularly adept at maneuvering on irregular terrain. Some Boarderlanders thought Astacans elegant and graceful creatures, but others—Blister among them, fellow Doomsine or not—thought them grotesque.

"I'm feeling a tad Maldoid-*ish*," Blister said, taking a couple of mind riders from his coat pocket.

Self-propelled darts with serum-infused tips, most commonly used by Boarderland's Maldoid tribe, mind riders could turn the most peace-loving citizen into a brawling lunatic.

"Haven't thrown one in a while," Blister said. "Good to keep in practice."

He and Ripkins stepped into view and the border guards paused in their patrol, surprised to see Arch's notorious henchmen.

"What're you both doing here?" one of them asked.

"Nothing much," Blister said, and with a forward thrust of his arm, released the mind riders.

Thump! Thump!

A mind rider lodged in the forehead of each border guard, tips penetrating their skulls, injecting the angst serum into the nooks and gulleys of their brains. Their neural pathways filled with static. Poison spiked their wits.

The serum never took long to produce its effect.

The Astacans looked about in a daze. Then, as if noticing each other for the first time, their glazed-over expressions morphed into visages of hate.

"Aaaagh!" one of them yelled.

"Yaaah!" the other shouted.

They fell together, punching and kicking at each other with a ferocity that would soon leave them both dead.

Ignoring the brawling pair, Ripkins and Blister stepped

up to the demarcation barrier—a tight, impassable mesh of lightning-like sound waves. To try and step through the barrier, even to venture a single limb tentatively into its mesh, was to invite a painful end. The sound waves would cause one's internal organs to vibrate, generating more and more heat until one burned to death from the inside out.

Ripkins removed a palm-sized medallion from his pocket. With a flick of his thumb, he launched it spinning into the air. Like a coin spinning fast on its edge, the remote eye became almost impossible to see. But unlike a coin, the thing *flew*. Emitting no more sound than the rapid flutter of insect wings, it spun through an opening in the demarcation barrier's mesh and into Wonderland, transmitting images directly back to Ripkins' visual cortex. He saw what it saw: the number and location of card soldiers on border patrol.

"A full hand," he said. "Pair of Threes. Pair of Fours. Lone Two."

The remote eye flew back through the demarcation barrier. Ripkins caught it and stowed it in his pocket. He called out to the card soldiers on the other side of the barrier:

"Pretty dull work, just pacing up and back all day, isn't it? Don't know about you cards, but I didn't sign up for this boring detail! Luckily, I've got something that helps us Boarderland guards pass the time! Come here and I'll show it to you!"

The two nations were not at war and the soldiers had no reason to think of Boarderland guards as enemies. The Three Cards ventured close.

"Yeah?"

They tried to get a view of Ripkins through the eye-squintingly bright sound waves, when—

Thewp! Thewp!

Ripkins harpooned them with kill-quills, yanked hard on the coils attached to the quills' blunt ends and pulled the soldiers into the demarcation barrier's mesh.

Tzzzzzzzzccckkkkkzzzkkkckch!

The dead card soldiers acted as shields, created a gap in the sound waves through which Ripkins and Blister jumped safely into Wonderland, tumbling and rolling because razor-cards were slicing the air and ground all around them, the Four Cards making the most of their AD52s while the Two Card tapped his ammo belt, about to transmit an emergency message via his crystal communicator, except—

Mid-roll, with effortless accuracy, Blister pulled the trigger of his crystal shooter and shot the Two Card dead.

Ripkins lobbed a whipsnake grenade at the Four Cards, and while they danced and hopped to avoid its deadly coils—sending razor-cards everywhere but at their attackers—he and Blister sprinted forward.

Suffering the nasty twistings of body parts that should never be twisted, the card soldiers fell, lifeless, and Arch's bodyguards were soon pushing through the tangles of Outerwilderbeastia, crunching twigs and leaves underfoot.

"Visit the labs?" Blister said, referring to the squat network of buildings in Wondertropolis' warehouse district, where a consortium of Alyss' scientists and engineers had tried to transform a host of captured Glass Eyes into a benign force. On lab grounds were the incinerator baths—large pits into which Glass Eyes were being herded and melted down, scorched into ash. There would be lots of Glass Eyes to choose from at the labs, but Ripkins shook his head.

"Too much security," he said.

"Find one that's roaming?"

"It'll be easier for us to avoid notice," Ripkins said.

"Yeah, but it'd be more *fun* to hit the labs."

The bodyguards knew where they had to go: Mount Isolation in the Chessboard Desert, Redd's former home and the birthplace of those they hunted.

Avoiding the notice of Alyss' card soldiers, who were themselves scouring the land for Glass Eyes still at large, became more difficult when they reached the desert. The alternating quadrants of black lava rock and sun-reflecting ice did not allow for much camouflage.

"Not surprising," Ripkins whispered when they came upon Mount Isolation.

Decks of card soldiers had the place under surveillance. Unable to return home, Glass Eyes might have been hiding nearby.

Careful to avoid detection, the bodyguards began to case Mount Isolation in ever widening circles, their course spiraling out from the dark palace while—

Not far away, behind a boulder that sat like an enormous lump of coal in the landscape, a pack of Glass Eyes was engaged in biological self-assembly. The vacant stare of crystal in their sockets; their eerie, waxwork stillness as if, all at once, they had suddenly paused in the middle of various activities: They were defragmenting their internal hard drives, healing wounds superficial and otherwise with the regeneration cell-buds that could develop into organs, limbs, tissue. But hearing the lightest of footsteps, their heads turned as one.

Ripkins and Blister were on their third time around Mount Isolation, approaching a quadrant of craggy rock formations, when—

Sssst!

A blade came slamming down toward Ripkins' shoulder.

"Humph." He sidestepped it with the calm of one avoiding a dollop of seeker droppings, pulled a crystal shooter out of his thigh holster, and fired.

The blade-wielding Glass Eye staggered, went down.

Blister was taking on two of them at once—hand to hand, blade to blade, defensive swivel countering offensive lunge in a ballet of violence. Ripkins sensed it more than saw it, the clash of activity to his left, because he'd become busy with his own pair of Glass Eyes, slashing at them with a forearm-length blade, using his crystal shooter to deflect their swords and knives, all while avoiding crystal shot from a third Glass Eye.

One after another, the Glass Eyes coughed their last breath, sent their last electrical pulse along wire-veins, fired the last synapses in their nanochip-infused brains. Carried away with the fighting, Blister seemed to forget the purpose of his mission.

"I'll take care of him," he said, stalking forward to put an end to the last remaining Glass Eye.

Ripkins quickly reached for his gossamer shot—a small, thin tube attached to his belt.

Fffshaw!

A large web bulleted out of the tube, fell over the Glass Eye. Frantic, it slashed and shot fruitlessly at the webbing. Blister, his adrenaline no longer getting the better of his duty, gathered the ends of the web in his fist and pulled; the web went taut, wrapping up the Glass Eye, rendering it helpless. Ripkins took the sword and crystal shooter from its pinned hands.

Ripkins heaved the imprisoned Glass Eye over his shoulder, and he and Blister ran off as—

Half a deck of card soldiers, alerted by the sounds of battle, entered the quadrant. In confused silence, they surveyed the scene: two Glass Eyes with blades sticking out of their guts, a couple more striped with the fatal burn marks of whipsnake grenades, the rest riddled with the puncture wounds of crystal shot. Judging by the weapons used, whoever had managed this carnage could have been anybody—although to defeat seven Glass Eyes, there must have been a lot of them.

For all the card soldiers knew, or ever would know, Ripkins and Blister had never been there, never retreated to their kingdom with a perfectly functioning Glass Eye as their prisoner.

CHAPTER 20

WEAVER HAD rushed to embrace her, and Molly herself had forgotten the effects of the drug-delivery system she wore, had jumped up and—

She'd woken up here, in this tent occupied by eight of Arch's wives, the place all plush and cozy and fragrant with the scent of crushed swamp blossoms. How could her mother—the woman she had dreamed about for so long, the single photo-crystal of whom she had stared at until she could have traced its image with her eyes closed—be alive? How could Hatter Madigan be her father?

"I want my homburg," she said to the two ministers guarding her. "And I want to talk to my mother."

"Do you, now?"

They didn't even turn toward her. They were watching

the newscast on the tent's entertainment crystal, where a Sirk reporter was describing the recent violence in Wonderland: the military outposts attacked; the mysterious contamination of the Crystal Continuum that had left the bulk of Alyss' army stranded around the queendom and Wondertropolis vulnerable to invasion.

"No," Molly breathed. Because Arch's words were starting to make sense. Too much sense. *Trying to protect your queen, you jeopardized the queendom itself.* Wasn't that what he'd said? How could she have been so stupid? So rash? She had contaminated the continuum with the Lady of Diamonds' weapon and the Diamonds had taken advantage of it.

"A general state of emergency has been declared in Wonderland's capital city," the reporter stated, "and authorities now say . . ."

She had let her worst impulses, her wounded pride, get the better of her. But now her pride took another hit, because . . . hadn't her failure, her lack of discipline, fulfilled Hatter's earliest suspicions of her? For a brief moment, she hated him. Him and Weaver. It was their fault that she was a halfer, a worthless halfer unfit to serve any queen, let alone Alyss Heart. It'd probably be better for everyone if she went off to lead a simple, boring life somewhere far away.

"I have to talk to my mother," she said. "You can't keep us here."

"We aren't 'keeping' Weaver anywhere," one of the ministers smiled. "She stays with us of her own will. However, I don't see why the two of you can't be reunited if you do one thing for me first." He handed her a brand-new diary. Like Weaver's, it was the size of a playing card but resembled a typical book from Earth. "Record a message to Queen Alyss—a confession, if you will—of everything that happened between you and Lady Diamond. All you have to do is tell the truth. Tell your queen how you *feel*." His eyes swiveled to the newscast, where the Sirk was reporting on the estimated number of Wonderland casualties.

Molly turned the diary over in her hands. She alone had brought destruction to the city that she loved. She had no reason to trust the minister. But it might be the last chance she had of ever seeing her mother again.

She pressed the sides of the diary, its cover popped open and—

"Dear Queen Alyss . . . " she started, recording her confession.

CHAPTER 21

IT DIDN'T take a genius tactician to see that failure was imminent, Alyss more powerful than Arch had supposed. He would have to focus on his contingency plan and let the Glass Eyes attack on Wonderland fizzle out—a circumstance mildly disappointing, but not worrisome. Such a strategist was the king that he had a contingency plan for his contingency plan, and even, if circumstances required, a contingency plan for his contingency plan's contingency plan. Besides, he had utilized the Glass Eyes as a lark. If he had truly believed that they alone might depose Alyss, why would he have bothered with the scheme involving Weaver and Homburg Molly, which was progressing as well as he could have hoped? If concluded successfully, it would provide him with invaluable military intelligence and no small addition to his special forces for the time he did make his ultimate move on Wonderland.

Resting in his quarters, Arch reached to the bedside table, slid the amoeba-shaped communication nodule into its appropriate slot as if inserting the final piece in a jigsaw puzzle, and a moment later his huddle of intel ministers appeared.

"How's our young guest?" he asked.

"As docile as any child could be, wearing a drug-delivery system as she is," said one of the ministers.

"She constantly demands to see her mother," said another, "and somewhat less constantly demands that we return her homburg to her."

Arch nodded. "Has she recorded the confession to her queen?"

"She has. But only because we promised to let her see her mother again."

The minister handed the diary to his king.

"Let her see her mother," Arch said, "but from a distance. They're not to speak to each other. What of the Diamonds? Are they still . . . occupied?"

The ministers grinned. "The Lady of Diamonds is relaxing at one of our imagination retreats. The father and son have as much wine, food, and music as they can desire, and they are surrounded by company. The pair are insatiable. Some have complained that, in addition to making everyone around him wear wigs of dried grass, the son is somewhat gross."

"Just make sure they're encouraged in their debauchery.

I want everything ready for the time when they will wake to find themselves in circumstances much altered for the worse."

"Everything *is* ready, Your Majesty. We wait only for your word."

"Fine. Now leave me. Send in Ripkins and Blister."

The bodyguards stationed outside the tent entered to find Arch dressing in the formal robe and mantle he wore to summits with tribal leaders.

"The mission I have for you requires that you journey to Boarderton," the king said. "The last I was informed, it was in the plains somewhere between the Bookie River and Duneraria. Don't concern yourselves too much with secrecy. The ministers will inform you whom you are to meet and what you're to do once you arrive. Go."

The bodyguards took their leave. Arch surveyed his reflection in a looking glass one last time, then readied himself for the dispatch he was about to make, pacing the length of the tent as he rehearsed what he would say in his role of the concerned king calling on a besieged neighbor.

CHAPTER 22

THE WALRUS-BUTLER toddled in and out of the palace's briefing room with winglefruit juice, flugelberry wine, wondercrumpets, and every refreshment he could think of to show his joy at Alyss' safe return from the battle at Wondronia Grounds.

"Have you seen Homburg Molly yet?" she whispered as he set a plate of mostly toasted oaties on the table.

"Oh no, my queen. No, still no sign of her."

She stared, frowning, at the food. *She should have gotten over her sulking by now. If she's trying to worry me by her absence . . .*

"Don't you like mostly toasted oaties?" the walrus asked with concern.

"I do." She crunched one between her teeth. "Please

send for the ranking families, walrus. We need to speak with them."

The creature bowed and waddled out of the room.

Hatter, Bibwit, Dodge, and General Doppelgänger were watching a skirmish play out on one of the holo-screens: Glass Eyes forcing Wonderland pawns to retreat under a barrage of razor-cards and crystal shot. Alyss raised a hand and caressed the air, as if gently feeling the contours of an invisible face. On the holo-screen, a construct of herself, a decoy, stepped out from behind a tarty tart vendor's cart. The Glass Eyes sensed it at once, abandoned their pursuit of the pawns, and trained their weapons on the decoy. Taking advantage of the opening, the pawns let rip with a slew of orb generators and—

Karooosh! Blooooomm!

Fireballs rolled over the Glass Eyes.

"I hope, Hatter," Alyss said, wiping her decoy from existence with a wave of her hand, "that the personal issues for which you left us have been resolved?"

Hatter nodded—once.

"You'll be pleased to know that the Millinery has been reestablished," Bibwit said.

But Hatter did not seem pleased or even curious as to how this had been accomplished.

"Well now," the scholar went on, "I'm just an old fuddy-duddy who could use a tan, so you needn't grant my opinion any authority, but I consider the queendom lucky that a handful of Milliners and their children lived incognito among the population during Redd's tyranny. With their ID chips removed, they established themselves as civilians and revealed their true identities only after Alyss became queen."

"They didn't join the Alyssian resistance?" Hatter asked.

"A few of them aided us in their way," said General Doppelgänger, "subtly sabotaging a number of Redd's directives from the inside, as it were. But their standing as civilians was too valuable to jeopardize. We considered it too much of a risk to have them join us openly, both because of the destruction Redd would have brought down upon us, but also for the future of the Millinery."

"No offense, Hatter," said Dodge, "I'm as glad as anyone to have you back, but isn't it time we start dealing with Redd?"

"She isn't responsible for the attacks," Hatter said.

Dodge and the general were speechless with surprise.

Bibwit caught Alyss' eye. "What makes you think that?" he asked.

"I'll show you. Queen Alyss, if you'll please construct a decoy of yourself on Tyman Way . . . I'll return shortly."

Within three wags of a spirit-dane's tail, the Milliner appeared on the holographic screen displaying a deserted expanse of Tyman Way. A construct of Alyss formed next to him. Barely a moment passed before a squad of Glass Eyes signaled their arrival on the scene with a volley of orb generators launched from arm cannons.

eeeeeEEEBRKCHRKKCH!

Amidst the smoke and flames and falling debris, Hatter positioned himself between the Alyss decoy and his attackers. There were five in all, though more were undoubtedly on their way. He activated his wrist-blades and sent incoming razor-cards clattering to the pavement as fast as the Glass Eyes could shoot them. He let the assassins approach to within a quarter of a block, then—*fwap!*—flicked his top hat into a flat pinwheel of blades and sent it zinging into them. He chased after the weapon, tumbled in a series of no-handed cartwheels, his arms held out straight to either side, wrist-blades spinning.

Thunk! Thunk!

The top hat blades sliced through two Glass Eyes and passed on, and the three remaining Glass Eyes succumbed to the deadly fans on his wrists. Clicking his bracelets shut, the Milliner caught his top hat blades as they boomeranged back to him and, with a deft flap of the hand, returned them to their more formal incarnation as headware. He dusted the hat's brim with his coat sleeve and plopped it on his head, found what he wanted among the lifeless Glass Eye parts that littered the ground, and returned to the palace's briefing room. He held up the severed arm of a Glass Eye for all to see.

"*This* is why I don't believe Redd is responsible."

After a long silence, Dodge cleared his throat. "I think I speak for all of us when I say, 'Huh?'"

Hatter showed them the maelstrom of its inner wires, its

lab-grown muscle and tendons. He showed them the words printed clearly on the polymer composite bone, *Manufactured in Duneraria, Boarderland.*

"Redd would never have left such evidence," General Doppelgänger observed.

Hatter nodded. "I noticed it while helping one of our outposts defend itself against an attack."

"It just means Redd's probably cooperating with Arch," Dodge complained.

"Since when has she cooperated with anyone?" Alyss said. "Bibwit, what are your thoughts?"

"Alyss, my thoughts are many and, for the most part, unfathomable. But I do agree with Hatter and the general. During the time I spent with your uncouth aunt, I found her to be extremely *proprietary*, forever fretting and worrying beyond reason that one of her diabolical inventions would be duplicated by the Alyssians. She took tremendous pains to eliminate all evidence of the manufacturing process in her finished products, be they Glass Eyes or anything else, in order to prevent our scientists from gaining too fine an understanding of their inner work—"

From the hall came a din of raised voices:

"Wait, ladies and sirs! Please, I must announce you first!"

"Out of our way, blubber face, we can announce ourselves!"

Into the briefing room marched the Lord and Lady of

Clubs and the Lord and Lady of Spades, the walrus flapping worriedly after them.

"Ooh hoo, I'm sorry, my most respected queen, but they—"

"It's all right, walrus," Alyss soothed.

"Does our queen think it proper to unnecessarily risk the lives of the highest-ranking families in Wonderland?" spewed the Lord of Clubs. "Does it amuse her to order them from the safety of their walled and gated mansions so that they can traverse dangerous streets, especially when she could have easily conversed with them via holo-screens? Didn't Bibwit announce that, while the nation is under attack, citizens should *remain indoors* for their continued health and well-being?"

"We demand extra crystal payments for the needless danger to which we've been subjected!" demanded the Lord of Spades.

Incivility I wouldn't show to the least-ranking citizen.

"As members of my cabinet," Alyss calmly explained, "you share in the responsibility of ensuring a safe future for Wonderland. I'm sure the four of you will agree that we're in a crisis and that trying times bring out the best in you. What queen wouldn't want such helpful cabinet members by her side in an hour of need? Forgive me for calling you here. I was thinking only of myself and others when I did it. But for the love of your rank if nothing else, advise me. How do you think we should counter this invasion?"

"Uh," said the Lady of Clubs.

"I know exactly how we should counter it!" said her husband. "First and foremost, a decree must be at once . . . decreed! All ranking families are to remain indoors and well-protected until it can be guaranteed that every threat of violence is past! It's imperative that nothing inconvenient happen to us, for the populace would then have no one to look up to!"

"Speaking of exemplars of society," said Alyss, "where are Lord and Lady Diamond?"

The walrus's whiskers trembled. "Not at home or anywhere else I could find, my queen. I have left messages for them."

Too coincidental to be a coincidence. Their absence is no accident.

The truth was, Alyss had never expected any flashes of brilliance or military insight to come from the ranking families. She had called them to the palace in order to observe them, to learn from their behavior if they knew anything of the attacks. *They would swear their support to Redd or Arch or anyone else if they believed they could gain from it.*

"By your sagacious advice, you've proved my wisdom in sending for you," she said to the Lord of Clubs. "I want the four of you to remain in the palace until I say otherwise. You'll be well-guarded so that no harm can come to you. Walrus, please show them to their quarters."

The walrus enlisted the help of six palace guardsmen to coax the complaining nobles out into the hall. General

Doppelgänger stepped over to the room's crystal control panel, which had begun to demand attention.

"We're receiving a communication from King Arch," the general said. "He would like to speak with you, Alyss, and he claims it's urgent."

"Then I suppose we'd better hear what he has to say."

The general pressed a button on the control panel and Boarderland's king, in his official robe and mantle, appeared on a holographic screen.

"Sovereign Heart," Arch intoned with a slight bow of the head, "I wish the reason for this communication was more pleasant, but I fear I'm to blame for the trouble your nation is presently facing."

"Nice of you to admit it," said Alyss.

"I assume you've discovered that Homburg Molly's been kidnapped by the Ganmede Independence Front and is being held as a political prisoner?"

He paused, letting this news take its full effect. Alyss tried to keep her ignorance from showing; as stiff-backed as Hatter, she merely nodded. But the others grumbled and shifted in their seats.

"Believing me to be a disinterested party," Arch went on, "the Ganmedes have asked that I serve as their liaison. I've agreed to do this only so that I can be of service to you. I don't fully understand what they want—something to do with munitions and their attempt to secede from Unterlan—but to prove they have no desire to hurt Homburg Molly, and that they will negotiate for her release in good faith, they have passed along this."

He showed her the diary given to him by his ministers. He laid it flat in his left palm and pressed its sides with the thumb and middle finger of his right hand. Its cover popped open and a 3-D image of Molly materialized, facing Alyss.

"Dear Queen Alyss," the girl's image said, "I'm recording this to let you know I'm all right and you don't have to worry about me anymore. I tried my best, but . . . I guess I don't deserve to be your bodyguard. 'Cause what happened to the Crystal Continuum is my fault. The Lady of Diamonds, she gave me this little wooden box I was supposed to deliver to you, saying she'd gotten it from Queen Genevieve. I figured she was lying, but instead of telling you or anyone else like I probably should've done, I tried to expose the lady's plot myself. I was mad at you and I wanted to prove . . . No, forget it. Who cares what I wanted to prove? I was inside the continuum when I opened the box and it exploded. So I guess the Wonderlanders who say halfers can't be trusted are right. I hope no one was too badly injured. I'm sorry. I never wanted to let you down."

Molly's image crackled to nothing.

"And this is where I too am at fault," Arch said, snapping shut the diary. "I have unknowingly allowed the Diamonds to indulge their machinations against you by providing them the space and secrecy to carry them out. The Lord of Diamonds recently paid for two lunar cycles' worth of servants and a convoy of tents. As I'd been informed that his encampment was one big party, and I don't care for his brand of frivolity, I chose not to visit him. But I see now that my ministers were being fed misinformation and that Lord Diamond and his wife were not hosting a celebratory affair but working to dethrone and even murder you. Lady Diamond has gone into hiding at one of our retreats."

"No harm had better come to Molly," Alyss said.

"I agree," said the king. "We must prevent a tragedy at all costs, which is why I suggest you do as the Ganmedes request."

"And that is?"

"Send Hatter Madigan to the Sin Bin Gaming Club in Boarderton, a city they view as neutral territory. Grant him the authority to negotiate on your behalf for Homburg Molly's release."

"Why Hatter?"

"As talented as he is in combat, they believe that he's the least likely to risk Molly's life in a rescue attempt. As to why they believe this, I think Hatter himself can best answer that question."

Alyss flicked her eyes toward the Milliner, but his face remained as inscrutable as a slab of quartz.

"Sovereign Heart, if I'd known sooner that you were being invaded," Arch said, "I would have offered aid before now, as befits a good neighbor. My doggerels of war are at your disposal. You need only ask for them."

"Thank you, Arch, but we have the attack under control."

"With your powers of imagination, I'm not surprised. Is it Redd?"

"Nothing is confirmed at this point. When do the Ganmedes expect Hatter in Boarderton?"

"In precisely half a lunar cycle. If he doesn't arrive in time, they will assume you don't wish to negotiate and Homburg Molly's fate will follow accordingly."

Arch ended his transmission without signing off and the holo-screen again aired the real-time scene of deserted Wondertropolis streets. The room was quiet except for the tinkling of General Doppelgänger's medals as he worriedly rubbed at his forehead.

"You don't believe Arch is an innocent intermediary, do you?" Dodge asked.

"No."

"I doubt Arch cares what Alyss suspects of him so long as she does what he wants," said Bibwit.

"I'd rather go myself," Alyss fretted.

The scholar shook his head. "That wouldn't be wise. It could be a ruse to lure you away from Wonderland, to distance you from the Heart Crystal and thereby weaken your imaginative powers. The queendom is too vulnerable and cannot sustain further attack. You must remain at home, close to the crystal."

He's right. But still . . .

"Hatter," Alyss said, "you've been more silent than usual. What did Arch mean when he said the Ganmedes believe you are the least likely to jeopardize Molly's life?"

The Milliner looked at her. His mouth opened and closed. He seemed too affected to answer.

"The girl obviously made inroads in your affections," said Bibwit. "I remember, it wasn't so long ago that you claimed halfers were—"

"Homburg Molly is my daughter," Hatter said.

Dodge nearly choked on the winglefruit juice he'd been sipping. The general, not knowing what else to do, split in two and then recombined. Bibwit's ears stood straight up, alert.

"When did you learn this?" Alyss asked.

"While I was away."

"But I remember the mother, Weaver, coming to the camp," Bibwit said.

"Do you remember her leaving it? Or her reasons for doing so?"

Bibwit spoke slowly and deliberately, not wanting to offend. "I wish I could answer in the affirmative, Hatter, but the night she disappeared, I'd stuffed my ears with putty and tucked them under my sleeping cap as I always do. It's the only way I can block out the world's noises enough to fall asleep. The next morning, she was gone."

"I will prepare to leave for Boarderland immediately," the Milliner said, and started toward the door.

"Hatter?"

Alyss' voice had none of the regal distance in it one would expect from a queen. It was soft and apprehensive, the voice of a concerned friend. Hatter paused.

"I hope you know that I care deeply for Molly," Alyss said, "and that I would never willingly do anything to harm her. But what Arch or his Ganmedes see as security against a foolish rescue operation, I can't help seeing as a risk. It feels odd saying this to you of all people, but . . . as this concerns your daughter's life, Hatter, your emotions might get the better of even *your* training. I worry that you'd jeopardize everything and anything to rescue her."

"I have never abandoned my training yet," the Milliner said. "I will not start now."

"I'll go," Dodge offered, but Alyss pretended not to hear him.

"Your past performances give me no cause to doubt you," she said to Hatter, "but then, as far as you knew, nothing you've done before has ever involved your daughter. I don't want to make a hasty decision. I want to use what little time we have to consider the smartest course of action."

"Perhaps we should send the knight and rook with a company of chessmen?" General Doppelgänger suggested.

"Yes, and you can monitor their progress in your imagination's eye," said Bibwit. "If there are Ganmedes to negotiate with, I doubt they'll refuse to talk with whomever we send."

Alyss agreed. "If they do, I'll be close enough to the Heart Crystal to combat them through my imagination. And while they're occupied with saving their own lives . . . " she directed her words at Hatter, " . . . you can then lead a force to rescue Molly."

The Milliner stood looking at his queen for a long moment. "If that is what you command, Your Majesty," he said. But something was welling up inside him, something he had never felt before and that at any other time he would have tamped down with all the force of his formidable will: disobedience.

CHAPTER 23

THE REMAINS of the well-heeled audience were piled in the corner, the waiters taking longer than usual to sweep up the dust that had been the bones of Sacrenoir's resurrected dead, too often pausing to glance at the man-cat and the ruinous woman in her dress of teeth-baring roses.

"Get to work!" Marcel scolded. "Unless you'd like Master Sacrenoir to treat his dead to a meal of your flesh?"

The waiters tried to focus on their brooms, but hardly a minute passed before they were again sneaking glances at the alcove next to the stage, where a scarlet cloud hung over the table, images flickering within it while the grim woman expounded to Vollrath and Sacrenoir:

"What you're seeing is the moment my ill-judging mother informed me that I would not be queen," Redd was saying.

In the cloud, images brought forth from her imagination flared and passed like lightning. A younger, less bitter-worn version of herself railed at Queen Theodora, who apparently didn't appreciate being talked to in such a manner and walked off, leaving her daughter to steep in futile anger. The scene shifted to Redd marching up a spiral hall. She had aged, grown haggard from years of disdain, the line of her mouth set in a permanent frown of disgust.

"There I am, festering on Mount Isolation, my home in the Chessboard Desert, heir to a queendom reduced to an heir of insult and outrage."

She watched herself step out onto a balcony atop Mount Isolation and begin to preach to the mercenary card soldiers and Black Imagination enthusiasts gathered below.

"Those are the nearly useless beings I called a military. It was all I could do to force them into a weak semblance of the army I deserve."

Again, the scene changed. The walls of Heart Palace tumbled. Queen Genevieve's card soldiers fell dead as Redd sauntered untouched through the battle of that long-ago day when her sister had been cut down from the throne. The Cat, sitting next to his mistress in the alcove, began to purr. But then the cloud revealed Genevieve's private quarters, the blades of Hatter's top hat catching the feline assassin unaware and costing him one of his lives. He saw what he'd not been able to see when it happened, lying there dead as he'd been: Hatter escaping into a looking glass with seven-year-old Alyss

Heart, Redd imagining her knotty scepter into a scythe and beheading Genevieve.

"My niece escaped through the Pool of Tears," Redd told Vollrath and Sacrenoir, "and for reasons I won't go into, I believed her dead." The next scenes passed quickly, as if she were growing impatient with the past. "After years of shaping Wonderland to my fickle will, as is my birthright, my niece had the gall to bubble up through the Pool of Tears, returning through a portal puddle she'd discovered here on Earth."

The vast rooms of Mount Isolation took shape around twenty-year-old Alyss Heart, now become a rebel leader and dressed in the coarse-fibered clothes of the Alyssians. Beyond a half-destroyed wall, the Heart Crystal was visible. Aunt and niece faced each other, razor-cards, orb generators, and cannonball spiders rocketing between them. Alyss shot an energy spear from her finger, snagged Redd on the end of it, and began smashing her around the room. With a heave of imagination, Redd freed herself and closed with Alyss like a fighter ungifted in imagination who physically attacks her foes. *Clangk!* Scepters clashed, and just when Redd's defeat seemed assured, she and The Cat dared what no Wonderlanders had ever dared before—a leap into the Heart Crystal.

"I'd had a cold that day and wasn't as powerful as usual, otherwise Alyss would never have done so well," Redd said as, in the alcove, the final image dissolved. She blew at the cloud and it drifted off into the crypt. "Has a malicious ruler ever suffered more? I think not."

"There have been rumors that one might travel to Wonderland through certain puddles," Vollrath said. "But until your mention of Alyss a moment ago, nobody, as far as I knew, had ever put the rumors to the test."

Redd scoffed. "Why would they? What would any of you have returned to in my sister's Wonderland but a skulking life in a society unappreciative of your talents? Nothing more than that awaits you even now, so long as Alyss remains queen. But your savior has arrived—me. For the first time, Wonderlanders reduced to living in this junk heap of a world have someone powerful enough to lead them back to their native home. And in exchange for helping me regain my crown, I will allow them to live free of whatever punishments were unfairly bestowed upon them by the narrow-minded courts of Wonderland."

"I can think of a hundred souls in this city alone who'll be eager to subjugate themselves to you," said Sacrenoir.

Redd pushed away from the table and stood. "Take me to them. They will either pledge their allegiance to me—and if lucky, live through my impending war with Alyss' forces—or I'll kill them where they stand."

"Your impatience is a virtue," said Vollrath, his long ears tilting forward in supplication, "but to prevent your attracting too much attention from earthlings, you might want to consider a change of clothes. It's unfortunate enough that you're somewhat blurry around the edges, but in addition . . . well, a gown of animate roses is not exactly the fashion of the times."

"You don't like my dress?"

The vines of Redd's couture stretched toward the tutor, the roses' petal-mouths chomping.

"It isn't that, Your Imperial Viciousness. The earthlings will not understand you. Not understanding you, they will be frightened and send their petty authorities to apprehend you."

"Ha!"

"Of course they'll fail. That isn't the point. But you'll have to waste energy dealing with them instead of concentrating on your niece's destruction. I doubt that the way to achieve your aim is to spread your strength across many fronts so that, when it's time to battle Alyss, you may not be at the peak of your powers. Your niece, I gather, shouldn't be underestimated."

Vollrath hadn't graduated from the Tutor Corps for nothing. "I don't like it when sound reasoning counters my wishes," Redd hissed.

"I apologize, Your Imperial Viciousness, and will try not to let it happen too often. But you might also want to camouflage this rather intimidating feline creature with whom you travel."

"The Cat is his own camouflage," said Redd. And to The Cat: "Show them."

The Cat shrunk down into a kitten, meowed, then morphed back into an imposing humanoid.

"Ingenious!" enthused Sacrenoir. "Your Imperial Viciousness,

I will find you something suitable to wear from the clothes of my recent audience. Something not too ravaged and bloody."

"I don't mind blood so long as it isn't mine."

The magician returned with a gown that bore the marks of its previous owner's demise: the lace was torn in parts, the once shimmering silk stained with dirt and worse.

"We will leave you while you dress," Vollrath said, and pulled the alcove's curtain shut to give Redd privacy.

At the foot of the stage, The Cat indulged a sudden urge to bathe himself. The waiters paused in their work to watch him, risking little now that Marcel was busy reviewing the night's receipts with Sacrenoir. And though Vollrath too was staring at The Cat, he hardly saw the creature. He was recalling everything Redd had divulged of her history, mining the narrative for tidbits he could exploit to make himself ever more necessary to Mistress Heart, and thus, ever more deserving of reward. A vital piece of information seemed missing from all he'd heard. He approached the alcove and addressed Redd through the curtain:

"Your Imperial Viciousness, for my own edification, would you mind telling me when your mother removed you from succession? Was it before or after you had navigated your Looking Glass Maze?"

"Before," Redd answered in a clenched voice. "But I *would* have navigated it if I'd had any underlings worth even a tenth of Bibwit Harte's intellect. The key to the maze was in my hands, but no one could get it to work."

Vollrath's ears took on the aspect of little beings huddled against the cold. "Where did you find this key?"

"My seekers snatched it directly out of Alyss' hands. *She'd* entered the maze. It's the only reason I'm here. If I had entered it too, she wouldn't have gotten the better of me at Mount Isolation. We would have both gained in strength from passing through it, instead of her alone."

Redd's lack of knowledge astounded the tutor. Did she really understand so little about how a Wonderland princess became queen?

"She doesn't even know what she doesn't know," he mumbled, and then: "Your Imperial Viciousness, perhaps we should speak face-to-face, without this velvet barrier between us. Are you decent?"

"I'm never decent!"

The curtain was flung open and there she stood, a clash of opposites—the hate-infused pallor of her blemished skin and her spaghetti-wire hair at odds with a dress that was meant to be seen in lavish parlors, and which, despite its rips and bloodstains, still retained an aura of delicate creaminess.

"The gowns of the privileged class suit you," Vollrath lied.

"If wearing this rag will in any way speed the process of gathering my future soldiers, then I will wear it. But if it doesn't . . . "

Vollrath bowed. "I will subject myself to your temper."

"You'll have no choice."

Again, Vollrath bowed. He knew how to humble himself before a potentially lucrative pupil.

"It's time to leave this tomb," Redd announced. "I want to be unofficially introduced into Earth society. Cat!"

The Cat devolved into a kitten and rubbed against her leg. She lifted him onto her shoulder and he perched with his claws digging into her skin to steady himself—the pricks of pain a comfort to this high priestess of Black Imagination. Sacrenoir issued instructions to Marcel for the disposal of his audience's remains and, torch in hand, led Redd and Vollrath out of the theater crypt.

"Every would-be queen has a Looking Glass Maze, which they and they alone can enter," Vollrath lectured Redd as they made their way through a catacomb to the open air of Paris. "Since you were in line to succeed your mother, there existed a Looking Glass Maze intended for you, and which, to tap the full potential of your imagination and become queen, you would have had to successfully navigate. You couldn't operate the key to the Looking Glass Maze because it was the key to *Alyss'* maze."

"Alyss' maze?"

"Indeed. Perhaps when my old colleague Bibwit tutored you as heir to the throne, he was remiss in his teachings. It wouldn't surprise me, although it would likely surprise most Wonderlanders. Only a handful of times in Wonderland history has a princess failed to complete her maze, but you are the first to be *removed* from succession. However, with regard to the fate of a Looking Glass Maze, the result of both must be the same."

"What force or being constructs these mazes?" Redd demanded.

"That is an important question, and the answer lies with those who can provide the answer to another, perhaps more pressing one: What happened to your Looking Glass Maze after you were removed from succession? I assure you, it did not cease to exist, and if you're able to locate and navigate it . . . "

Redd understood. A maze intended solely for her, designed specifically to unharness the full power of her imagination? Alyss had gained surprising strength and skill by passing through her Looking Glass Maze. Yet she, Redd, had nearly conquered Alyss without passing through her own. The maze was everything. She would storm through as many of its false passages as necessary to complete it; she would become invincible.

"Earn your life, tutor. Where do I find my maze?"

"In the Garden of Uncompleted Mazes, of course. But where this garden is, I have no idea. You have to ask the oracles of Wonderland."

"The caterpillars," Redd sneered as a staircase of uneven stone came into view ahead of her. "I hate the caterpillars."

Sacrenoir dropped his torch to the ground and kicked dirt over it to extinguish the flames. A slant of light shone down on the stairs from above. Redd led the way up to the street. It took several moments for her eyes to adjust to the harshness of the morning sun, but even then—

"What's this?"

Everywhere she looked: Parisians enveloped in hazy nimbuses, some gray, others as purple-dark as bruises, while still others were more or less radiant with a whitish glow.

"To some Wonderland eyes," Vollrath said, "those gifted in White Imagination glow brightly while those given to Black Imagination glow darkly. It's more difficult to notice the dark glow at night time. It's an excellent thing to be able to discern friends and enemies at a distance. The dark glow will make it easier for us to find the soldiers you desire. You should see the cloud that hovers around *you*, Your Imperial Viciousness. It's a wonder you're visible at all."

Redd examined herself—her arms, her feet. Everything appeared as it had since she'd stepped from the painter's canvas. No bruise-dark aura.

"Wonderlanders can't see their own glow," Vollrath explained, "for the same reason that they're usually not good judges of their own behavior. They do not see how they actually are, only how they perceive themselves."

Redd stared out at the passing clouds of people. The Cat, his tail swishing, nimbly crossed from her right shoulder to her left.

"You needn't tramp about the city with us, Your Imperial Viciousness," said Sacrenoir. "Let Vollrath and me gather our acquaintances so that you can review them as a group. This will save you labor and give you time to plot a search for your Looking Glass Maze."

"An idea worthy of my tutelage," agreed Vollrath. "Mistress Heart, you will, I think, be intrigued by the Hall of Mirrors in the Versailles Palace. Why not take in the sights Paris has to offer?"

"Because, tutor," Redd snorted, "I'd sooner kill you."

CHAPTER 24

DODGE, NOT usually one to linger over tokens of the past, was in his guardsman's quarters picking over the few items he had salvaged from the former palace: a portrait of his father he'd drawn when he was eight years old, a dented broach that had belonged to his long-dead mother, and a packet of letters he'd written during Redd's reign but never sent.

He set the portrait prominently on the mantel and moved the dining table in front of the glowing hearth, laying out two place settings and a pitcher of winglefruit juice. There was nothing left to do but wait.

"No talent for waiting," he said to himself.

He had volunteered to go after the Diamonds and Alyss had ignored him. In front of everybody. He thought it important for her to understand a couple of things. He surveyed the room again, hoping to find some final preparation that needed doing, but all was in order.

Bleep, bleep bleep bleep, bleep.

His crystal communicator sounded with the agreed-upon signal. Any moment Alyss would be passing down the hall to the sovereign suite. He pulled smooth the sleeves of his guards-man's coat and squared his shoulders, to appear as official as possible. He stepped to the door and out into the hall.

"Queen Alyss, my guards have discovered something I think you should see."

Her face had relaxed at the sight of him, but her brow at once contracted, her lips thinned with tension.

"We've found evidence of suspicious activity in the palace," he said.

"What sort of activity?"

"You might want to step this way and see for yourself. I apologize in advance for your having to set foot in a guards-man's quarters."

He led her into his rooms. The boyish portrait of Sir Justice, the fire crystals in the hearth, the elegantly arrayed table: Alyss blinked in puzzlement.

"What *is* all this?"

"My best guess, Your Majesty, is that it's breakfast, but I can't be sure until we taste it."

Which was when she realized. "Dodge," she said quietly.

A guardsman entered carrying a pair of covered serving dishes, set them on the table and departed. Dodge pulled out a chair for Alyss and, once she was seated, assumed the role of gallant host.

"On platter number one," he said, "we have what I believe is your favorite—Chef Blanchaud's mysterious hash, which I agree is delicious even if we don't know what's in it." He lifted the cover of the serving dish and steam escaped toward the ceiling. "On platter number two . . . " he removed the cover of the second dish with a flourish, " . . . we have half-baked cakes with choco-nibblies."

"Mmm."

He transferred one of the cakes to her plate, ladled out a spoonful of hash for her and filled her glass with winglefruit juice, then served himself and sat down.

"You did all of this?" Alyss asked.

"I wouldn't even let the walrus help me. And he wanted very much to help."

"It's all so lovely, Dodge. And delicious."

He watched her cut a small piece of cake with the side of her fork and lift it to her mouth. There were lines under her eyes, silhouetted crescent moons cupping the underside of her eye sockets.

"Are you tired?"

"I'm almost always tired."

He nodded. He had yet to touch his food. "Alyss, do you remember back when we were . . . I guess I was nine, so you must've been six, and we used to play Guardsmen and Maidens?"

"I remember everything."

"We used to make up a lot of games, didn't we?"

"I enjoyed them more than I do the real thing . . . until now."

"Well . . . I think you're old enough now to hear the truth, Alyss. I used to let you win."

"Ha! You thought that whenever I *did* win, it was because I'd cheated, I'd used my imaginative powers."

"It was."

She smiled. "If it pleases you to think so."

Dodge shifted the hash around on his plate. "Besides bringing me close to you, the purpose of some of those games was to improve my combat skills so that I'd be able to protect you whenever the need arose, as befitted a palace guardsman. Funny then that now it's you who are trying to protect me."

He looked at her. She paused, her glass of winglefruit juice held at her lips.

"What do you mean?" she asked.

"I survived for thirteen years in your absence with wrath and vengeance in my heart—it might even have been these that kept me alive. I'd rather not be governed by these passions, but you can't hope to rid me of them by putting yourself between me and The Cat."

Alyss said nothing and stared at the fire crystals in the hearth.

"You think I was too quick to blame Redd for the Glass Eyes' attack?" Dodge asked.

"Yes."

"Well, it's been confirmed that The Glass Eyes were manufactured in Boarderland. Maybe I did rush to judgment. If so, it was a mistake and I admit it. I'm trying my best not to let revenge dictate my actions, Alyss, but . . . I don't know. I can't promise what's going to happen if I see The Cat again. I only know that if I *am* to conquer these vengeful feelings, I have to be the one to do it, not you or anybody else."

"I'm sorry."

"You don't have to apologize, it's just . . . everybody knows I was angry after our parents were murdered. But there was also . . . something else. I came to believe that I'd spend my life alone."

"Dodge, I'm—"

"There was nothing to pity in this," he said quickly. "It was just the way things were. But when I found out you were alive . . . " he shook his head, " . . . you have no idea what living under Redd's rule can do to you, Alyss. It was unbearable."

"We have all borne things we never imagined."

"Most of life is unbearable. It's unbearable but we bear it. That's what I believe. But right now, Alyss, here with you, I don't *feel* it."

She'd been trying not to cry almost since she'd stepped into Dodge's rooms, but she could no longer stop herself. "Maybe one day," she said, "when Homburg Molly is safe and things are peaceful enough that the queendom can run itself, we'll take a trip to together. Somewhere quiet. There's no reason we can't do that, is there?"

Dodge didn't say what he knew to be true: The queendom would never run itself. There would always be some emergency that required the queen's attention. There always had been. And he knew that Alyss knew it.

"You're the queen and can do you as you wish," he said. From his inside coat pocket, he removed his packet of letters and handed it across the table. "These are for you."

"What are they?"

"Letters I wrote to you during Redd's rule, when I believed you were dead. There aren't many. I didn't have much peace for writing."

Alyss stared at the packet.

"I still think it's possible that Redd is involved," Dodge said. "It'd be just like her to do something we'd never expect her of doing, such as leaguing with Arch. What will you do about the Diamonds?"

"Have them taken into custody."

Dodge rose from his chair and walked over to her. "That's enough of unpleasant topics for now. Did you enjoy your breakfast?"

"I loved it," she said, turning her face up to his.

"Good. I hope you'll forgive me, being just an upstart guardsman and all, but . . . " He leaned down and kissed her lips.

"I could have you reported for that," she smiled.

"Yes, you could."

He lifted her to him and kissed her again, was still pressing his lips against hers when Bibwit Harte, four General Doppels, and an equal number of General Gängers stampeded into the room.

Dodge stepped away from his queen, stood at attention.

"He's gone!" the Doppels cried. "Hatter's gone!"

"What do you mean 'gone'?" Alyss asked.

"We think he's on his way to Boarderland—" started the Gängers.

"—to rescue Homburg Molly!" finished the Doppels.

"He wouldn't."

"All card soldiers patrolling the demarcation barrier have been notified," said Bibwit, "but I'm not sure how much good it'll do."

The more Alyss considered it, the more she believed it likely: Hatter had gone after his daughter in direct opposition to her commands. *I was right not to send him. His emotions are already getting the better of him.*

Bibwit, Dodge, and the generals were waiting for instructions. Alyss quickly scanned along the demarcation barrier with her imagination's eye, seeking Hatter until—

There. He was stepping out from the trees of the Everlasting Forest and approaching the barrier with determined strides. Busy with their luggage and passports, the civilians waiting to cross the border didn't notice him until he reached into his backpack with both hands and—*fli-flink! fli-flink flink flink!*—pinned the patrolling card soldiers to the ground like specimens on display for a curious giant, blades piercing their uniforms but not their flesh. The Milliner passed his hand over the control box that was at every official checkpoint; a door-sized opening formed in the impassable weave of sound waves that separated Wonderland from Arch's kingdom. Without slowing, Hatter M. stepped through it and crossed to the other side.

CHAPTER 25

FOR GENERATIONS, Boarderton had attracted those who felt foreign among their own kind, those wanting to escape the suffocating customs of their birth tribes to enjoy the more varied, expansive life one inevitably finds in a major metropolis. With the exception of Arch's royal entourage, Boarderton was the only city in the kingdom that consisted of mixed tribes. While a Maldoid would never be caught socializing with a Kalaman anywhere else, inter-tribal doings were commonplace in the capital city, where one didn't survive long without being tolerant of otherness.

Nowhere was the array of the populace more apparent than in the Sin Bin Gaming Club, a ratty establishment usually located in a ratty quarter of laborers' tents. On any given night in Sin Bin, a stranger could find Onu mingling with

Astacans, Awr tippling with Scabbler, Gnobi engaged in philosophical debates with Sirk. Such Boarderlanders might have been born into warring tribes, but they now belonged to a single tribe: Boardertonians, foremost and above all.

When Hatter set foot in the Bin, representatives from each of the nation's twenty-one species were there, along with several from the remote regions of Morgavia and Unterlan. Loud and raucous, four-fifths of them were drunk, the remaining one-fifth working hard to get drunk. Hatter wouldn't have cared if there were twice as many and they were all hopped up on artificial crystal. He'd have fought the entire crowd for even the slightest chance of securing Homburg Molly's release.

In the corner, seated on low benches and sharing a bottle of viscous liquor with a couple of Maldoids and a Scabbler: four Ganmedes.

Were they his contacts? Hatter waited but they paid him no attention, so he passed on, made his way around the drinkers packed three deep at the bar to the seating area beyond, where too many tables scarred from the bottles and goblets of former carousals were crammed into too small a space. When he reached the far end of the tent, he started back. A male from the Fel Creel tribe stepped away from the bar and faced him. Hatter had no way of knowing that the tribesman was actually a former Fel Creel who now traveled with Arch as a member of the Doomsines.

The Boarderlander stood with his arms at his sides, his palms facing out. He flexed; the serrated blades of his fingerprints pushed through the skin and caught the light. Hands moving faster than shuttering eyelids, he snatched a cap off a sullen Astacan at the bar and shredded it into countless scraps. The Astacan spun around, ready to fight, but thought better of it when he saw what had become of his cap. He turned back to his drink, and Ripkins thrust his chin at Hatter, challenging.

Fwap!

Hatter's top hat was off his head and flattened into spinning blades, the Milliner's arms moving like those of an Earth-ninja expertly wielding nunchucks, his blades zinging up and down and around his body in tight, artful circles, then—

Fwap!

He was again wearing his top hat.

The club's regulars made room for the fighters, then went back to blearing their senses, accustomed to these sorts of disturbances.

"Hunh!"

Ripkins lurched forward, his right arm extended, and a pair of kill-quills arrowed toward Hatter.

Flangk!

Hatter snapped open his wrist-blades and stepped aside, but the move was anticipated by Ripkins, who had already yanked on the cords attached to the kill-quill's tail ends. The weapons were tumbling back to him as—*fip fip fip fip*—he fired off half a deck of razor-cards and—

Moving to avoid the kill-quills, Hatter stepped directly

into the path of incoming cards. Wrist-blades or no wrist-blades, he would have been sliced to death if he hadn't fallen flat to the ground with twice the speed of gravity.

Ripkins leaped for him, was in the air about to come down when—

Shwink!

Hatter punched his belt buckle and his belt sabers sprung open. Ripkins changed direction in midair and somersaulted clear, which gave Hatter time to jump to his feet and shrug open his backpack, its corkscrews and daggers at the ready. Shielding himself with the coptering wrist-blades of one hand, he launched his backpack's weapons at Ripkins.

"Yah! Yah! Yah!"

But Ripkins' hands were creating a cyclone in front of him, invisible with speed, shredding *air*. And whether it was their centrifugal force alone or he was actually catching the incoming blades and flinging them back at Hatter, every blade and corkscrew that threatened him went hurtling back toward the mythic Milliner, who more and more found himself on the defensive until it was all Hatter could do to twirl, spin, duck, and jump to avoid being hit.

"Aaah!"

Hatter charged at Ripkins, his wrist-blades pushed out in front of him. Arch's bodyguard jerked his shoulder as if to adjust the hang of his coat: A pointed stick the length of a writing crystal slid out the end of his sleeve and into his hand. Pressing his thumb against its nub end, Ripkins extended the stick to the length of a spirit-dane. Hatter, closing the gap between them, recognized the weapon: a telescoping javelin.

"Hngh!"

Holding the javelin horizontally, gripping it with both hands near its midpoint, Ripkins pushed it into Hatter's wrist-blades and—

Krchkkkrchk!

Both sets of blades jammed to a halt, the ends of the javelin caught within their spin. Hatter's hands were effectively pinned to the ends of the javelin, and Ripkins held a fistful of kill-quills poised at his jugular.

Hatter nodded, impressed. Then—

"Nguh!"

He shrugged hard, flapping both arms down and away as if he were shaking off water. Ripkins went staggering backward and the javelin clattered to the floor. His wrist-blades gearing back to full speed, Hatter sent his top hat flying into the hookah haze gathered thick over patrons' heads.

Clink! Clangk! Clonk!

He and Ripkins went at each other, Ripkins starting to have trouble when—

The top hat blades came boomeranging out of the haze, spinning toward Arch's bodyguard from behind, veering up at the last moment.

Smack!

The flat sides of the blades knocked Ripkins in the back of

the head and he tumbled to the ground. Hatter caught hold of his weapon and slammed it down, two of its blades embedding in the dirt on either side of Ripkins' neck like a pair of open scissors, pinning the bodyguard on his back.

Ripkins grunted, impressed.

Hatter clicked shut his bracelets, took up his top hat blades and, with a flick of the wrist, transformed them back into innocent headware. Ripkins stood, pocketed his weapons, and brushed himself off.

"Where's Homburg Molly?" Hatter demanded.

Ripkins jutted his chin: *Look behind you.* Hatter half turned, saw another Fel Creel in elbow-length gloves standing with his hands clasped in front of him, waiting politely. Ripkins slipped back in among the customers at the bar while Blister peeled off his gloves, held up his bare hands, both front and back, for Hatter to see. Like a magician about to perform a magic trick, he showed Hatter the inside of his shirtsleeves—*Nothing up my sleeves.* Without further preliminary, he pressed a finger against the neck of an unsuspecting Onu.

"Aahaahaahaaaagh!"

The Onu writhed and squirmed. Blister kept the finger pressed against the bubbling flesh of his neck.

"Aaaaaahaaaaaaghrgh!"

Blister at last pulled his finger away, the Onu sopping with sweat and exhausted from pain. He flicked open a knife, lowering its point toward the balloon-skin of the Onu's swollen neck. Pop! Pus poured out of the wound and the Onu collapsed.

Blister grinned. "For me," he said to Hatter, "weapons like yours are unnecessary. Although I'm no mediocrity when it comes to using them."

Hatter again had recourse to his entire arsenal. Top hat blades, wrist-blades, belt sabers, backpack weaponry—all clashed against Blister's pikes, pickets, and swords. But after an extended combination of slashing and twisting, Hatter found himself on the ground, cornered against an overturned table, Blister's deadly index finger a chest hair's length from his exposed heart.

Hatter raised a respectful eyebrow. Then—

Flink!

Out sliced his belt sabers. Blister jumped back, laughing even though his finger was bleeding from a deep cut.

"What do I care if you chop it off? I have thirteen others."

Again they sparred, Blister sometimes reverting to the more traditional weapons of swords and shooters to fend off Hatter's aggression, other times relying solely on the threat of his touch.

"Ungh! Ungh!"

Hatter sent two C-shaped blades coptering toward him. The blades caught Blister's hands, pinioned them to two poles supporting the tent. Hatter let two more blades fly and Blister's feet were suddenly pinioned, his four limbs extended in the form of an X like a volunteer who has risked his life as the target of a knife thrower.

"Pretty good," the bodyguard mumbled, as effusive as he'd ever be regarding the skill of another.

Hatter flung his top hat blades. *Dink, dink, dink, dink!* They ricocheted off Blister's restraints, knocking them loose, and boomeranged back to him. Blister rubbed his wrists and shoved his hands into their long gloves. His finger was still bleeding.

Ripkins stepped out of the crowd at the bar. "Come with us if you want to save your daughter's life," he said.

CHAPTER 26

IN HER tent at Boarderland's most exclusive retreat, the Lady of Diamonds was flexing her imagination under the guidance of a trainer, or enabler.

"You can't imagine yourself able to fly and then—poof!—you're flying," the enabler was explaining. "But you can imagine wings on your body and, if they're large enough, you'll be able to fly by virtue of their motion. Like everything in our universe, imagination has its laws."

Eyeing the modest swirl of imagination energy before her, the Lady of Diamonds didn't seem to be listening. She was trying hard not to blink.

"Imagination's laws have been gleaned from the study of the strongest, most talented imaginationists throughout history. A talented imaginationist can transform an inanimate object into a simple life form, such as a gwormmy. But for more complex creatures, such as doggerels of war or jabberwocky, even the most talented can only create an illusion of them, not the actual life forms themselves. Therefore, when I speak of conjurings, I am referring mainly to inanimate objects, to successfully complete which, you must first envision your chosen object in intricate detail. And this . . . " the enabler turned a doubtful eye on the Lady of Diamond's hovering amoeba of imaginative energy, " . . . is what you should be doing now. First construct the object in your mind. The better you understand the object, the more knowledge you have of it, the more successful you'll be. Which is why I wanted you to choose something you know well."

The energy swirl was beginning to solidify, but into what was unclear.

"Good!" said the enabler. "Excellent! Keep concentrating on the jewelry case in your mind and, by dint of your obvious talent, you will transfer what you see into the physical realm."

"I've always told my husband I was talented."

"Conjuring is nothing more than focus, Lady Diamond. Imagine—ha ha, I amuse myself—but really, imagine that the light of our suns is Imagination. On any given day, the sunlight is all around us, diffused and shining on what it will without any influence from us. Now suppose your imagination is a magnifying crystal that channels the sunlight to a specific point with increased intensity until it creates a flame. The flame is your conjured object."

The Lady of Diamonds' neck muscles were tensed and trembling. She had gone from trying not to blink to squinting hard, as if the slit of her eyes determined the degree of her mental focus. But her conjured jewelry case resembled nothing so much as four pieces of wood glued together by a toddler.

"The more complex an object," the imagination enabler said, "the longer the process takes and the more energy that is required. More energy requires a greater imaginative gift. To conjure a chair is easy; to conjure a meticulously engineered aerial craft is significantly more difficult. Those with powerful imaginations seem to intuit complex objects, as they can conjure instantaneously what it would take lesser imaginations days or weeks to conjure, if at all. But anyone can see from this display of your strength—just look at the jewelry case you've produced!—that you have a particularly powerful imagination."

The Lady of Diamonds gazed proudly upon her creation. "It looks exactly like the 104 I have at home," she said. "Put them side by side and I wouldn't be able to tell them apart."

"Of course you wouldn't," enthused the enabler. "Being from Wonderland, the name of Alyss Heart will obviously be familiar to you. But what you cannot know, as I don't like to mention it lest it seem like bragging, is that I was your queen's imagination enabler when she was a child. Since that time I have enabled many other highly gifted imaginationists, but you, Lady Diamond, are easily the most gifted imaginationist I have ever coached."

"Well," the lady said. Was this not further proof that she should be queen instead of Alyss Heart or any of Wonderland's other ranking ladies? Should someone as gifted as she *not* lose herself in reveries of her own stupendousness? Absolutely she should. So the Lady of Diamonds floated away on musings of her magnificence, which was why it took her a moment to realize that her tent had been invaded by the white rook and his small force of pawns and card soldiers.

"Lady Diamond," the rook said with a sarcastic bow, "by order of Queen Alyss Heart, I hereby take you into custody, to be carried back to Wonderland, where you're to stand trial for treason and conspiracy to murder the queen."

"What?!"

The pawns and card soldiers surrounded the lady.

"This is outrageous!" she raged. "Someone's clearly playing a trick on you, chessman! Do you have any idea how much my vacation package at this retreat costs? Get out of here before I have *you* arrested!"

The rook threw a grenade at the lady's feet. She flinched, but instead of a bone-shattering explosion, the grenade's detonation produced a small cell, one just large enough to contain her.

"But you don't even have jurisdiction here," she whined, shaking the porta-prison's bars.

"King Arch is aware of my mission and has granted me all the authority I need."

"King Arch? That deceitful . . . Arrest *him*, why don't you?

225

He's to blame for everything. I'm warning you, chessman! Let me out of this thing or proceed at your own risk! I can stop you with the power of my imagination!" The lady squeezed her eyes shut, balled her hands into fists and—

Poosh! A piddling little jewelry case formed. The rook, soldiers, pawns, and imagination enabler stared at it, wondering what miraculous means of escape it would provide. Then it fell apart.

"Hup," one of the card soldiers said as he and the others lifted the Lady of Diamonds' porta-prison between them and carried it out to the waiting smail-transport.

"Somebody notify Lord Diamond!" the lady shrieked, shaking and rattling the bars of her cell. "Lord Diamond knows how to put chessmen in their proper places! Just you wait, Mr. Rook! You'll face a punishment worse than any you can fathom for this mistake!"

"You and your husband will have plenty of time to discuss my punishment while you await your trials," said the rook.

~

Their memories of the previous night were unreliable, befogged and sketchy, entire chunks of time blacked out by overindulgence. Still, Jack of Diamonds was pretty sure that he had fallen asleep atop a mattress-sized pillow stuffed with the first-growth feathers of tuttle-birds. The Lord of Diamonds was likewise certain that platters of tasty treats and decanters of mind-fuzzing libations had been within arm's reach when *he* had drifted to sleep beneath the canopy of an antique Kalaman bed. And both father and son remembered tiring themselves out with dancing, their ears even now ringing from the loud volume of the Boardertonian deejay's music. How then had they become surrounded by so much blatant *industry*?

"What's all this?" the Lord of Diamonds asked, waking from a heavy slumber and reluctantly opening his throbbing eyes.

They appeared to be in a factory. The signs of mass production were all around: conveyor lines, automated assembly arms, laser-solders, racks of intel chips, an army of steel skeletons, some fitted with wire-vein armatures and lab-grown muscle, others plain. On the billowing tent walls: blueprints for building Glass Eyes.

"Where are the ladies and servants?" Jack of Diamonds yawned.

Which was when the white knight, leading a contingent of pawns and card soldiers, marched into the tent. The knight gazed around at the Glass Eyes manufacturing facility—overwhelming corroboration of King Arch's story, if ever there was.

"Lord Diamond," he said, "by order of Queen Alyss Heart, I hereby take you into custody, to be carried back to Wonderland, where you are to stand trial for treason and conspiracy to murder the queen."

"Arrested?" the Lord of Diamonds murmured, backing

away and shaking his head. "Treason and murder?"

The knight turned upon the Jack of Diamonds. "And you, sir, being an escapee from the Crystal Mines, are also under arrest. I intend to personally deposit you back where you belong."

The knight lobbed a pair of grenades—one at Jack's feet and the other at the lord's. *Foosh!* Porta-prisons shot up at the grenades' points of impact, but—

They contained nothing. Jack could be surprisingly quick for his size, and he'd jumped behind the machine that screwed Glass Eye heads onto Glass Eye bodies. The Lord of Diamonds, meanwhile, was ducking under mechanical arms and stumbling across loading bays. The pawns and card soldiers split into two groups and gave chase, but the lord ran a serpentine course, erratic and nonsensical enough to avoid capture until he sighted an unobstructed path to the tent's exit. He sprinted toward it, was just a couple strides from freedom when—

"Ugh!"

The white knight dove off a storage rack and tackled him. Out came another grenade and—*foosh!*—the Lord of Diamonds was encaged in a porta-prison.

The pawns and card soldiers gathered round, congratulating one another on a mission accomplished. Or *mostly* accomplished. For in all the rumpus, he of the oversized rump, Jack of Diamonds, had quietly slipped away.

CHAPTER 27

HATTER FOLLOWED Arch's bodyguards out of the Sin Bin Gaming Club and across a dusty street to a tent repair shop that was itself in need of repair. Blister took up position on one side of the entrance, Ripkins on the other, and the Milliner pushed aside the tent flap and stepped inside.

"Hatter Madigan," King Arch said.

He instinctively calculated his odds: Arch; the nervous proprietor hunched over a patching machine; the two assassins out front; probably reinforcements nearby. Not the greatest situation, but Hatter had faced worse.

"Where are the Ganmedes I'm to negotiate with?"

"They couldn't make it. But I have the power to deal on their behalf. I assume you have the power to negotiate for your queen?"

Hatter gave no indication either way.

"Ripkins!" Arch shouted, and when the called-for guard entered the tent: "Escort our host across the street for a drink."

"N-no, that's all right," said the proprietor, "I'm not thirsty." But Ripkins had already stepped up to him and taken hold of his elbow. "I mean, I'm not *not* thirsty. Sometimes I don't realize how thirsty I am until I have a drink, and then it's as if I could drink an entire . . . "

The proprietor's words were lost to the world outside. Hatter and Arch were alone. Reinforcements would never make it in time. All Hatter had to do was flick his wrist and the king would be dead.

"I wonder how Alyss and the others reacted to hearing that the great Millinery man had secretly fathered a child," Arch mused.

"And I wonder how the great King Arch knew about it."

Arch laughed. "*That* is a question that will soon be answered, my Millinery friend. I prefer questions that have definite answers, don't you? As opposed to abstract ones concerning the meaning and purpose of life, blah blah blah. You'd probably like to know that your daughter is being adequately taken care of."

"I want to see her."

"As would I, were our places reversed. Unfortunately, I'm unable to accommodate your request. The Ganmedes are clever. They've asked me to negotiate for them, but they haven't told me where they're keeping her."

"There are no Ganmede kidnappers," Hatter said through tightened jaw. "Not unless they're working for you."

"No? Well, they'll be surprised to learn of their nonexistence. But if you're so sure, why don't you take me prisoner and force my hand?"

Hatter was wondering the same thing.

Arch assumed a look of benevolence. "Do you know, Hatter, that I often worry about you? I fear you're not making the most of your skills and intelligence. You've worked closely with two queens and so know the ins and outs of governing. You have the respect and loyalty of all who serve in Wonderland's military. It's a surprise to me that you haven't become Wonderland's ruler yourself."

"I was born a Milliner."

"Don't be so old-fashioned. You were born to reinvent yourself as many times as you like. We all were. What was it Queen Genevieve used to say? 'In imagination lies freedom'? It's rare that I agree with any female, but in this case I'll have to lend authority to Genevieve's little maxim by seconding it. Why not be a Milliner *and* a ruler? You're not being very imaginative, Hatter."

"I'm not here to discuss my personal failures with you."

"But wouldn't you consider Homburg Molly among those failures?"

Hatter reached for his top hat as if he'd been physically

attacked. He ran his fingers along its brim, Arch's life saved by the hesitation. The king would have to wait for what he deserved until Hatter could be sure of Molly's safety.

"Having been away from your official duties," Arch said as the Milliner's hand lowered to his side, "you might not have heard, but I've developed a weapon capable of destroying all of Boarderland, Wonderland, Morgavia, Unterlan, and who knows what else. I call it WILMA, which stands for Weapon of Inconceivable Loss and Massive Annihilation. It also happens to be the name of one of my former wives, who had to be put down on account of her feisty temper. I'm sure you can guess that I have no desire to obliterate myself or my nation. I do, however, know that for the betterment of all life and the inflation of my self-worth, my nation must expand to include yours and the others. But for this to happen, WILMA must be fully operational and the threat of my employing her genuine, otherwise your queen and the 'rulers' of Morgavia and Unterlan will have no reason to subjugate their governments to me. The interesting little wrinkle in all this, Hatter, is that in order for WILMA to operate at her full power, I need you. How and why I need you will be explained in the near future. But first, I'd like to invite you to join my tribe. I don't ask everyone. You should be flattered."

"Are these the terms for Molly's release? I 'join' your tribe and you'll let her go, unharmed?"

Arch, pacing throughout his talk of WILMA, had paused at the tent's entrance. He now waved for someone outside to approach. "I think you'll find that you have more reasons to join with me than merely securing Molly's safety."

With that, the king stepped outside. In his place stood an apparition, an illusion, a wish: Weaver. How long the ensuing silence lasted, Hatter didn't know.

"I thought . . ." he murmured finally, unable to finish. *I thought you were dead.*

"Did you get the diary I left for you?" she asked.

He nodded. "But I don't under—"

"Oh, Hatter!"

She ran to him and he held close the much-loved body he thought he'd never hold again, breathing in the smell of her and waiting to be overwhelmed by the joy and relief of finding her so unexpectedly alive. But he had too many questions, the same, nagging, prickling questions he'd had since his reclusive days atop Talon's Point.

Gently, he unclasped Weaver's arms from around his neck. Tears were in her eyes. She guessed what he was thinking.

"I wasn't as irresponsible as it seems," she said. "The Alyssian camp in the Everlasting Forest . . . I knew Molly would be in excellent care. I just . . . I *had* to leave you word of our daughter, and I had to leave it somewhere safe where I knew you'd get it no matter what happened to me or Molly or the Alyssian cause."

"But what are you doing here, with Arch?"

"That," she said, smiling, "was a lucky accident. One of his guards, Ripkins, happened to see me enter the tunnel leading up to our cave at Talon's Point. He followed me and overheard me recording the diary. I thought he was one of Redd's troops come to kill me. But without saying a word, he gave me one of his communicators. Arch was waiting to talk to me and said he knew about Redd, that she was hunting down everyone connected to the Millinery and that, if I'd let him, Ripkins would bring me to Boarderland, where I'd be protected. I wasn't going to go at first, but then I thought . . . I worried that if Redd found out who Molly was, she would kill us both, so I thought the best way to save our daughter was to stay away from her. Tell me I made the right decision. Tell me I did."

She was crying afresh. Hatter reached up and cupped her face between his hands, wiped her tears with his thumbs.

"You made the right decision, Weaver."

She put her head against his shoulder. "I'd assumed the worst after Redd destroyed the Alyssian headquarters. But Arch came to me as soon as Molly was abducted. He promised to do everything he could to get her back. We're lucky the Ganmedes chose him as their intermediary."

"You really believe Molly's been kidnapped by Ganmedes?"

"I've seen them. I've seen *her*."

Hatter was taken aback. "Where? When?"

"In Boarderland. I don't know exactly *where* we were camped, but . . . it was during the last eclipse of a Thurmite moon. She's grown so much. She was confused more than

234

anything else. About us. I didn't get to spend much time with her."

Hatter was no longer listening. Molly was in Boarderland, probably not far away. Arch would want to keep her close. Arch, who was probably monitoring his and Weaver's every word. Unless the king knew something about Weaver that Hatter didn't, and there was no need to bug the tent.

"Before I met with Arch," the Milliner said, "I suspected there were no Ganmede kidnappers. Now that I've met with him, I'm sure there aren't any."

"What are you talking about? I just told you I saw them."

"They're working for Arch."

"That's ludicrous! You think, after all he's done for me, Arch took her? Why would he—"

"He's using the two of you to get to me for some reason. Who else knew she was our daughter? You said his guard heard you record the diary."

"He found me by accident, Hatter!" The folded arms, the head tilted slightly forward while she eyed him from beneath the overhang of her brow: She was getting mad. "I owe Arch my life," she said. "He's been nothing but kind and helpful."

"When has King Arch ever been kind and helpful without an ulterior motive?"

"Being a Milliner makes you suspicious of everybody. You're so smart when it comes to military things, why doesn't it translate into being smart about *others*? I don't want you to accuse Arch again. He's my friend."

He would get nowhere arguing with her. Either she'd been brainwashed or the stress of the past years, of giving up her daughter, had made her susceptible to a faith in the goodness of others, even in those who'd exhibited no special affinity for goodness.

"You truly believe we need Arch if we're to get Molly back safe?" Hatter asked.

"Yes."

"And you trust him?"

"Almost as much as I trust you."

He kissed her. "Wait here."

He hadn't decided what he was going to do even as he stepped outside the tent, where Arch, Ripkins, and Blister were waiting. Kill or defer, kill or defer, he couldn't make up his mind. But then he was standing in front of the king and his body seemed to decide for him. Just as he had done in the past, whenever showing reverence for Genevieve or Alyss Heart, he prostrated himself.

"If your invitation still stands, Your Majesty," he said, "I would be honored to join your tribe."

CHAPTER 28

REDD HEART had been born to attract attention, and no garment from any universe, known or unknown, could have prevented the eyes of lesser creatures from being drawn to her. Finding that all attempts to blend in with the sorry specimens of Earth were futile, she stopped trying. In London's Crystal Palace, she donned her dress of flesh-eating roses and twirled before a reflective glass, a renegade Heart pleased with what she saw.

"I now consider myself *officially* introduced to Earth society," she pronounced.

A cheer went up from her recruits—a cheer more akin to grumbling thunder than a hearty outpouring, which for the thousand or so earthlings and ex-Wonderlanders enlisted to Redd's cause in the past months, was the closest they could manage.

"Scatter," Redd commanded.

So they did, dispersing to explore their new home and to idle away the hours with petty scams and abuses, eager for what Redd had promised would be the most unwholesome adventure of their lives—their attack on Wonderland, when whatever cruel talents each possessed were to be indulged to their fullest. They were still spilling out of the palace's Italian court when Vollrath offered himself up to his pupil.

"It isn't clear that your Earth clothes have helped in our recruitment process, Your Imperial Viciousness," the tutor said. "Therefore, I'm ready for whatever death you have in mind for me. Whether mercifully quick or agonizingly slow and torturous, I readily give myself up to it, as I said I would."

Redd stared at the bald head bent down before her. How refreshing Vollrath's sacrifice was. He didn't beg for his life. He didn't embarrass himself with groveling or sniveling, or appeals to her nonexistent mercy. Thinking that he might still be helpful in finding her Looking Glass Maze, she said, "I'm feeling generous today. You get to live."

"I thank you for your leniency, Your Imperial Viciousness."

"Leniency is for the weak-minded. Do not goad me with leniency."

Vollrath bowed. "I apologize, Your Imperial Viciousness. But if I may overstep my bounds and impose further on your by no means lenient generosity: Since you are going to let me live, could you perhaps imagine for me . . . oh, let's say a fistful of money, with which I and a few others can celebrate?"

"You'll find it in your pockets. Now leave me to my brooding."

The recruitment search had taken Redd across the European continent—to Africa, Asia, Russia, and back to Europe, Vollrath and Sacrenoir serving as her constant companions, her guides and recruitment officers. And just as had happened with Hatter Madigan during his thirteen-year search for the exiled Alyss Heart, wherever Redd went, stories began to circulate that in time would become legend, myth. Redd passed through Germany and tales of a *kobold* resembling her description were whispered. In Scandinavia, she was turned into a *trollkonor* with a bit of the *huldra* about her, and like every trollkonor, she was said to have a tail. In Spain, she became an evil temptress of Moors. In Constantinople, she was transformed into one of the most powerful *alkiris* ever heard of, immune to steel and particularly spiteful in her killing of newborn babies and their mothers. In Egypt, she was said to be a female demon, a devourer of souls. In Hong Kong, a new goddess cursed her way into the immortal pantheon, to be trusted less than Lei-zi, the goddess of thunder, and to be feared as much as Chu Jiang, king of the hell reserved for thieves and murderers. But as these stories passed from lips to lips, imprinting themselves on the public consciousness of various cultures, so too through derelict districts and select upper-class salons did the truth become known: Redd Heart, displaced evil Queen of Wonderland, wanted soldiers to fight with her for her queendom.

"P-Potential recruits seem more than w-willing to come to you, Your Imperial Viciousness," Vollrath had noted, shivering on a street corner in Saint Petersburg. "All you n-n-need do is choose somewhere to r-reside until we return to W-Wonderland so that would-be s-s-s-soldiers will know where to f-find you."

Redd, unlike her followers, was immune to the cold, the stinging wind. "Then we will live in the same city where my niece once lived," she had said, "to sour whatever lingering effects of White Imagination her presence might have had on the place."

So Vollrath and Sacrenoir had carried Redd to Oxford, England, where they escorted her around the provincial streets, the quads of Oxford University. It hadn't taken long for Her Imperial Viciousness to see that she couldn't live there.

"I'm nauseous from all of these picturesque lanes and quaint shops," Redd had announced. "It suits my niece perfectly. She can have it."

Soon thereafter, Redd had arrived on the streets of England's capital city. A haughty-faced woman with cottony edges, a purring cat riding on her shoulders, and over one hundred international rogues massed behind her, Londoners had gaped and gawked as she called Vollrath and Sacrenoir to her side in Trafalgar Square to discuss where to live.

"There's always Buckingham Palace."

"Beneath me," Redd had scorned. "I won't acknowledge their 'queen' by taking over her hovel."

"Then you'll no doubt find the mansions of their dukes and duchesses beneath you."

"No doubt."

"There is another possibility," Vollrath had said. "It's an enormous structure, predominantly of iron and glass, the size of which suggests to many the strength of a mighty empire as well as boundless imagination. They say it houses the marvels of the age, from steam hammers, hydraulic presses, firearms, furniture, pianos, pottery, perfumes, diving suits, fabrics, and—"

"Enough!" Redd had commanded. "I expect nothing great from Earth imaginations, but to shut you up, I will suffer you to take me there."

The Crystal Palace was located on Sydenham Hill in the south of London, an Erector set of elaborate ironwork and 350,000 square yards of glass panels. But its palatial courts— examples of technological progress and human ingenuity— were almost overshadowed by its painstakingly landscaped parks, their terraces and gardens complete with waterfalls and man-made lakes in the center of which jets of water shot twenty feet into the air.

"What do you think?" Vollrath had asked as they stood by the Lower Lakes whose grounds were home to statues of actual-sized dinosaurs.

"Eh," Redd had grunted. "I suppose it'll have to do."

It was Sunday, the Crystal Palace closed to the public. Much to the disappointment of Redd's soldiers, aside from a few broken windows and a scuffle or two with lonely security guards, they had commandeered the palace without incident. And it was now, as Her Imperial Viciousness was passing through the Italian Court, that she glimpsed her reflection in a bit of decorative glass—a charismatic and (she thought) crystal-genic leader stuffed into an unflattering Earth dress. With a dismissive sweep of her arm, thread became rose vines, the weave of silk became rose vines, frills of lace became rose blossoms whose petal-mouths opened and closed, clacking their teeth.

The Cat sprang off Redd's shoulder and morphed into a humanoid assassin, which caused a murmur of awe to pass among those recruits who'd never seen him at his most dangerous.

"Earth's high society will have to contend with us in earnest now," Redd said.

"Good," purred The Cat.

~

Redd might have declared her entrance to Earth society official on Sunday, but it wasn't until Monday that Earth society learned of it. Palace employees—cashiers, ticket takers, tour guides, and security guards—showed up for work that morning as usual, but instead of the customary church-like quiet, they found Redd's soldiers roaming about amidst shattered glass, broken statues, smashed furnishings, and decimated art. The sight of Redd's horde was enough to make even the most courageous ticket taker go whey-faced and run, but when Redd and The Cat themselves appeared, attracted by the sound of troops terrorizing fresh victims, the more fragile among them took one look at the queen's ghastly visage and the assassin's glinting claws and fainted where they cowered. A fleet of bobbies arrived. But sighting the motley trespassers, none of the officers charged forth with the bravery they might have displayed against a more recognizable enemy.

"Who are these foolish-looking men with their round hats?" Redd smirked. "They've nothing but clubs for weapons."

To exercise her imagination more than anything else, she flicked her fingers at them. *Thimp, thimp thimp thimp!* The bobbies felt the sting of scatter shot through their uniforms, against their flesh; not the usual scatter shot of steel or metal balls, but *pennies*. Paper money began to rain down from the ceiling. The bobbies stuffed their pockets as fast as they could and ran from the palace. The authorities were powerless; Redd and her followers would not be dislodged from their new abode.

Men from the press soon ventured to Sydenham Hill, risking their lives to interview the woman who could conjure storms of money at will.

"Yes, let them inform the pathetic public that Redd Heart has come," Her Imperial Viciousness said when Vollrath explained what they wanted. "I have allowed myself to wallow in anonymity long enough."

Whenever a new article was printed in the newspapers, Redd took her pet assassin out for a stroll, amusing herself with the chaos she and The Cat caused—Londoners fleeing in every direction at the sight of them.

She organized her troops along conventional hierarchical lines, the least talented divided into companies of fifty-two, each company captained by a recruit with greater imaginative gifts than those beneath her. The captains reported to battalion commanders more gifted than they. Each commander had five captains reporting to her while they themselves reported to the most gifted recruits, those who reported directly to Redd. Among this last, powerful rank was Baroness Dvonna, who had a talent for draining imagination from young and inexperienced Earth children not yet in full control of their abilities, leaving them forever lethargic, withered, glum. How this talent might fare against Wonderlanders was unclear, but Redd enjoyed the fact that the woman had littered Earth with a generation of sourpuss children. Plus, the baroness had a great many of these children under her control and, if nothing else, they could be thrown on the front line against Alyss' forces.

Redd's top military rank also included Alistaire Poole, a self-taught surgeon-cum-undertaker with a penchant for performing autopsies on people not in the least dead. His weapons of choice were scalpel and bone saw. There was Siren

Hecht, an ex-Wonderlander whose imaginative gift lay in her ability to imagine her voice into such shrill, piercing registers that bank managers would fall to the ground, writhing with pain, while she helped herself to their vaults. And rounding out Redd's crew of direct reports: the Marquis and Marquise X from the Basque region of Spain who, unfortunately for the local goatherds, were adept in hypnosis and occult spells; Mr. Van de Skülle, a slave trader originally from the Dutch West Indies who'd made a menace of himself during America's civil war and was particularly skilled with a spike-tipped whip; and, of course, Sacrenoir.

Whereas this crowd of elite Black Imaginationists had been wooed into Redd's service by Vollrath, those who made up the lower ranks—foot soldiers, grunts—traveled from all over the world for an opportunity to line up before Her Imperial Viciousness, subjecting themselves to her inspection and interrogation. Twice a week, Redd enlisted new recruits from this mass of hopefuls, passing before each of them while Vollrath related his or her particular talents.

"As you know, Your Imperial Viciousness," the tutor explained one night, "most imaginationists are good at a single thing only, as an ordinary Wonderlander might be gifted in math but not poetry. Take this one here." Redd and the tutor were standing before a sunken-chested man whose tattered clothes and unruly beard made him look as if he'd just been rescued from a deserted isle. "This former Wonderlander can do nothing but shoot pellets from his elbows."

"His *elbows?*" Redd frowned. "Show me."

The man bent his arms and, after a moment of concentration, tiny disks zipped out from his bony elbows and plunked against the wall.

"Tsst," Redd said, unmoved. She made her choices. The perimeter of the room was suddenly lined with soldiers and, with Vollrath and her commanders at her heels, she started for the exit, calling out, "As for the rest of you . . . good-bye!" By the time she convened with The Cat in the hall, the rejects—including the elbow shooter—had been summarily dispatched.

Redd's feline assassin had just returned from one of his late-night forays into the city. Where he went on these excursions, or what he did, not even Her Imperial Viciousness knew. But he inevitably returned with a load of bird carcasses, which he would drop at his mistress's feet. Amid the carcasses tonight, however, there was also a book.

"Think you're posh, do you?" Redd fumed when she saw it. "Want to improve yourself with *reading?*"

"Look at the title," said The Cat.

The book flew up to her hand. *Alice in Wonderland.*

"A-L-I-C-E?" Redd said.

"It's about your niece," said The Cat. "It's filled with idiotic lies about Wonderland, but it's famous here."

"Someone wrote a book about my niece?" Redd turned on her tutor. "Did you know about this?"

"I swear I didn't," Vollrath lied.

She let the book fall open in her hand. She riffled through its pages from first to last with her imagination. To think that Alyss had been immortalized by some Earth scribbler! She slammed the book shut. She tapped a long finger against its cover, under the author's name. "Find this Lewis Carroll and bring him here!"

The Cat hurried off. Sacrenoir and the rest of the commanders loped away to discipline their troops.

Redd scowled in the direction of the palace's Renaissance Court, where her rejected recruits lay dead on the cold hard floor. "At this rate, it will take a lifetime to amass even half the soldiers I'll need."

"Perhaps," suggested Vollrath, his ears genuflecting, "a few of us should return to Wonderland to search for your maze while Sacrenoir and others continue to gather an army here?"

Redd knew, despite her many displays of imaginative strength, that her powers had weakened. She would never have admitted it—she was still a hundred times stronger than anyone around—but she was too far from the Heart Crystal. She had to get close to it again, to feel a fresh influx of its energy, and sooner rather than later . . .

CHAPTER 29

IN HEART Palace's memorial wing, Alyss was sitting on an exact replica of her mother's favorite settee, gazing expectantly into a looking glass as if hoping to find the wisdom of the ages in its quicksilver.

So many rulers become tyrants, partaking more of Black Imagination than White. Is it because being a queen or king makes you selfish? When everyone around you does as you tell them, never speaks their true minds for fear of upsetting you . . . How can a ruler not grow increasingly less tolerant of anyone or anything that frustrates her? But mother wasn't like that . . . was she?

"Queen Alyss."

She hadn't noticed Bibwit and General Doppelgänger enter the room. How long had they been standing there?

"A curious thing has been discovered," Bibwit said.

"I'm almost afraid to ask what you mean by 'curious.'"

"And I'm almost afraid to tell you, my dear Alyss. But it appears that imaginationists who were in the continuum at the time of Molly's—what shall I call it?—her mishap, yes, well . . . it seems that these imaginationists have found themselves *unable to perform*. We've had reports of conjurers unable to conjure, writers unable to write, musicians unable to play their instruments or compose, and inventors unable to invent. Just as the mysterious NRG that Homburg Molly unwittingly released has rendered the Crystal Continuum unusable, so too has it rendered the abilities of imaginationists."

"The NRG does seem to be dissipating with time," General Doppelgänger offered. "Whenever one of my soldiers tries to enter a looking glass portal, the NRG knocks him back, but not as forcefully as it once did. The continuum should shortly be available to citizens. We do hope that some remnant of the weapon that caused all of this will be found once the continuum is viable again, but we're not counting on it."

Alyss remained silent, staring into the looking glass. Bibwit motioned with an ear and the general took the hint.

"Queen Alyss, if you will excuse me, I must tend to . . . something. Please accept my congratulations."

Alyss was startled. "For what?"

But the general's footfalls were already echoing down the hall. Bibwit swiveled his ears away from the door, the better to focus them on his immediate surroundings. He peeked into the looking glass that had so held Alyss' attention. He saw nothing but the room's reflection.

"Have you located him?" he asked.

Hatter. Alyss had, in her imagination's eye, spotted the Milliner less than half a lunar hour ago, but it had been exactly the same as all the other times: Instead of finding him deep in negotiations with Arch to secure Molly's release, he was tagging along with the king as one of his attendants—at banquets, speeches, gaming events, military exercises. Hatter's behavior was, in the worst sense of the word, curious.

"No," she lied. "I still haven't found him."

The Milliner's disobedience had necessitated a change in strategy: She'd had to direct the knight and rook, already on their way to rendezvous with Arch at the Sin Bin Gaming Club, to arrest the Lord and Lady of Diamonds instead, leaving Hatter to try and secure Molly's release as he thought best. Nothing else seemed feasible. Whether or not the Milliner would face consequences for his disobedience depended, to some degree, on what happened with Molly, as well as his attitude when—*if*—he and his daughter returned.

"I've also been searching for Molly," she said. "In Boarderton and the Ganmede province . . . "

Bibwit sat down beside her on the tufted bench. "But you don't see her either?"

"No."

She'd been contacted by Arch soon after Hatter's arrival in Boarderland. "Queen Heart," the king had boomed, "I am thankful—for Homburg Molly's sake—that you've sent the Milliner to negotiate on her behalf, as the Ganmedes requested. Mr. Madigan is a keen negotiator and I have every confidence that he and the Ganmedes will shortly agree to terms assuring Homburg Molly's release. But why hear it from me when you can hear it from Hatter himself?"

The Milliner had then come online, Alyss hoping for a clue to help interpret his behavior. But looking as blank as a fresh sheet of papyrus, Hatter only corroborated what Arch had already told her—he was negotiating for Molly's release; there was cause for optimism.

He must have known she would look for him with her imagination's eye; which meant he must have known that she had seen him gallivanting about with Arch; which in turn meant he knew that Alyss knew that he was lying about his negotiations. And yet he had lied anyway. Why? Even if Arch had been eavesdropping, with a timely dip of the head or shift of the eyes Hatter could have communicated the precarious-ness of the role he'd assumed. With a patterned blinking of eyelids, he could have reassured her that all she'd seen him doing, he had done for Molly and the queendom. Had his love for Molly made a deserter of him?

"I think perhaps I too should congratulate you," Bibwit said.

"Why does everyone keep wanting to congratulate me?"

Bibwit winked and nudged Alyss several times. "Why, indeed. I can understand your not wanting to make a grand announcement of it, Alyss. But I have not lived through untold generations for nothing, and I believe that even if the queendom weren't dealing with its present problems, you would not have chosen to flaunt your disregard of a royal practice that Wonderland queens have abided by since at least the time of my birth." He winked and nudged her some more, his ears flopping friskily atop his head.

"Bibwit, *what* are you talking about?"

"Although," the tutor qualified, "if you do plan to marry below your rank, I think you can outrage history even more by choosing lower than a guardsman."

Alyss blushed.

Bibwit leaned closer and spoke soothingly, sincerely. "Your recent displays of affection have been admirably subtle, my dear, but no longer hiding your feelings from yourselves, it's impossible that you could hide them from the rest of us—or, at least, from me. I congratulate you on your engagement to Dodge."

"Well, technically, I'm not sure we're—"

"Technicalities are for engineers, Alyss. I approve your choice of Dodge for a husband, even if, technically, it isn't my place to do so. But humor a wise, ancient albino, will you, and don't chastise me for my approval."

After some time, Alyss said, "Thank you." Her thoughts had led her back to Hatter, to the possible reasons for his troubling behavior in Boarderland.

It has everything to do with Arch, I know it does.

Throughout their trial, the Lord and Lady of Diamonds had asserted their innocence, claiming that they had been set up by Boarderland's king. The evidence said otherwise: So damning was it that even the Diamonds' connections in court hadn't saved them from being sentenced to the Crystal Mines for twenty lunar years.

"I doubt Lord and Lady Diamond were as innocent as they claimed," Alyss said, "and yet . . . "

"You think there may be some truth in what they alleged of Arch?" asked Bibwit. "That it had been his idea to give Molly the mysterious weapon?"

"Yes."

"We've discussed this, Alyss. As helpless as it makes you feel, when it comes to King Arch, nothing can be done. It wouldn't be wise to accuse him of aggression against Wonderland, especially when we have only the Diamonds' accusations to support the claim."

"I know."

Bibwit smiled—one of those sad smiles suggestive of a lifetime of accumulated knowledge, not all of it heartwarming. "But what you know and what you feel are two different things?"

She nodded.

"It's a hard lesson," said the tutor, "one of the hardest, to learn that with all of your imaginative powers, there are times when you can do nothing."

CHAPTER 30

ARCH HAD long ago found that his best defense against enemies was to guard against what he would do if he were his own adversary. Putting himself in Hatter's place—shockingly reunited with Weaver, his daughter held prisoner—Arch would have made the same choice the Milliner had made; he too would have joined the tribe. But, the king reminded himself, Hatter's joining the tribe should not be mistaken for genuine allegiance. If he were Hatter, he would use it as a means of gaining time to learn what he could of Molly's whereabouts, and to get reacquainted with Weaver. He would do all he was told until such time as he could effect Molly's rescue. Convicting Hatter of his own counterplots, Arch did not allow the Milliner to go anywhere unobserved. Hatter took his meals with Ripkins and Blister and was given a cot in their tent. On the occasions he was granted leave to visit with Weaver, an intel minister was always close by, watching, listening. Was it reckless to let the Milliner converse with Weaver? Arch didn't think so. If anything, the care he himself had shown to Weaver, and the "friendship" that had formed as a result, might confuse Hatter, chip away at his steadfast loyalty to the Heart clan until, for the security of his own family, he became more accepting of Arch as his king. Hatter might go from feigning allegiance to sincerely embodying it.

"Do you know what this is?" Arch asked.

He held the silken thread aloft, stretched taught between his hands. The thread glinted in the light. If the Milliner knew what it was, he didn't say.

"It is silk produced by one of Wonderland's six caterpillar-oracles," Arch explained. "This one, I believe—it's hard to see in this light—is orange. I know you're familiar with the power of caterpillar silk, Hatter, so there's no use pretending."

"My hat is, in part, made of them."

"Yes. Your hat contains threads from the blue and purple caterpillars and it is these that account for the hat's remarkable characteristics as a weapon. You see that I know things you would not expect me to know. The spinster who taught Milliners to manufacture their hats in just such a way, what was her name?"

"Miss Hado."

"Miss Hado, that's right. Poor Miss Hado. Once Redd took

control of Wonderland, she didn't survive much longer than Queen Genevieve. But as determined as Redd was to eliminate Milliners from existence, she was somewhat lax in the disposal of their headgear. Had you managed to avoid Redd's Glass Eyes after her coup, Hatter, you could have gone around to Wonderland's many purveyors of contraband and bought up the headgear of your assassinated Millinery colleagues. You would've had to be quick about it, though, as you wouldn't have been alone. The supply of Milliner hats, never abundant, became more and more limited as Wonderlanders unraveled them, trying to discover how the caterpillar threads worked. No one succeeded in this, I assume, or we would've known it by now."

"You must have succeeded, Your Majesty," Hatter said, "or I wouldn't be here."

Arch toyed with his caterpillar thread, coiling and uncoiling it around a finger. "You will not provoke me into telling more than I wish. I unspool this information to you a small amount at a time, much as one of your caterpillars spools silk out its spinneret. You will be told as little as is necessary for you to perform the task I require of you. Now let's see, what else do I know that might surprise you?"

In trying to surmise the details of Arch's plan, Hatter had concluded that it *had* been an accident. Arch could not have lured Weaver to Boarderland as part of his present scheme. To do that, the king would've had to know about his and

Weaver's relationship *before* she left the Everlasting Forest's Alyssian headquarters for Talon's Point. The king would have either had to induce Weaver to abandon Molly at the headquarters and risk a journey to Talon's Point, or he would've had to know, not only that she *would* do such a thing, but *when* she was going to do it. And as clever as Arch was, none of these was possible. Ripkins had stumbled upon Weaver at Talon's Point and Arch, learning who she was, had cultivated a relationship with her in case it might one day prove useful. Which it obviously had.

"I know," Arch resumed, "that when using caterpillar silk to make a Milliner's hat, the mix of colors and the amount of each color used have everything to do with the powers produced. I know that the stitch in which the threads are bound are equally important. I suppose what I'm saying is that different combinations of caterpillar silk produce different weapons. For example, were you to take a bit of green thread and a pebble-sized wad of yellow thread and weave them together in a butterfly stitch, you'd better be sure to have a zincon-lined container to put them in, because you'll have produced something not unlike what recently upset Wonderland's Crystal Continuum. I also know that each of you Milliners was taught to manufacture your own hat, as it was believed you should give birth, so to speak, to the weapon that would become an extension of yourself."

"Your knowledge befits your authority, Your Majesty," Hatter said.

"And every Milliner's hat contained no more than a couple shreds of caterpillar thread. Often they contained no more than one color. Isn't that right?"

"As far as I know. I only have experience with making my own hat."

"Hatter, what if I told you that I had enough silk from all six of Wonderland's caterpillar-oracles to produce many generations' worth of Millinery hats?"

Hatter said nothing, hoping Arch would answer his own question. It couldn't be that he wanted the foremost Milliner of the age to sit around manufacturing top hats for Boarderland forces, could it? "Are you sure they're not counterfeit, Your Majesty?" Hatter asked.

"I'm sure."

They sat looking at each other.

"You haven't asked me how I came to possess so much caterpillar silk, Hatter."

"It's not my business, Your Majesty. My business is for me to do as you command, to prove my loyalty to you and thereby earn my daughter's freedom."

"I don't know why you insist on believing your daughter's freedom is mine to grant, " Arch said with a scowl. "One thing remains to be done if WILMA is to be fully operational. You'll soon serve your purpose, Mr. Madigan, and then we'll see how far your loyalty to me extends."

~

The bodyguards' tent was typical of Boardertonian bachelors—the cots covered with quilts of unicorn skin, the furniture all silver alloy and animal hides. Taking up most of the tent was an entertainment matrix, complete with virtual reality booth, 360-degree holo-screens, a game-controller body suit, and enough buttons, knobs, and switches to dizzy even the most technologically savvy.

Hatter was washing up at the water basin, in preparation for a night out, while Ripkins watched him, lounging on his cot with feet crossed and hands clasped behind his head.

"You sure she doesn't have any friends?" Ripkins teased, swinging his feet to the floor and reaching for Hatter's top hat, which rested innocently on the Milliner's cot. He examined its lining as if he were a haberdasher inspecting a competitor's wares. "'Cause I'd give anything to find a meaningful, long-term relationship like the one you and Weaver have. Wouldn't you, Blister?"

Blister, sitting at the dining board amid take-out containers and dirty plates, pinched dead the last leaf of an olive branch poking out of a vase. "No," he said.

"How do I look?" Ripkins asked, plopping Hatter's top hat on his head.

Hatter spun, slapped at the hat's front brim; it flipped from Ripkins' head to his own. "It looks better on me."

"You should probably know," Blister said to him, "we took it easy on you back at Sin Bin."

259

"Did you?" Hatter said. "That's ironic, since I took it easy on *you*." And with that, the Milliner stepped from the tent, out into the Boarderton night.

Weaver was waiting for him outside the Living Room Tavern, so-called because its tables and chairs were as alive as its patrons. Hatter held the tent flap open for Weaver and—

"Ah, the Madigans," their usual table said as they entered. "Where should I position myself this evening? We have some space by the mullet-hawk buffet."

Made of hydroponic barks particular to the marshy regions of Boarderland, the furnishings at the Living Room Tavern used the exposed roots at the bottom of their legs to get around, steeping these root systems in tubs of water whenever they weren't catering to customers. Two chairs approached. Crossing paths with other similarly engaged furniture, one of the chairs carried Hatter to the riverfront buffet, which featured thirteen different species of fish from the Bookie River, while the other chair carried Weaver to the salad bar. They then convened at the usual table, which had stationed itself near the mullet-hawk buffet.

"Has there been any progress concerning your daughter?" the table asked.

"Not enough," Weaver said, with a pointed look at Hatter.

"I'm very sorry to hear it," said the table. "But I'm sure things will turn out all right, particularly with King Arch aiding you. Now what would the two of you like to drink?"

Hatter and Weaver were again carried into the traffic of crisscrossing chairs and tables to fill their glasses. When they were returned to their meal, their table stayed quiet, respecting their right to privacy while they ate. But Weaver seemed bent on respecting her own privacy, silently forking salad into her mouth until her utensil at last clanked down on her plate.

"I know you've been doing your best and these Ganmedes are being ridiculous in their demands . . . "

Hatter's face showed surprise.

"Arch keeps me informed," Weaver explained. "Anyway, I know you're not used to negotiating as much as you are to . . . fighting, but I think we should at least have daily proof of Molly's well-being, don't you? Especially *because* the Ganmedes' demands are so extreme."

"I'll arrange it," Hatter said, not daring to tell her that the only Ganmedes he'd seen were a couple of Arch's tailors and that, as yet, he'd negotiated with no one, not unless he counted his recent meeting with Arch. So while Weaver did her best to be upbeat, talking proudly of Molly's maturity and good looks, and of how nice it would be when the three of them were living as a family for the first time, the Milliner retreated into his thoughts . . .

Assuming that Ripkins had come upon Weaver by accident at Talon's Point, the question was, What had the bodyguard been doing there in the first place? Spying on the nearby military post? Possible, but not likely—not when there were so many other Wonderland outposts Arch would have deemed of equal or greater strategic value.

"Why're you shaking your head, Hatter?" Weaver asked. "Won't you even consider living in Boarderland? I know you have responsibilities to Queen Alyss and the Millinery, but maybe we could live here part of the year?"

"Maybe."

Hatter guessed that it had to do with WILMA, that Ripkins had probably been on Talon's Point preparing WILMA to go online. He himself had seen nothing irregular when he'd lived on the Point, but then, he hadn't exactly been on the lookout for caterpillar silk. But why was he even thinking about this? It wasn't as if he could set out on a reconnaissance mission to Talon's Point; *that* would bring Arch's displeasure down on him and jeopardize Molly's life.

"I'm sorry," Weaver was saying. "I don't mean to whine and crab at you, it's only . . . I'm so worried about Molly. Our lovely little Molly."

"I know," Hatter said. "I know. Me too."

He had no choice. He had to stay here, trapped between duty to his family and duty to the queendom, at present unable to fulfill either.

CHAPTER 31

EVER SINCE Redd and The Cat had leaped into the Heart Crystal, card soldiers had been posted at the Pool of Tears in case anything from Earth resembling them, physically or in spirit, were to surface. But card soldiers were not enough to deter inconsolable Wonderlanders from throwing themselves *into* the pool. Criminals, runaways, bankrupts— every so often, down-and-out Wonderlanders made runs for the pool, sprinting past the patrolling soldiers and plunging into the water.

Before Jack of Diamonds used the last of his pocket crystal to bribe a border guard and reenter Wonderland, he passed through satellite encampments of the Gnobi and Scabbler tribes where, on repeated newscasts and to his extreme humiliation, he learned that both of his parents had been convicted of conspiracy to murder Queen Alyss Heart. The moment the white knight had shown up to arrest him and his father, he'd known King Arch had been setting them up the entire time—using them to deliver his weapon to Homburg Molly, disposing of them once they'd served their purpose.

"Probably never intended to give us back the Diamond Hectariat," Jack grumbled. "If I had even four pocketfuls of crystal, *I'd* set *him* up! I'd show him what happens to anyone who plots against my family!"

But that was the problem: Though he was now in Wonderland, he had no access to the family accounts, the vaults of rubies and emeralds and crystals. As a fugitive from the law, he could not return to the family's estate, nor was there a single Wonderlander he trusted to offer him refuge.

"Why'd I ever bother coming back here?" he groused.

Without riches, he could not help his parents escape the Crystal Mines, nor could he avoid the authorities for long. Not knowing what else to do, Jack of Diamonds sulked his way to the Whispering Woods and stood peering out at the card soldiers who patrolled the cliff overlooking the Pool of Tears.

"Why, why, whyeeee!" he moaned. "Why'd Arch have to ruin my life? What'd I ever do to him?" After a considerable time spent pulling his hair in disbelief over his reduced state, he sighed, "Here goes," and made a break for it, running as fast as his flabby legs could carry him toward the cliff's edge.

Strange. Here he was, a high-ranking escaped convict, and not only were the soldiers not trying to stop him, they didn't even notice him, too intent on staring down at the Pool of Tears with their crystal shooters and AD52s at the ready. Jack slowed to a jog. Still no one noticed him. When he reached the edge of the cliff, he stopped. Together with the soldiers, he looked down at the bubbling, roiling water. Whirlpools were forming—first one, then another and another.

Someone was coming.

PART THREE

CHAPTER 32

REDD WAS in the Medieval Court at the Crystal Palace, reclining on a stone bench and flipping idly through the pages of *Alice in Wonderland* while she exercised her imagination; all around her translucent Redd Hearts performed knee bends, toe touches and hamstring stretches, but they were shooed into nonexistence when The Cat bounded in with a large burlap sack over his shoulder. Without so much as a meow, the feline assassin untied the sack and dumped its contents at his mistress's feet. A man tumbled out, glancing wildly every which way and cowering as if he expected to be hit. At the sight of Redd, he hugged his knees to his chest, making himself as small as possible, and began mumbling in constant prayer.

"Are you Lewis Carroll?" Redd asked him.

"I-I-I am Charles D-D-Dodgson."

Redd's eye twitched—a precursor to violence, as The Cat well knew. He pawed Dodgson in the back of the head. "Explain," he ordered.

The Don of Mathematics at Christ Church college rubbed his head and spoke in a pout. "I am Ch-Charles D-Dodgson, also known as L-L-L-Lewis C-Carroll, author of the volume y-you hold . . . in your hand."

"So you can't tell the truth even when it comes to your own name?" Redd said. "How perfect." Circling him, studying him as if to be certain the timid creature before her could really be responsible for immortalizing her niece on Earth, she asked, "Do you know who I am?"

"A somewhat blurry woman w-wearing a desp-p-picable costume?"

Taking this as a compliment, Redd trounced about like a dame at her ball. "Yes, it's horrendous, isn't it?" Several roses snaked out from the thicket of the dress and directed their mouthy blooms at Dodgson. "I am Redd Heart. Did my niece ever mention me?"

"I have never met your n-niece."

Redd laughed. "Mr. Dodgson, I think we have established that you are a gifted liar, both in person and . . . " she thumped *Alice in Wonderland*, " . . . in print. Your talent is the reason I brought you here. Your talent and your ill-advised decision to write a book about Alyss Heart, which, doubly unfortunate for you, became popular in this bland world. But do not lie to me, you inconsequential man. You have met my niece and I will not allow myself to be eclipsed by her in Wonderland, on Earth, or anywhere else. You are going to write a book about me, Mr. Dodgson. You will immortalize me, just as you have immortalized Alyss. And my book had better sell more copies than that drivel you scribbled about her."

"B-B-B-But I know nothing about you."

"You will start by writing down anything my niece told you about her dear old aunt Redd. As for the rest . . . *make it up*." Redd then turned to her lieutenants, who were lined up against a wall, waiting for when she might find them useful. "Mr. Van de Skülle, take my biographer here to the Greek Court, where he is to live until his manuscript meets with my approval. You'll find the necessary writing instruments waiting for you," she said to Dodgson. "You might notice that once you enter the court, thick bars will form on the doors and windows. But don't worry yourself. They're only there to prevent you from escaping."

Shortly after Van de Skülle shoved Reverend Dodgson from the room—

"I've found one, Your Imperial Viciousness," Vollrath said, breathlessly entering the court. "It's not far from here, on Cockspur Street."

Redd turned to her lieutenants. "Sacrenoir, you're in charge until we return. As for recruits, I expect you to enlist only the worst of the worst—which, for my purposes, are the best. Alistaire, Siren, come with us."

Out on Cockspur Street, pedestrians scattered like nervous rats as Redd marched at the head of Vollrath, The Cat, Alistaire Poole, and Siren Hecht.

"There!" Vollrath said, pointing to a puddle where no puddle should have been—in the window display of a stationer's shop.

Without slowing or hesitation, Redd shattered the window, stepped into the stationer's display and dropped into the puddle.

Sfoosh!

She was sucked down and out of sight. Vollrath, The Cat, Alistaire, and Siren quickly followed. If the eardrum-popping descent through the multidimensional waters had any effect on Redd, she showed no sign of it. Her face was firm, expressionless, and she kept her eyes wide open as she torpedoed deeper and deeper . . .

Then came the brief suspension in the lightless depths, and the portal's reverse gravity began to take effect, drawing Redd and her underlings up with increasing speed until—

Sploosh! Fablash! Splashaaa!

They exploded out of the Pool of Tears into the open air. Instantly, razor-cards were slicing down around them, muzzlefuls of crystal shot whizzing past their heads. Before Redd splashed back into the water, she was spinning, her arms held out to either side, orb generators spraying out from the tips of her fingers.

Waboooshkkktsh! Ba-ba-booozzzztshchkshkchtt!

The last of the enemy's crystal shot whistled past. The card soldiers patrolling the Pool of Tears were no more.

"They'll know we're coming," Vollrath said, bobbing in the water.

"No, they won't." Redd had, by the power of her imagination, routed to the void every warning the soldiers had tried to send to General Doppelgänger on their crystal communicators.

On dry land, The Cat hissed at the pool and shook the detestable wet from his fur. Redd, being in the same dimension as the Heart Crystal, felt stronger than she had in a long time. She gestured violently, and the not-so-distant white noise Alistaire and Siren had been hearing ceased.

"The Whispering Woods," The Cat said.

"There'll be no whispering about *me*," Redd declared. "Alyss is not to know of my return until I pass through my Looking Glass Maze, by which time Sacrenoir better have amassed the Earth army I'll need to battle her forces, or he'll wind up as a midnight snack for his skeletons."

"But they'll know we've come," Vollrath said again.

Redd looked at him as if she might rip the tongue from his head.

"The caterpillars," the scholar clarified. "Being able to see into the past and the future, they'll know we've come and why."

The Cat brushed at his whiskers. "Back when Her Imperial Viciousness was last in power," he remembered, "she ordered

273

us to destroy those outdated worms, but every time we tried, they saw us coming and slithered off to wherever outdated worms go when they want to be safe."

"I hate truth," Redd spat, "but The Cat is speaking it. Why *should* the caterpillars sit still and let me approach them after what I've done?" she asked Vollrath.

"You don't believe in their prophecies?" the scholar asked, surprised. How could a Heart, one whose family had for generations most gained or lost by the prophecies, not believe in them?

"I see no use for the caterpillars or their fortune-tellings," Redd said. "Whether I believe in them or not is irrelevant when I'm in possession of the Heart Crystal."

"Not if the prophecy has to do with your *having* the Heart Crystal," Vollrath humbly submitted.

"Shut up, tutor. But console yourself with this: I *do* believe that, if anyone can tell me where to find the Garden of Uncompleted Mazes, it's the caterpillars. Now answer the question I put to you: How do we ensure they'll let me approach?"

Vollrath searched his albino brain for an answer, his ears rubbing together like the worrying hands of an earthling. The six caterpillars of Wonderland: servants of the Heart Crystal, the power source for all creation. For the most part, they kept aloof from government intrigues or political rivalries, involving themselves only if they thought the Heart Crystal was in danger of being destroyed. They didn't much care who possessed the crystal, so long as it was left to disseminate imagination, the creative urge and the spirit of invention, to Earth and other worlds.

"When you were last in power," Vollrath asked, "you didn't in any way try to disrupt the Heart Crystal's energy flow, did you?"

"Of course not, fool! It would be no good to me if its power were compromised."

"Well then," Vollrath said happily, and loud enough for the clairvoyant caterpillars to take note. "So long as you promise not to destroy or harm the crystal or in any way disrupt its flow after you resume power, I'm sure the caterpillars will meet with you. Do you promise this?"

"I promise," Redd steamed.

"Good." But in case this wasn't enough to secure the caterpillars' presence, and knowing that there was one thing the oracles couldn't resist, Vollrath added, "When we go to meet them, we shall arrive bearing tarty tarts!"

The Cat, hearing the snap of a twig behind them, twirled around ready to pounce.

"In Redd I trust! The Redd way is the right way!"

Having dropped flat to the ground the moment Redd burst from the pool, Jack of Diamonds had survived her bombardment as card soldiers fell dead to the left and right of him. As soon as he'd recognized who was swimming to shore, he'd hurried down to meet them.

"Wherever Redd leads, I follow!" He now saluted, stepping from the nearby scrub and approaching her imperial viciousness.

"Except when it involves leaping into the Heart Crystal," Redd snarled.

"We shouldn't leave any witnesses," The Cat said.

"No, we shouldn't," Redd agreed, and with that, The Cat swatted Jack to the ground with a paw.

"Let me have him," Alistaire Poole smirked, taking scalpel and bone saw from his instruments case.

"No, me." Siren Hecht opened her mouth to let loose the weapon of her voice.

"Wait!" Jack cried. "Your Imperial Viciousness, please! Do you want to kill the one man in Wonderland who can most help you?"

Redd signaled for The Cat, Alistaire, and Siren to wait a moment. "What, in that fatty head of yours, makes you think I need anybody's help?" she asked.

Jack clambered to his feet. "Your Imperial Viciousness, I couldn't help overhearing you when you came onshore. I don't pretend to understand your talk of gardens and uncompleted mazes, but I did hear you say that your army on Earth isn't large enough to battle Queen Alyss'—I mean, your traitorous niece's. But *I* can fill your ranks to bursting with the tribes of Boarderland, the most fearsome troops this world has to offer . . . besides Milliners. And Glass Eyes. And maybe certain chessmen and—"

"Get on with it," Redd demanded.

"Well, if the twenty-one tribes of Boarderland were to cooperate and together attack Arch, his forces wouldn't be able to defeat them. But they'll never do this so long as Arch is king because he keeps them constantly at odds, feeding them the assorted lies he calls privileged intelligence and cultivating hate among them."

"And for that, I respect him."

"Yes, but *I'll* convince the tribes to come together under *your* command and rise up against Arch. I'll say that you've promised to leave Boarderland to them all equally—which you can do or not, as you choose—if they will fight the forces of Wonderland as your army. You could be queen of Wonderland *and* Boarderland."

Redd remained silent, thoughtful.

Jack glanced uncertainly at Alistaire's glinting bone saw. "And, uh, I heard you mention that you're off to visit the caterpillars," he said, "but if you wish, I can get you into Boarderland without Alyss or her forces discovering you . . . a certain guard who can be bribed. I know where Arch's royal convoy is presently camped and it's a short journey from there to the Valley of Mushrooms."

"I have powers enough to enter Boarderland without resorting to bribes," Redd sniffed.

"Of course you do. I just meant . . . " Growing more desperate, Jack fell to whining. "Mistress Heart! In a scheme to wrest power from Alyss, my parents were betrayed by King Arch and sentenced to the Crystal Mines. I'm broke, friendless, and without any wigs whatsoever! I have only one reason to remain in this world, a single guiding principle by which to steer my life, and that is to bring utter ruin down on Arch's head, just as he has brought to my family!"

"Why didn't you say so? For that motive alone, I'll let you live to try your plan."

The Cat, never fond of Jack of Diamonds, rolled his eyes.

"But I *do* doubt your ability to convince the tribes to fight under me," Redd observed.

"And I live only to prove your doubts unfounded, Your Imperial Viciousness."

"Let's hope you do." Turning to the others with what was supposed to be expansiveness, Redd said, "You see, I'm not above helping an unfortunate soul find new purpose in life . . . so long as it benefits *me*."

~

The next day, Jack of Diamonds led Redd and her entourage out from the shadows of Boarderland's Glyph Cliffs. Arch's royal encampment was visible in the middle distance.

"I'll leave you to introduce yourself to the king," Jack said, bowing to Redd. "It's best if he doesn't see me."

"You have exactly seven cycles of the Thurmite moon to carry out your plan," Redd informed him. "If you cherish consciousness, do not fail."

"The next time we meet, the tribes of Boarderland will be

at your disposal," Jack promised, bowing several more times and hurrying off.

Redd watched him trot back toward the Glyph Cliffs, then turned and, with Vollrath, The Cat, Alistaire, and Siren in step behind her—

"Come," she said, starting for Arch's camp. "It's time to visit one I called a friend, back when I had use of friends."

CHAPTER 33

THE TWIN Wonderland suns had risen full above the horizon, the Wondertropolis skyline gilded, backlit, with their morning rays. In the palace courtyard, the sunflowers planted around the war memorial were yawning and shaking off the dew. Dodge—wide-awake despite having been up the entire night—was standing at his father's grave.

"In everything, father, I aspire to do as I believe you would have done. I know that my behavior reflects on you and, despite my failings, I hope I've made you proud."

The Hereafter Plant growing from the mulch of Sir Justice's grave—its blossom the perfect likeness of the beloved guards-man—bobbed on its stem.

"But this idea that I'm supposed to maintain my proper place in relation to my queen . . . " Dodge went on, "I love

Alyss, father. Why should her title demand her to favor the affections of ranking sons when they've done nothing but win the lottery of birth? I won't ignore my heart just because it's not considered proper for a guardsman to love his queen. I hope you understand."

For the first time this morning, Dodge looked directly at the Hereafter Plant's complicated blossom—the overlaid petals that formed the familiar cheekbones, the pistil-eyelashes. Even the buds of the eyes were accurate; Sir Justice's irises had been precisely that shade of turquoise blue.

"I miss you, dad."

It sounded so weak, so inadequate. Words given the impossible task of conveying a family's tragedy. *I miss you.*

He wiped his eyes. The sunflowers were sniffling in sympathy and one of them lifted its voice in song, the melody somehow evoking the melancholy beauty of loss, of surviving in the face of seemingly unbearable loss.

"Give me the wisdom and courage to face the future, whatever may be coming," Dodge prayed.

~

The kitchens and servants halls were buzzing with news of Hatter's defection, but Alyss, alone in the palace's sovereign suite, had stopped spying on him. She'd learned little from her numerous remote viewings of the Milliner, in which, inevitably, she'd see him attending some leisure event with Boarderland's king, apparently unconcerned for Molly's safety.

Which means either that Molly's safe or that he's doing what he must to ensure she becomes so. I will not give up on him, not when he has so often risked his life for my mother's as well as my own.

Her mother. Alyss stared into the looking glass hanging above the hand-chiseled water basin.

You said you'd always be with me. On the other side of the glass.

"I must be staring into the wrong mirrors," Alyss said aloud. In one of the parlors, she lowered herself into a floating chair. Dodge's packet in her lap, she took out the first of his letters.

Alyss,
You would have been fourteen today if you'd lived. Happy birthday. I'm not so mad about what's happened to us right now, I don't know why. Bibwit would probably say it's because it's impossible to be angry all the time, but he's wrong. Tomorrow or even sooner all of my rage and hurt will return. Total. All-consuming. I believe in my rage and hurt. I need them if I'm to survive long enough to kill The Cat. After that, I don't care what happens. Especially now that you and father are gone.

The letters were not dated; it was impossible to tell in what order they were written. Alyss chose another at random.

Best friend,
I can't live according to the principles of White Imagination or even by the guardsman's code my father and I used to value. Try to understand. It isn't that I don't believe in them, but I can't allow room for belief. The Cat must, and will, die. Wonderland isn't a city that cares about honor codes anyway. If I lived by some code, my actions would become predictable. The enemy would take advantage of this and I'd be killed. An honorable death doesn't exist. Death is death. But it's funny that survival and revenge require the same thing: no honor codes, no supposed higher principles to aspire to, no mercy. Would you still recognize me, Alyss? I avoid looking glasses, not wanting to see my own reflection.

Another letter was stained with what might have been tea or something worse.

Alyss,

There are those who still think me young, but I feel as old as Bibwit after everything I've been through. Early this morning, a platoon of Alyssians was ambushed while carrying supplies to HQ. I was with them. I thought I was used to the sight of blood, but when it belongs to your friends . . . I lost more than a few today. What kind of life is this, that I live only to take the lives of others? I don't want to believe I could have changed so much. I want to believe that somewhere beneath all this anger there is still the Dodge Anders you used to tease for his love of guardsmen and Milliners, and who felt absolutely giddy to have your attentions—you, heiress to a queendom and keeper of my heart.

Tears were trickling down her cheeks. Alyss folded the letters and returned them to their packet. *Queens aren't supposed to cry as often as I do, especially warrior queens, but how can I—*

"Alyss."

284

She shot a glance at the looking glass on the wall behind her: nothing but the expected reflections. Nothing but the usual reflections too in the looking glass above the water basin.

"You must be mistaken," a male voice said. "I don't see her."

"I'm not mistaken. She's here."

The voices—her parents' voices—seemed to be coming from a compact lying open on a side table.

"Once children have grown," Nolan mused, "they want as little to do with their parents as possible. Woe are we whose only daughter finds us an embarrassing spectacle."

Alyss approached the side table and saw her mother's face occupying the whole of the compact's palm-sized mirror. "I don't think you're an embarrassing spectacle," she said.

Nolan thrust his face into view. "Alyss!"

"Father. I miss you both every day. I've been staring at my own reflection for so long, hoping to see you, that I'm beginning to hate the way I look."

"Impossible!" Nolan exclaimed. "You're beautiful. And I understand that a dashing guardsman thinks the same."

Alyss glanced at her skirts, bashful.

"You look tired," Genevieve said.

"I'm fine."

"Even in times of crisis, you must rest. And you've been crying."

"I'm fine, mother."

Nolan was squeezed out of view. Genevieve's face again filled the compact's glass, her voice tender. "Alyss, I *am* sorry you've had these tremendous responsibilities thrust upon you."

"It's not your fault, mother. You were *murdered*."

"But perhaps I should have been better fortified against Redd's coming. There are moments when I wish you'd been born with no extraordinary ability, into an average Wonderland family. It's a weakness in me, I know. To wish for a past that can never be. What would have become of Wonderland if you were not who you are?"

"*I* have more weaknesses than you know, mother. Lately, I've been thinking that my sacrifices—all of our sacrifices—haven't been worth it."

"You cannot ignore the gifts with which you were born. Your duty is to the queendom, above all else."

"To secure the greatest good for the greatest number," Nolan added, crowding his face into view. "You can't put Wonderland at risk to save a single citizen, not even your favorite guardsman."

"Since when has wearing the crown meant being told what I *can't* do?" Alyss muttered. But when her mother looked on the verge of a lecture, she quickly added: "Wouldn't you be more comfortable in a larger glass? Maybe the one by the floating chairs?"

Genevieve shook her head, knocking temples with her husband. "We're all right."

"Perfectly comfortable," Nolan agreed. "Smell." His nostrils expanded to take in the sweet, earthy fragrance that had drifted into the room.

"That means it's time for us to go," Genevieve sighed.

Turning from Alyss, the couple walked hand in hand into the far reaches of the glass, shrinking in the distance until they were gone from view altogether. The smell had grown pungent. A funnel cloud of blue smoke was coming from the bedroom, where Alyss found the blue caterpillar curled snugly around his hookah at the end of her bed.

"Blue," Alyss said. "I'm honored to have your company and wish only to have it more, that I might not interpret your coming as an ill omen."

"Ahem hem hem," Blue burbled, exhaling a cloud that formed the words *Oh well*. He puffed on his hookah for a time, the soft *peh peh peh* of his lips the only sound in the room. "I, an unnaturally large caterpillar, will reveal to you that of yourself which yet you know not," he said at length. He exhaled a cloud, which briefly took on the shape of a butterfly before transforming into a jumble of scenes: Redd, struggling with a crystal in the shape of a locksmith's key, with Bibwit at her side—or no, it was just a member of the tutor species; King Arch tugging on the whisker of a colorless caterpillar; Redd taking hold of a dusty, time-ravaged scepter. The cloud then resumed the form of a butterfly, which folded its wings and—

Alyss awoke. Only a faint hint of sweetness in the air. Blue was gone, Dodge sitting on the edge of her bed.

"Do you smell that?" she asked.

He nodded. "A caterpillar was here."

Alyss sat up, annoyed. "If Blue has something to tell me, why can't he just come out and say it? Why does he have to bother with all of his inexplicable scenes and symbols? No wonder so many Wonderlanders think the oracles are useless."

"But you don't, Alyss. What did he show you?"

Despite her parents' warnings, despite agreeing with Dodge about the impossibility of protecting him from his own worst impulses—

I don't want to tell him. No, because, at the very least, the caterpillar's warning meant that Redd would soon return to Wonderland. Or that she already had.

"He said he would reveal myself to me and then I saw King Arch trying to pull a whisker off a caterpillar." She sought Redd with her imagination's eye, but since she didn't know where to look, it was like knocking on any random door in Wondertropolis and hoping her aunt would answer it.

"That's all?" Dodge asked.

"Yes."

"We should inform Bibwit and the general," he said, standing. But on his way out, he paused in the doorway and delivered the news that had originally brought him to the suite: "None of the card soldiers at the Pool of Tears has checked in with Central Command. Not one is answering his crystal

communicator. The knight and rook have been sent to the pool and will soon report back."

Redd. So Dodge knew she'd been lying, was already preparing himself for a confrontation. She wanted to explain—*explain what, exactly?*—but words wouldn't come, and her lie hung heavy between them like a fog.

CHAPTER 34

THE ENCAMPMENT was as rowdy as ever when it happened: the air rent by a scream of such pitch and intensity that every Doomsine fell to the ground in pain and slapped hands, paws, or hoofs over their ears. Wives, soldiers, servants, animals, tailors and tavern keepers, everyone devoted to serving Boarderland's king collapsed as if punched. And no matter how desperately they tried to stop up their ears, still the unending scream penetrated their skulls.

Having conjured earplugs of appropriate density, Redd Heart walked unperturbed along the encampment's temporary streets, accompanied by the equally unperturbed Vollrath, Cat, Alistaire Poole, and Siren Hecht. The group might have passed for a wicked ex-queen and friends out for a bit of sightseeing if not for Siren, whose mouth was open to twice its normal size, her vocal cords issuing forth their life-paralyzing vibrations.

Redd sighted Arch's tent in her imagination and paraded her troops to it. Outside of the tent, two figures were bent to the ground in wincing agony, one of them in elbow-length gloves.

"Knock, knock," Redd said at the entrance.

Inside, Arch and his intel ministers were foundering on the floor, holding anything within reach to their ears—pillows, decorative crystals, coats. Redd flashed Siren a look; the assassin shut her mouth and the hideous shrieking stopped. Slowly, the intel ministers raised their heads. Arch was squinty-eyed with doubt when he saw his visitor.

"Redd?"

"I realize it's been a while, Arch, but did I mean so little to you that you don't even recognize me?"

The king reached a hand out to touch her. "No. But you seem . . . out of focus."

She was about to slap his ring-laden hand away when Ripkins and Blister stormed in, Ripkins with sword drawn and Blister stretching his bare hands toward The Cat and Alistaire Poole. Without turning from Arch, Redd imagined the handle of Ripkins' weapon too hot to touch—"Ah!" he cried, and dropped it—and she hurtled both bodyguards backward, out of the tent and across the street, through a wives' tent, across a second street, through a shoemaker's tent, across a third street and into a glassblower's hutch. They crashed through the hutch's back wall, the whole structure collapsed, and they landed hard in the rubble of an alley, prevented from getting up by the heavy, iron-like slabs Redd had conjured on top of their limbs and torsos.

Back in Arch's tent, Her Imperial Viciousness pushed out her bottom lip in an exaggerated pout. "The way you avoided me after mother thought she'd stop me from being queen," she whined to Arch, "it makes an heiress suspect you'd only been interested in her power and influence."

"You know that's not true, Redd," Arch said, struggling to his feet. "I was as unimpressed with your parents and their government as you were. While you were in line to succeed your mother, they assumed our gallivanting was not-altogether-harmless fun you would outgrow, and I could be as rowdy with you as I liked. But for me to have contact with you after they removed you from succession . . . " He shook his head. "They were my most powerful neighbors. For reasons of diplomacy and national stability, I couldn't do it."

"And what of my hateful time on Mount Isolation and the thirteen years I ruled Wonderland? What are your excuses for not seeing me then?"

"I should ask about *your* excuse for not seeing *me*. I think we've been equally guilty in neglecting our relationship—or equally innocent, whichever you prefer."

Redd grunted, unconvinced. Arch's intel ministers were still recovering from Siren's screams, fingers at their ears to try and clear the ringing out of them, but the king himself had taken on his usual aplomb, acting as if he'd never suffered at all.

"You've returned at an opportune time," he smirked. "Alyss has been facing difficulties, Wonderland having recently defended itself against an attack of . . . Glass Eyes."

Redd looked painfully gaseous all of a sudden, her face taut in an expression of pleasure. "If anyone else had dared to copy my inventions . . . " she said. "I see you've taken advantage of my absence."

"Would you care for me if I didn't? Don't think I presumed to tamper much with your creations, Redd. Of the Glass Eyes produced here, the only difference was in whose voice they recognized as their authority. But in honor of seeing you again, and in lieu of a fruit basket, allow me to offer you what is left of the manufacturing facility that Lord and Lady Diamond were overseeing in Boarderland."

Redd cackled. "Arch, it's impossible to stay angry at you when you're so devious. But what makes you think I need my old Glass Eyes? I have a formidable army on Earth already assembled—you're acquainted with the talents of some of my soldiers." She indicated Siren Hecht. "And I shortly intend to navigate my Looking Glass Maze, which I should have done long ago. It will make me the strongest Heart in history, and I will then reduce my young niece to an irksome memory. So you and I will again be neighbors. I trust your masculinity isn't too offended?"

"Wherever a female must be in power, Redd," Arch

293

smiled, "you are, and have always been, my only choice. For how long can I expect to have the current displeasure of your company?"

Again, Redd laughed. "Not another minute. I'm off to the Valley of Mushrooms."

"Well then," Arch said, "let me provide you with an escort to the border, both military and pleasurable, consisting as it will of soldiers and chefs. You don't need the military help, I know, but it pleases me to offer it."

One of the intel ministers hurried from the tent to assemble the escort.

Adopting a more intimate tone, Arch stepped closer to Redd and said, "I have Boarderland more thoroughly under control than I once did. After you are again ruling your nation, I hope we can see more of each other."

"Oh, Archy warchy," Redd said in a grotesque approximation of tenderness, "we *will* see more of each other, I swear it."

~

Redd and her assassins had been escorted out of the Doomsine encampment, and though Ripkins and Blister were still several blocks away, trying to wrestle out from under Redd's iron weights, the intel ministers had reconvened in Arch's tent.

"Is it really wise," a minister asked, "to try and befriend such a one as Redd?"

"I lose nothing by pretending it," Arch said, "whereas I risk everything if I don't. As long as she lives, Redd will cause serious trouble for whoever possesses the Heart Crystal."

Unseen by the king or his ministers, a shadow flitted past the tent's entrance, a shadow belonging to someone about to enter but who stopped suddenly when Arch asked, "Homburg Molly is secure?"

"As ever, my liege."

Moments ticked away as Arch schemed in silence. Then—

"If I had to bet," he said, "I'd bet that Redd may yet turn out to be stronger than her niece."

"But even her strength," one of the ministers offered, "maze or no maze, is nothing compared to WILMA."

Arch nodded. "It's sooner than I'd like to put Hatter to my purpose. I wanted to string him along awhile, make him desperate for Molly's life and weaken whatever rebellious resolves he has in his head. But Redd makes it necessary to take action now."

The shadow at the tent's entrance disappeared, the eavesdropper secreting away.

"Bring Hatter Madigan to me," Arch ordered. "It's time he met WILMA."

CHAPTER 35

PRETENDING TO be out for a stroll, Hatter passed through bazaars, promenades, and food courts, well-to-do and not so well-to-do neighborhoods, scanning the various scenes with a trained eye and hoping for some evidence of Molly's whereabouts. He made these excursions whenever possible, sometimes with Weaver at his side, though she thought they were simply a means for him to better familiarize himself with life in Boarderland.

An intel minister whose duty was to keep Hatter under constant surveillance approached. "The king requires your presence," he said.

Hatter fell in step with the Doomsine and was soon seated in the royal tent, Arch pacing back and forth before his usual pack of intel ministers.

"As Queen Alyss' bodyguard—" the king began.

"Homburg Molly is the queen's bodyguard, Your Majesty," Hatter said.

Arch smiled. "Yes, I forgot. You're with us now. As the *former* bodyguard then, of both Queen Genevieve and Queen Alyss, you have privileged access to every gwormmy-length of the queendom—more privileged perhaps than anyone except Bibwit Harte or Alyss herself—and you can travel anywhere within Wonderland's borders without attracting suspicion. For obvious reasons, I could not have recruited Alyss for the task I'm about to assign you, and Bibwit Harte is not physically capable of performing it. You are the only Wonderlander with both the access my task requires and the Millinery skill to accomplish it." To his ministers, he commanded, "Give it to him."

Hatter was handed a skein of thread wrapped in cloth.

"What you now hold," Arch said, "is silk from Wonderland's green caterpillar-oracle, in total weight equal to that of a gwynook's wing. You are to return to Heart Palace with it. Once there, you are to scale the palace's tallest spire. At the top, you won't fail to recognize my Weapon of Inconceivable Loss and Massive Annihilation. You are to weave the entirety of green silk onto the weapon in this pattern." Arch handed the Milliner a pocket holo-crystal, which showed what looked like the center of an Earth spider's web. "You must follow the pattern exactly. If, for any reason, you fail in what I ask of you, if you tell anyone what you're about, neither you, Weaver, nor anybody else will ever see Homburg Molly alive again. Once the mission is complete, you're to contact me immediately. But there is a time limit. If I have not heard from you after two revolutions of the Thurmite moon, you will never afterwards hear from your daughter." Arch glanced at his wrist, on which there was no timepiece. "Now, Mr. Madigan, I suggest you get going."

~

Suspecting that he'd be under surveillance so long as he remained within Arch's borders, Hatter passed into Wonderland before giving over all pretense of carrying out the king's mission, hiding in the brittle scrub of Outerwilderbeastia and waiting until the last traveler had proceeded through the official crossing. As soon as the card soldiers were alone, he shrugged daggers from his backpack and flung them at one of the demarcation barrier's pylons.

Clank! Clunk clang!

The soldiers whirled, at the ready. Hatter sprinted up behind them and, with his bare hands, rendered them unconscious before a single one glimpsed him. On the Boarderland side of the barrier: five guards.

Fthap!

Hatter's top hat was flattened into spinning blades and he was about to eliminate the guards when he realized: A disturbance might alert Arch. Better to leave as little trace of his reentry into Boarderland as possible.

Remaining on the Wonderland side of the demarcation barrier, Hatter walked two hundred paces in the direction of the Valley of Mushrooms, then activated the blades on his right wrist and pushed them into the ground. Dirt and clay and pebbles churned loose. He pushed the rotating blades deeper and deeper into the ground, using his left hand to clear away the debris until he had tunneled under the demarcation barrier and emerged on the Boarderland side. He made the fastest time he could back to Arch's camp, approaching from the direction of the setting suns so that he would be unrecognizable, a silhouette, to any Boarderlander who happened to spot him. Within a hectare of the camp, he took his top hat from his head, flattened it with a jerk of the wrist, and folded the blades into a compact stack, which he secured in the inside pocket of his coat. He then slipped off his coat and buried it with his backpack, marking the site with a melon-sized rock scarred by a spin of his wrist-blades.

Hatter glanced up at the sky. Already half a revolution of the Thurmite moon had passed and he wasn't even back where he'd started. But he proved lucky. Entering the Doomsine encampment, he came across a load of washing on a clothesline and made away with the loose-fitting pants, many-pocketed blouse, and hooded coat favored by day laborers: necessary camouflage, because if anyone recognized him, he and his daughter were dead.

CHAPTER 36

WHEREAS OTHERS would have stood gazing down upon the valley in silent awe at the gigantic, multicolored mushrooms and remarked that even the quality of the valley's light seemed more vibrant than it did anywhere else, Redd started the final descent into the caterpillars' habitat without pause or murmur. Vollrath, The Cat, Siren, and Alistaire tramped after her—Siren and Alistaire muting their amazement at a vista unlike any they had ever seen, The Cat stewing in worry because the valley had fully recovered from the devastation his mistress had ordered in her first months as Wonderland's queen. It wasn't supposed to have recovered and Redd might punish him.

But Her Imperial Viciousness had other concerns as she stepped along the valley's spongy floor, searching for the caterpillar-oracles in her imagination. The mushrooms were serving as a sort of cloaking network, deflecting her imaginative sight every which way so that all she saw were mulch and stalks and mushroom tops.

"We'll have to draw them out," she said, conjuring a vendor's cart filled with fresh, aromatic tarty tarts in a variety of flavors.

Vollrath, The Cat, Siren, and Alistaire fanned the delicious scents out in all directions, and in less time than it would have taken a hungry Wonderland child to eat a single tarty tart—

"There!" Vollrath exclaimed, pointing to a blue smoke cloud that formed a beckoning hand.

They followed the hand to a nearby clearing, where the members of the caterpillar counsel sat with their bodies coiled beneath them as they puffed on the same antique hookah. Each of the caterpillars occupied a mushroom as distinct in color as himself: blue, orange, red, yellow, purple, and green.

"Mmm, tarty tarts to munch," Blue said.

Vollrath, The Cat, Siren, and Alistaire began handing out the treats.

"I get the vanilla ones with gobbygrape filling!" called the yellow caterpillar.

"I want vanilla!" whined the orange caterpillar.

"Anything with choco-nibblies is mine!" the purple caterpillar cried.

"*I* get the choco-nibbly ones!" complained the red caterpillar.

"Ahem hum, I'll trade two caramel tarties for one of the sugar-dusted winglefruit-filled," Blue offered.

"No way!" rebuffed the green caterpillar.

It was one of the most difficult things Redd ever had to do: stand polite and respectful while the larvae bickered like brats and stuffed their wrinkled faces, dropping crumbs and jellied filling onto their mushrooms. When they were no longer shoving three tarts into their mouths at once but nibbling one at a time, she said, "Wise, ancient caterpillars, my tutor, Vollrath, has informed me that for many years I've been remiss in not passing through my Looking Glass Maze."

The red and yellow caterpillars were mouthing Redd's words as she spoke them, and the orange caterpillar motioned with his numerous right legs for Her Imperial Viciousness to *get on with it*.

"It's a circumstance I want to correct," Redd said. "I already know that my maze is located in the Garden of Uncompleted Mazes, but I need you to tell me where the garden is."

"Yadda, yadda," said the purple caterpillar. "Yadda, yadda, yadddda."

"The question is not *where* the Garden of Uncompleted Mazes is but *when*," Blue grumbled, his mouth full of caramel.

"When the Garden of Uncompleted Mazes is?" the orange caterpillar asked, doubtful.

"That's the question!" exclaimed the red caterpillar.

The oracles giggled and fell silent, alternately munching their tarty tarts and puffing on their hookah. Finally, with a look of exasperation, the yellow caterpillar said to Redd, "Du-*uh*. We're waiting for you to ask the question!"

Redd balled her hands into fists. "When is the Garden of Uncompleted Mazes?" she rasped.

"Oh, now and then, now and then," Blue answered, upon which all of the caterpillars shook with loud laughter—all except Green, who continued to munch a tarty tart and blink at Redd with an appraising, curious expression.

Unable to hold back any longer, Redd aimed her crooked stick at them as if it were a rifle or bayonet and—

Foo-foo-foo-foo-foo-foosh!

Fireballs shot out. The caterpillars' six mushrooms erupted. Flames licked the sky, sizzled out as quickly as they'd come. The mushrooms had been charred black, but there was no sign of the caterpillars.

"Idiots! Useless idiots!" Redd shouted.

Vollrath, The Cat, Siren, and Alistaire dropped to the ground and covered their heads as she lashed out at the landscape, conjuring orb generators, crystal shot, and flaming spears. A shadow fell over them as an enormous scythe formed in the air and began to swing, lopping mushrooms flat. But at the very height of the violence—the exploding fungi, the thousand razor-cards shredding mushroom stalks—Redd felt a tap on her shoulder. She turned and there was the green caterpillar, nonchalantly puffing on a small hookah. Redd held up a hand; the outsized scythe paused mid-swing, the orb generators and razor-cards and flaming spears hung suspended in mid-flight.

"The Garden of Uncompleted Mazes exists in the could-have-been," the oracle said. "What could have been was *then*. But it is also *now*. Do you understand?"

"I don't want to understand. Tell me where the garden is or you will lose the valley forever."

The caterpillar pulled at his water pipe and considered the renegade princess before him: the hate-infused creases of her toughened skin; the knotty hair; the gown of rose vines in constant slithery motion. At length, he said, "To get there, it is necessary for you to think back to the precise moment when your becoming queen—a thing to be—became a could-have-been. Let your mind be wholly absorbed in that moment. Give yourself up to it. Reexperience it in all of its emotional devastation. Once you accomplish this, you will see, somewhere in the rear of the memory, a small door. Through this door, you will find the garden."

Redd was suspicious. "Why are you telling me this when the others didn't?"

"Let's just say, it gives me something to do."

The caterpillar exhaled a cloud of green smoke. It enveloped Redd and the others, and when they awoke, they were alone.

CHAPTER 37

PARTING FROM Redd, Jack of Diamonds had lumbered breathlessly into the first encampment that fell in his way.

"Your leader!" he'd said to the Gnobi tribespeople lolling about. "It's important that I speak to your leader immediately! Your future freedom depends on it!"

The Gnobi, when not roused to violence, were a sluggish clan, the least nomadic of Boarderland's tribes. Not sensing any immediate threat to their freedoms in the person of Jack Diamond, they had responded to his urgency with characteristic listlessness.

"Myrval's tent is somewhere that way," one of them had said with a vague wave of the hand.

"Follow the sound of the snoring and you'll find it," another had suggested.

But there had been a fair amount of snoring to be heard in the camp, and not until Jack had roused several civilians from their naps did he catch sight of the only tent with a pennant flying from its roof and two males asleep on stools at its entrance.

"Guards," he'd said to himself.

He had marched past the slumbering guardsmen and, in the tent's front room, discovered five more sleeping guards—two slumped on chairs, two curled up on floor mats, and one snoring on his feet. What Jack had come upon was no less than a festival of snoring, a riot of honking inhalations, snotty exhalations, and inarticulate mutterings. But louder than all of these, coming from the back room: the wail of an ailing jabberwock. Jack had stepped into the back room and seen a lone figure asleep on a cot.

"Myrval!" he'd called, unsure, which had caused the sleeper to groan and roll toward the wall.

"I'm an emissary of Redd Heart, former and future queen of Wonderland," Jack had said, shaking the Gnobi leader awake. "She has sent me here with a proposal that can guarantee future peace and freedom for the Gnobi tribe—for *all* of Boarderland's tribes. But it's a—"

"That's nice of Miss Heart to think of us," Myrval had mumbled, and again closed his eyes.

"We must arrange a gathering of the tribal leaders to discuss the details of Mistress Heart's proposal, a summit."

"*You* can arrange what you like. I have nothing against

nineteen of the twenty other leaders, but Gerte, who heads the Onu tribe, insulted my daughter. He's an abomination and I will never meet with him unless he is to apologize."

Jack had been about to promise this and anything else when Myrval yawned, "The Gnobi and Onu are on the verge of war."

Jack had had similar trouble with the rest of the tribal leaders, each citing one of their number with whom they refused to have any dealings that did not involve bloodshed. Several of them also took offense at Jack's not having physically visited their camps to request their attendance at the summit, seeing in this his favoritism of the Gnobi tribe. But Jack of Diamonds had exercised his powers of persuasion to the utmost. At last able to convince the twenty-one leaders to talk, he was now in one of Myrval's conference tents, with Myrval seated on his left, a fire pit glowing in front of him, and the faces of the other leaders on screens around the pit.

"What I have already said to each of you singly," Jack began, "I repeat to you now that we're together. You are made subordinate to King Arch by the antagonisms he invents to keep you at war with one another. He does this to prevent you from joining together to fight his forces, knowing that he doesn't have the military power to defeat you if you formed a coalition against him."

"That's insane," said the Sirk leader. "Just yesterday, I got word from a reliable spy that the Fel Creel are gathering beyond the pale hills in preparation for an attack against us."

"That's your justification for the attack *my* reliable spy says *you* are planning!" shouted the Fel Creel leader.

"We planned no attack until we learned that you were."

"Ditto!"

"This proves what I've been saying," Jack interrupted. "It's obvious that neither of you would be attacking the other if not for the 'intelligence' you received. The Sirk tribespeople would go about their peaceful business and the Fel Creel would go about theirs."

"Right!" said the Sirk and Fel Creel leaders.

"But the intelligence you both received was false," Jack explained. "It came directly from King Arch in order to put you at deadly odds. Just as the 'intelligence' the Catabrac received of an impending ambush by the Shifog was false, as was the report the Shifog received of the Catabrac stockpiling weapons to annihilate them."

The Catabrac and Shifog leaders mumbled in surprise; neither had mentioned these intelligence reports outside of their own tight-lipped clans.

Jack turned to the Gnobi leader. "And Myrval, I assure you, Gerte of the Onu tribe never said your daughter looks as if she's been put together out of spirit-dane droppings and that her personality is just as foul as her person. I was there when King Arch thought up that particular bit of ugliness."

Myrval said nothing. Each tribal leader was glancing at every other, unsure what to believe.

"He might be speaking the truth," said the Maldoid leader.

"How else could he know the exact wording of the insult?" Myrval answered. "I have never repeated it, not even to Gerte, who I assumed recalled his own foul words."

"I'm glad to see that I'm gaining credibility," Jack said. "Now, as Redd Heart's emissary, I've come to propose that you all unite under Redd to battle Arch. King Arch will be defeated and, in exchange for helping you take control of Boarderland to govern equally among you, Redd asks only that you fight under her command for another teensy little war with the forces of Alyss Heart, so that she can regain control of Wonderland."

"Excuse me," said Myrval, "but now that you have informed us of Arch's methods, why should we fight under Redd's command when we can battle Arch without her help?"

"Because," Jack said, "to fight Arch on your own, you will be required to choose a leader from among you. I'm just guessing, but I think there'll be more than a little argument over which of you is best fit to lead the others. With Redd at your head, you are all equal."

"With Redd at our head, we are all equal," repeated the Maldoid leader, encouraged.

"Redd Heart is not known for being trustworthy," said the leader of the Awr tribe. "But even supposing that we agree to this proposal, and that she leaves Boarderland under our control as she promises, we would still have to contend with her as our neighbor. She would make a dangerous neighbor."

"She ruled Wonderland for thirteen years without causing Arch much trouble," Jack said. "I urge you not to let this opportunity for true freedom pass."

"And why is Redd suddenly so concerned about *our* freedom?" asked the Kalaman leader.

"Her Imperial Viciousness is primarily occupied with regaining her crown. The easiest way to accomplish this is to engage you all as her mercenary army. Happily, you stand to benefit from the arrangement as much as she does."

"We would like to discuss the matter in private," said the Glebog leader.

"Of course." Jack rose to depart. "But allow me to say one more thing before I leave you to your decision. If you accept Redd's proposal, you face the uncertainty of a future that you will, at the very least, have some power to shape. But if you reject the proposal, you're doomed to remain as you are, with only the freedom to fight against one another for as long as Arch lives."

Jack stepped from the tent, his words—the wisest he'd ever uttered in his life—lingering after him.

CHAPTER 38

ALYSS AND her advisers were gathered in the palace's war room, Alyss shifting uneasily in her seat as Dodge and the others tried to decipher what they thought was the entirety of Blue's message.

"He said he would teach you about yourself," Bibwit questioned thoughtfully, "but then you didn't appear in anything he showed you?"

Alyss nodded.

"Most curious."

"I don't like it," General Doppelgänger said, and began punching buttons on the crystal communicator's control pad strapped to his forearm.

Zzzz! Flink! Zzzz! Flink!

From the vision nozzle on the general's ammo belt, real-time images of Ten Cards stationed at outposts throughout the queendom were projected onto the air. No sign of trouble, every lieutenant reported, or of anything unusual. But then a Ten Card posted in Outerwilderbeastia caught sight of Bibwit.

"Back already, Mr. Harte? I knew the tutor species was fast, but not *that* fast."

"Whatever do you mean?" Bibwit asked.

"Just one quarter of a lunar hour ago I saw you hurrying toward the demarcation barrier. I assumed you were on some scholarly pilgrimage to Boarderland, as you were headed directly for gate crossing 15-b."

Bibwit's ears danced a dance of perplexity atop his head. "Was I . . . alone?"

"I didn't get much of a look at the others. Being so pale, you stand out against Outerwilderbeastia's vines, you know."

"Yes. Yes, I'm sure I do," Bibwit said absently.

"Your Majesty." The Ten Card bowed to Alyss. "General." The Ten Card saluted and his image dissolved.

"I'm starting to get a bad feeling," the tutor said.

"*Starting* to?" Dodge guffawed.

The general's crystal communicator beeped. He pressed a button on its keypad and an image of the white knight formed in front of him.

"General, all the soldiers guarding the pool are dead," the knight reported.

Dodge was instantly on his feet, checking his weapons—

the ammo clip in his crystal shooter, the trigger of his AD52. "Any evidence of The Cat?" he asked. "Slash marks or anything like that?"

"Hard to tell *what* exactly killed them."

Beep, beep beep. The general again pressed his communicator's keypad and an image of the white rook appeared next to the knight.

"Listen," the rook said.

After several moments the general frowned. "I hear only silence."

"Yeah, and I'm standing in the *Whispering* Woods," said the rook. "Every mouth here has been glued shut."

Bibwit was tugging on an ear, his brow as furrowed as a rumpled bedsheet. "In the scheme of all that is conceivable," he said, "it's possible that another villain might be responsible for the deaths at the pool, but it would irresponsible of us not to assume the worst—by which I mean, that Redd has returned."

"Already there, Bibwit." Dodge was checking his supply of razor cartridges and whipsnake grenades. "What's the plan, General?"

"It's difficult to prepare adequately when we don't know where the front line is. Or the enemy."

"All of Wonderland is the front line," Dodge countered. "The enemy could show herself anywhere at any time."

He was being careful not to look at Alyss—the exact opposite of Bibwit, who was watching her intently, almost as if, with his acute hearing, he could hear her mounting dis-comfort.

A responsible queen would probably be searching for Redd in her imagination. But a responsible queen wouldn't have let her advisers believe she'd told them the whole of Blue's message.

Her parents' words nagged at her conscience: Her duty was to secure the greatest good for the greatest number; she could not put Wonderland at risk to save a single citizen.

I must own the truth. For the queendom. For myself.

"I think," Alyss said suddenly, "I would like to go over again what Blue presented to me."

Confusion showed on the faces of Dodge and the general, but Bibwit looked as if he'd been afraid of this. "Yes?" he said.

"Blue told me that he, an unnaturally large caterpillar, would reveal to me that of myself which yet I know not. I'm pretty sure those were his exact words. He showed me Arch pulling on the whisker of a colorless caterpillar, but before that . . . " her eyes swiveled to Dodge, " . . . he showed me Redd."

"Why didn't you say so before, Alyss?" Bibwit asked.

"I don't know." She and Dodge were looking steadily at each other now. "It was wrong of me not to say anything."

"What did he show you of Redd?" asked General Doppelgänger.

Dodge had turned away, needlessly adjusting the hang of his thigh holster.

314

"I saw her fumbling with a crystal shaped like a door key," Alyss said. "She was with a tutor. And I saw her gripping something that looked like an old, much neglected scepter."

Bibwit groaned. "It's worse than I thought," he said. "Much, much worse. Alyss, I haven't had the luxury of educating you as fully as I would've done in a time of peace. Certain finer points of monarchical theory I either summarized or skipped altogether. As I did with certain historical details or facts I have hoped would be irrelevant. Of this last sort are particulars related to Looking Glass Mazes. I neglected to tell you every little thing about them—everything that is known, I should say. But I see now that my neglect was the result of my own wishful thinking. I've been hoping that if I did not name the possibility, if I ignored it, it would not exist."

"The possibility of what, Bibwit? No one has any idea what you're talking about."

"I was certain that if Redd returned in a recognizable form, she would never discover it on her own. I hadn't counted on her uniting with one of my species and actually *learning* anything. But assuming Redd has returned, I fear that the tutor the Ten Card mistook for me was, in fact, Vollrath—one of my kind who long ago succumbed to Black Imagination and had to fling himself into the Pool of Tears. I've always assumed that he's been causing trouble on Earth, and Blue's warning to you, Alyss, makes it plain: If Redd has not accomplished it already, she intends to enter her Looking Glass Maze. The tutor must have told her about it. She will retrieve her scepter and, in doing so, become stronger than before."

"I don't understand," Alyss said. "I've already navigated the maze."

"What difference does any of this make?" Dodge asked Bibwit. "Redd is back and we're not going to surrender to her, no matter what. As long as we don't underestimate her capacity for blood and mayhem—"

"It might be impossible for us to do anything *but* underestimate her, such could be her strength. Alyss, I will explain all, but we must confirm whether or not Redd is among us, and whether what Blue showed you of Redd with her scepter is the future or the past. If the future, it may still be prevented. If the past . . . I'd rather not think about it. General?"

"It should be coming online now, Bibwit."

Doppelgänger had activated the holo-crystals embedded in the demarcation barrier's pylons at gate crossing 15-b. Real-time images of both Boarderland and Outerwilderbeastia appeared on screens in the war room.

"What's that?" Dodge asked, seeing movement in the distance of the Boarderland terrain.

General Doppelgänger directed the holo-crystal to zoom in, and there, by an outcropping of rock as if waiting for someone, were a male and female of no known Boarderland tribe. They might have been Wonderlanders. Then again, they might have been earthlings. The third figure, however, with his long ears and nearly translucent complexion, was unmistakable.

"That," Bibwit said, "is Vollrath."

Just then, Redd's only feline assassin stepped around a boulder into view.

"The Cat," Dodge whispered. He had thought himself prepared, but the actual sight of his father's murderer—smudged somehow, as if seen through a greasy window—made all of his earlier professed hopes for self-restraint now sound hollow, false.

"Dodge?" Alyss said, watching the hand with which he gripped the handle of his father's sword. It was shaking.

"Dodge?"

But he was no longer with her. His world could fit only two: himself and The Cat.

CHAPTER 39

REDD WOULD have preferred to be in the Chessboard Desert, within sight of Mount Isolation, the better to recall that long-ago day in all its heart-twisting gall. But every moment she remained in Wonderland without an army to support her was a risk; Alyss could sight her at any time. So she made use of the corrupt border guard introduced to her by Jack of Diamonds, and led Vollrath, The Cat, Siren, and Alistaire back into Arch's kingdom.

She wanted a location unexposed to elements and enemies alike, a refuge where she would not be bothered with present threats or concerns. Half a lunar hour's walk from the demarcation barrier, she found it: a natural sculpture of heavy granite slabs and boulders thrown up by the land's shifting tectonic plates.

"No one had better disturb me," Redd warned.

"No one will," said The Cat.

"We'll be standing watch, Your Imperial Viciousness," Vollrath promised. "You'll have all the time and peace you need."

Redd slipped between a pair of boulders into a sort of room—roofless, with walls of pockmarked rock. She sat on the ground and closed her eyes. It took awhile; to forget or mentally shunt aside all thoughts of the present, the *now*, was not so easy. But after a few superficial dips into the well of memory, she was there again, living it—a seventeen-year-old princess, wild-eyed and tipsy from indulging in artificial crystal, sneaking home from forbidden fun with young Arch of Boarderland. Her parents, Queen Theodora and King Tyman, were waiting for her in her bedroom.

"It's late, Rose," Theodora sighed.

"It's so late, it's early," said Tyman as he pulled back a curtain to let in the morning sun.

"Always so quick with the blatantly obvious, aren't you, father?" Redd began to undress, turning away from her parents to avoid having to explain her bloodshot eyes.

"Rose," Theodora said to her backside, "I don't know if we've somehow failed you as parents or if your behavior comes from chemical imbalances brought on by your ferocious decadence. But your constant disobedience—not only of me and your father but of the queendom's most basic laws, as if these should apply to everybody else but not to you—your disregard of even common civilities, and your utter lack of respect for how government *works* . . . you're far beyond merely alienating those you would need to help you govern effectively."

"It is they who've alienated *me!*" Redd shouted, spinning round.

"Raising your voice will accomplish nothing."

"Rose, have you been . . . ingesting artificial crystal?" Tyman asked.

"Don't be stupid, father."

"In any case," Theodora went on, "I don't see how you can effectively govern a nation when you are unable to govern yourself. I'm sorry. But you're not to be queen."

Redd laughed. "Of course I am, mother. I'm the eldest; I'm the heir. Nothing can change that."

"*I* can change it. Your imagination might be as powerful as you believe—certainly you would have made a formidable monarch. But partaking more of Black Imagination than White as you do, I'm removing you from succession. Genevieve is to be queen."

"Genevieve!"

Objects in the room became suddenly kinetic—jewelry cases, books, holo-crystals, and end tables shot from their usual places and smashed against one another.

"And we think it best," Tyman said, ducking to avoid a flying lamp that shattered against a wardrobe, "if you live on Mount Isolation for a time."

"That rotten old place?"

"We're hopeful that living in relative isolation will have

a sobering effect on you," Theodora explained. "You will not have the same amenities there as you enjoy here and, we hope, less opportunity to indulge your ruder appetites."

A phalanx of chessmen marched into the room.

"What's this, an *escort* to my new home?" Redd jeered. "I could send these mediocrities to oblivion with a single strike of my imagination."

"You forget, Rose, that I have powers of imagination too," Theodora warned. "And I am more practiced in the use of them. You will kill no one, though if you so much as try, I assure you, for all intents and purposes, you will be as good as dead to your father and me."

"This hurts us as much as it hurts you," Tyman said.

"Not yet it doesn't, my dear dim father. But it will. It will hurt you both much worse, I swear."

Redd threw her clothes back on and was about to stomp out of the room and through the palace halls, exploding bookcases, vases, statuettes, candelabra—everything she passed—with her imagination. This was what she'd done in actuality, but now, reliving the scene in her memory, she turned and saw, past the chessmen waiting to escort her from the premises, a door where no door had ever been. It was connected to no wall—to nothing, in fact—and the top of it reached only as high as her bosom. She elbowed through the chessmen and approached it. She pushed it open, unable to see what lay beyond. No matter. Her whole future was staked on stepping through . . .

~

Most gardens are recognizable by their array of flowers and other plantings, but whoever or whatever had named the Garden of Uncompleted Mazes obviously hadn't set foot in it. What passed for sky was blackness, void. The ground was as smooth as some never-seen-before gemstone and resembled the surface of a petrified sea. Eleven crystal cubes, identical to the key to Alyss' Looking Glass Maze in everything except size, were rooted in the curious ground, each at a single point so that they seemed to be balancing precariously. Even the smallest of the cubes was taller than Redd.

Her Imperial Viciousness approached the one nearest her, reached toward its glossy surfaces and—

Plink! Her fingers came up against its cold solidity. She punched and knocked at the cube's six sides. Nothing. It would not let her in. At the next four cubes, she did the same—pressed and knocked on their sides, explored every sparkling cranny, every luminescent crevice in search of the lever or button that would provide access to her maze.

Then she realized: Her impatience had made her dim. Her key would be the smallest of the eleven, the one that had had the least time to grow.

It was several spirit-dane-lengths in front of her. She started to run. Not knowing why or what she planned to do, she ran directly toward the cube.

Fssst!

She was standing in her maze, her own face sneering back at her from the countless, dust-filmed looking glasses that surrounded her.

"I've come!" she yelled, the words ricocheting off the cloudy glasses without cease or loss of volume. Consonants jarred, vowels overlapped. The noise pained her ears, but what did she care? She would endure anything. She had made it this far. She would not leave until she had found what she'd come for.

In every direction, mirrored corridors branched off into the maze's dusky reaches. She tried to locate the scepter in her imagination's eye, but her powers were useless. She would have to find it the old-fashioned way, by scouring every gwormmy-length of every corridor.

"Not much of a maze, are you?" she muttered, because she had discovered that she could step through the looking glasses without consequence. It was as if she were in a giant room, the mirrored halls the ghostly residue of the intricacy it had once contained.

"How dare you, when I'm smarter and more imaginative than you!" a girlish incarnation of herself hissed. The night she'd murdered her mother played out in a glass. But mostly, phantasms of the past kept to the edge of her senses, half heard, half seen.

Then she spotted it, lying up ahead as if it were nothing but a useless stick someone had dropped in her hurry to leave. A once brightly colored staff, it had rotted black with age.

The heart at its top was shriveled and gray, its filigree flaked and rusted—the scepter's abandonment like that she had suffered from her parents.

"And they had the impudence to blame me!" Redd shouted, her mind again spiraling into the memory of that distant day that had changed everything.

"It's your own fault, Rose," Theodora had said. "You refuse to listen to anyone's counsel but your own, and you insist on being so undisciplined, disregarding the most basic principles of White Imagination."

"Perhaps I have discipline in other things!" Redd had spat.

"That's what I'm afraid of. You've already scared a number of important Wonderlanders."

Redd shook the memory out of her head. Her fingers closed around the scepter, giving her access to the full potential of her imaginative powers. She was the strongest Heart alive. Soon, she would be the only Heart alive.

CHAPTER 40

SHE HAD stopped trying to fight, only daring to move her mouth so as not to be knocked flat by the drug-delivery system the ministers refused to remove. Her brain was still woozy from the last dosing, when she'd tried to prevent one of King Arch's wives from clipping a bauble to her ear.

"You should let your hair grow," the wife said now, flicking at Molly's short-cropped bangs with a manicured hand.

"I like my hair the way it is."

She had kept it short because of her work as Milliner and Queen Alyss' bodyguard. It could have compromised her; a combatant might have snagged hold of long hair in a fight. But she didn't have to worry about any of *that* now, did she? She'd given up her post. She probably deserved this humiliation for the deadly mistake she'd made—having to sit unmoving with Arch's wives gathered around her, applying rouges and powders to her cheeks, coloring her lips, and dolling her up in their bracelets and necklaces.

"You could be pretty if you tried," said another wife, coming at her with an eyelash brush.

The wives stepped back to appraise her.

"Much better," one of them said.

"Now maybe you won't scare prospective husbands off," said another.

But Molly couldn't care less about prospective husbands. She had noticed, in the rear wall of the tent, a slit that hadn't been there before . . . as if made by the skillful swing of a blade.

~

Before being sent to engage WILMA, Hatter had already searched most of the Doomsine encampment for evidence of his daughter. Disguised as a day laborer, he now did quick reconnaissance of the few unexplored neighborhoods that still remained, but found nothing, Molly's whereabouts as unknown to him as ever.

He would have to start over. He'd never be able to search the entire camp a second time. He squinted up at the sky—little more than one revolution of the Thurmite moon before the time allowed for his WILMA mission expired. All he could do was hope. And move fast, but not so fast that he attracted suspicion.

Head lowered, making the most of his peripheral vision, Hatter huffed along recently visited streets and alleys. At a market stall selling fresh herbs and vegetables, he saw two of Arch's personal chefs. The sight of them, royal servants out among the common folk, served as a jolt to his senses. How could he have been so remiss? He had searched everywhere for Molly *except* the royal enclave in which he himself had been living—among the tents of Arch's personal retinue. He had always assumed that the king would keep Molly close, but *that* close?

He made his way to Arch's tent at the center of camp, where the threat of being recognized was greater than anywhere else, and had barely begun his hunt when—

"Are you in need of work, laborer?"

It was Weaver. He bowed his head to indicate that he was, not wanting to risk letting his voice be heard.

"I have some furniture that needs to be moved. I can pay you a necklace of beaded quartz and a hot meal."

He followed Weaver out of the main thoroughfare to her tent. Swallowing her sobs, she spoke in a desperate whisper.

"They said you'd gone, and I . . . You were right. You've been right all along. I overhead Arch talking about Molly. I should've believed you sooner, I—"

"Sshh, Weaver. Sshh, you wanted what you thought was best for Molly, for all of us. You have no cause to blame yourself. Do you know where she is?"

Weaver stepped back and wiped her cheeks. "I'm not sure. His ministers take turns visiting one of the wives' tents. I doubt Arch would let them if their business had anything to do with his wives."

"Show me which tent."

She was about to step out to the street, but he touched her arm to stop her. "How did you recognize me?"

"I'll always know you. The way you walk is as familiar to me as my own thoughts, even after so many years."

Hatter nodded. But if she could spot him so easily, others might not have a difficult time of it. Still, there was nothing he could do about it now.

"Show me where Molly's being kept."

Weaver, walking ahead of him as instructed, indicated the wives' tent with a slight turn of the head and continued past. Hatter ducked around to the back, to a small space with enough room only to stake and unstake the tent supports. He tapped his belt buckle, the sabers of his belt snapped open, and he quickly sliced a small gash in the canvas. He tapped his belt buckle again and the sabers retracted. He peered through the slit he'd made into the tent. Among the thirteen wives who lounged on voluptuous pillows and lush silks, he saw her: guarded by a pair of intel ministers, sitting glum and alone in the corner. She was without her homburg and dressed in pink clothes he'd never seen before.

Weaver was waiting for him in her tent.

"She's there," he said. "I've only got my wrist-blades and my belt. Do you have access to weapons?"

"I've heard of a dealer in the Kyla district. Contraband. But—"

"If our daughter's to live, we have to find him."

CHAPTER 41

CHESSMEN GUARDED the palace's perimeter, card soldiers had been dispatched to key points in Wondertropolis, and military outposts throughout the queendom were put on alert. In the palace's war room, the screens showing Vollrath, The Cat, and the two unidentified strangers blinked on and off as if from a momentary power failure. Before the failure, Vollrath and the others were visible; afterward, they were gone.

"I'll find them," Alyss said. Directing her imaginative sight to the outcropping of rock where the enemy had just been, she scanned the surrounding Boarderland terrain. When she located them, they were farther away than she would've thought, speeding headlong in a vehicle unfamiliar to her, as it had been freshly conjured by Redd—a three-wheeled machine built to cover rugged land, in which her aunt sat above and behind the others in a throne-like seat, a staff topped with a long-dead heart in her hand.

"I see them," she announced. "Redd's with them. She has her scepter."

"We should attack before she attacks us," Dodge urged.

"Attack Boarderland?" The general looked doubtful.

"We'd have Redd *and* Arch to contend with," said Bibwit.

"We already do, I'd bet."

"She's traveling *away* from Wonderland?" Alyss murmured.

Racing deeper into Boarderland, her steel-wool hair buffeted by the wind, Redd turned and seemed to stare right at Alyss, as if she could sense her niece's imaginative eye upon her. The corner of her lips curled in a sneer, she swung her scepter and, in Heart Palace's war room, Alyss jumped, startled; her imaginative sight had gone black.

"What is it?" Bibwit asked.

"She blocked my sight."

"Not good," the general fretted, splitting in two. "Not good at all," said Generals Doppel and Gänger, each entering coordinates on their crystal communicators, ordering troop deployments to the demarcation barrier.

Alyss tried again to settle the eye of her imagination on her aunt. She flashed on images of Redd in a valley and on a hill. Then she realized, there were hundreds of them: Redd in her three-wheeled transport trundling across an open plain; Redd in her three-wheeled transport bouncing up a rocky escarpment; several Redds spread out on the Glyph Cliffs; an untold number of Redds along the banks of the Bookie River; innumerable Redds marching along Boarderland's side of the demarcation barrier.

"We're getting reports!" Generals Doppel and Gänger cried.

"She's conjured doubles of herself," Alyss said. "Hundreds of them, if not more. From this distance, there's no way for me to know which one is real. I'll have to attack them all at once."

She conjured a spikejack tumbler for every Redd she saw. The tumblers would pass harmlessly through the constructs, but the legitimate Redd would have to counterattack to survive. The weapons went hurtling toward their targets—and through *all* of them.

"I don't understand. Not one of them is real?"

"How can *that* be?" Dodge steamed. "Where could she have gone?"

Alyss had no answer and Bibwit's ears shrugged in apologetic ignorance. Generals Doppel and Gänger were shouting into their crystal communicators:

"The demarcation barrier itself is the *front* of the front line!"

"Our border soldiers are the *back* of the front line!"

Bibwit hopped to his feet. "We need to get you to the

crystal chamber, Alyss. Your imagination will be strongest there."

"Great," said Dodge. "So if Redd happens to remote view her, she'll know where the Heart Crystal is."

"If Alyss cannot defeat Redd while standing next to the crystal—a necessity Redd's apparent strength is calling into question—it won't matter if we try to hide it from her."

Whether this convinced Dodge or he had simply resigned himself to the worst, he turned toward the door. "I'll be with my men." He was already halfway to the hall when—

"Wait!"

Alyss was standing, a pleading, concerned look in her eyes. But for what was she pleading? She could say nothing to keep him from going—she *should* say nothing—and she knew it.

He returned to her, but only for a moment. "I forgive you, Alyss. For lying to me. That's something, isn't it—a guardsman forgiving his queen?" He kissed her. "Please stay safe. I'll try to do the same."

He spun on his heels and was gone, and Alyss allowed Bibwit to lead her from the room.

CHAPTER 42

THE ARMS dealer was a scurrying creature, a former Glebog who kept his merchandise beneath false drawer bottoms, behind artwork that popped out of frames, and inside clocks and cooking appliances whose mechanical workings had been removed. Hatter waited outside his tent while Weaver purchased as much as she was able with the gems he had given her. She emerged carrying a duffel, inside of which were a couple of AD52s with several additional projectile decks, a quiver of mind riders, and a scorpspitter.

Hatter armed himself in a nearby alley, latching the quiver and scorpspitter to his belt so that his laborer's coat hid them from view. He pocketed the projectile decks, strapped one of the AD52s to a thigh and reached for the other.

"I'm keeping this one," Weaver said.

"I don't think you should."

"I know."

The luxury of arguing was not an option. "At least wait until I'm inside," Hatter said. "We only have a chance if I get to Molly before the worst of the fighting starts."

As they entered Arch's street, Weaver drifted off alone, loitering at a propaganda stall while Hatter slipped around to the back of the wives' tent. He peered in through the cut in the canvas he'd made earlier. Nothing had changed inside: still just the thirteen wives, two ministers, and Molly.

From the distance, a rumbling approached, growing in volume.

Hatter pulled the scorpspitter out from under his coat and dropped it into the tent. *Sploink! Splish!* Bullets of poison splattered against the inside walls, and before the last of the wives ran screaming to the street, Hatter flicked open his wrist-blades and rammed them hard against the tent's canvas. He stepped through the shreds. The ministers on either side of Molly unloaded their shooters at him, but he moved toward them, his blades deflecting the onslaught of their deadly crystal. He had gone just a step or two when the guard posted outside the tent's entrance ran in, and behind him, Weaver.

"Hey!" Weaver shouted, and when the guard turned, she dealt a quarter-deck of razor-cards into him.

Shwink! Hatter snapped open his belt sabers, twirled and sliced the life out of the ministers. Weaver was rocking gently on her knees, holding her daughter.

"Your homburg?" Hatter asked.

"I don't need it anymore," the girl answered, ashamed.

This wasn't the time to ask what she meant or to look for it. "We should hurry," Hatter said.

"I can't move in this."

With her eyes, Molly indicated her outfit. Hatter slashed the tight-fitting material with his wrist-blades and it fell in tatters without a single knife edge so much as scraping her skin. Weaver ferreted out something for Molly to wear from among the wives' things. Hatter folded shut his wrist-blades, unlocked one of the bracelets and tossed it to his daughter along with the quiver of mind riders.

"I shouldn't . . . " she said, looking glumly at the weapons. "I can't be trusted. I've already messed up enough."

Hatter stepped over and snapped the bracelet onto her wrist. "No more than any one of us," he said, then unstrapped his AD52 and—

Fi-fi-fi-fi-fith! Fi-fi-fi-fi-fith!

He spun 360 degrees, dealing razor-cards at the surrounding tent, severing it in two—the wind blowing away the top half, the bottom half dropping to the ground.

Arch's warriors were filling the street and adjacent tents. Hatter slammed projectile deck after projectile deck into his AD52's ammo bay, dealing razor-cards at them until the last of his limited supply was gone and the weapon clicked empty. He used his one set of wrist-blades as a shield, their high-powered rotary action knocking the kill-quills, crystal shot, poison bullets, and razor-cards of his enemy toward unsought-for targets. Molly, wearing his other set of wrist-blades, apprehensively shielded their backside, and Weaver kept snug between them, firing her AD52.

"Follow close behind me!" Hatter yelled.

He charged straight at the Doomsine warriors in the street, his whirring wrist-blades held out in front of him. *Doink! Patingk! Ping!* The enemies' missiles ricocheted off his blades, which stuttered and slowed when one of the warriors failed to get out of his way. But now they were on the move, he and Weaver and Molly hurrying down the street, and the Milliner might have considered this an improvement in his family's situation if enemy fire hadn't been coming at them from every direction, blasting out of heavily covered positions.

A flash of light: An orb generator came rocketing toward them.

"Take cover!"

Father, mother, and daughter dove to the ground as one.

Krachboooooooooooooooooooooooooooofffffsh!

The quiet that settled after the explosion might have belonged to the grave, but soon they heard the thump of debris raining down around them. Every tent in the camp had collapsed. The Doomsines they'd been battling just a moment before were standing in stupefied silence, looking off at the horizon.

Hatter motioned for Weaver and Molly to crawl under the nearest tent and he crawled in after them. Whatever was going on outside, if it lasted long enough, they might be able to slip from one tent to another, unnoticed, and escape to the edge of camp.

~

Arch was being entertained by wives numbered nine, sixteen, twenty-three, and thirty-two when a minister rushed in and—

"Your Majesty," the minister said, the rest of his words lost in the roar and rumble of an engine that grew increasingly louder until it was directly outside the tent. The minister finished speaking, the engine cut off, and Redd flounced in followed by The Cat, Vollrath, Siren Hecht, and Alistaire Poole.

"What, back already?" Arch said, not quite hiding his annoyance.

"Grouchy because I interrupted your family frolic, Archy?" Redd smirked. "I think I feel a pang of jealousy."

"They're *my wives*, Redd. They mean nothing to me."

"Really? Then you won't mind if I . . . " Redd made as if to throw her scepter as she would a spear. Boils and hairy cysts and mustaches shot out from its shriveled heart and lodged on the faces of the four wives, spoiling their pretty looks. "There, that's better." Redd turned back to Arch and wiggled her scepter. "Do you know what this is?"

"It looks like a rotten bedpost that should have been incinerated long ago."

"Close. It's the scepter meant for me as queen, retrieved from my Looking Glass— "

Gunplay erupted outside. Arch whistled for Ripkins and Blister, but they were not at their usual posts.

"Looking for these two?" Redd asked, and in rolled the bodyguards, contained in a ball of clear, impenetrable glass she had conjured. "I assume they have special talents if you've made them your personal guards, Archy. I'm going to keep them secure until I know what these talents are and how I can exploit them to my own purposes."

The battle outside was gaining momentum: the warrior calls, the overlapping grunts of the dying.

A bloodied minister stumbled into the tent. "My liege, Homburg Molly has escaped."

"What do you mean *escaped*?" Arch shouted. "How could she have *escaped* when her every movement sent her dizzy to the floor?"

"Pardon, my liege," said the minister, "she didn't escape so much as she was rescued. By her mother. And Hatter Madigan."

"Hatter Madigan is *here*?" Redd asked.

But Arch was too busy railing and cursing to answer. He stomped and punched the air, and after a particularly forceful flogging of his invisible foes, Redd said, "Your rage is impressive, Archy, but the pressures of ruling are clearly too much for you. I think I'll take control of Boarderland and let you get some rest."

Arch's tantrum was gone in a moment. When he spoke, he had the tone and manner of an indulgent uncle. "Redd, I ask this with utmost respect to your imagination, but . . . " He made a show of counting The Cat, Vollrath, Siren, and Alistaire. ". . . I see only four supporters. Even with your imagination, you can't defeat my forces."

"Quite right," Redd said, and with a dip of her scepter, the tents of the entire Doomsine encampment fell to the ground.

They were surrounded. Armed warriors from all twenty-one of Boarderland's tribes had encircled the camp and stood awaiting their orders.

Redd raised her voice loud enough to be heard by all. "Arch, I introduce you to my army! Army, this is your former king!"

"With Redd at our head, we are all equal!" the tribes called in unison.

"This isn't possible," Arch breathed. "It's one of your imaginative tricks."

"Is it?" With the speed of an orb generator exploding from a cannon, she shot a black and thorny rose vine from the raisin-heart crowning her scepter. Seeking a victim at random from amid her new army, the vine wrapped around an Onu and strangled him.

"Constructs of my imagination are not able to die," she said. "So you see how wrong you are, Archy."

"But how?" the king whispered. "How did you—"

"You have me to thank," said a voice, and out from under a collapsed tent crawled Jack of Diamonds.

"You?" Arch said.

Jack bowed. "I'm ecstatic to be the instrument of your ruin, Your Former Majesty. It's the least you deserve for betraying my family."

"Yes," Redd sighed, "as much as I like to take credit for other people's accomplishments as well as my own, in this instance, Archy, I have to admit, it *was* Jack's idea to convince the tribes to fight for me and his efforts that brought it about. But all annoying fops must come to an end. I have no more use for Jack, and so—"

"No more use?" Jack of Diamonds said in disbelief. "But I've always been useful to you, Your Imperial Viciousness! I can and always will be! I'll—"

Without a twitch of exertion, Redd sealed his lips with glue. "Who wants to kill him?" she asked.

The Cat raised his paw. Siren and Alistaire raised their hands.

"Mmmmm mmm mmm," protested Jack.

Arch was breathing as heavily as an overworked spirit-dane, the glint of hatred in his eye directed at Jack. Redd noticed this and said, "In view of his recent demotion, it seems appropriate to let my friend Arch have the honors."

In desperation, Jack started to run, but Redd conjured a thick black rose vine that tripped him and bound his wrists and ankles.

An assortment of weapons appeared before Arch: AD52, scorpspitter, Hand of Tyman, whipsnake grenade, basket of mushrooms. Arch recognized a deadly fungus when he saw it. He could sate Jack's appetite once and for all. He took a mushroom from the basket and stood for a time over the squirming Wonderlander.

"Any last words?"

"Mmm!" Jack begged, eyes wide. "Mmmmmmm!"

Arch knelt down and pressed the mushroom against his mouth. "Good. Because I didn't want to hear them anyway."

The roots of the fungus forced Jack's lips open. Fed by his saliva, they worked their way down his throat and strangled his heart. Arch stood and wiped his hands. A mushroom cap poked out of Jack of Diamonds' mouth: his heart had stopped beating.

"And now," Redd said, "for war."

CHAPTER 43

ALYSS HAD taken up position in the crystal chamber, standing on the viewing platform halfway to the floor and facing the pulsating glow of the Heart Crystal, reaching toward it every so often for a fresh surge of imaginative energy. Behind her, Bibwit sat at a control desk. By means of viewing screens and speakers and talk-back controls embedded in the desktop, he was able to monitor enemy progress, troop movement, and communications among Doppel and Gänger, the Ten Card lieutenants and chessmen. "The demarcation barrier!" the tutor called.

"Yes," Alyss said, because she had already viewed it—a large segment of the barrier had been knocked out of commission, and Redd's mercenaries were pouring into Outerwilderbeastia.

Redd was attacking with her usual intelligence, sending Glass Eyes at card soldiers and chessmen in a kamikaze-like first wave and immediately following it with a massive battering by orb cannons and cannonball spiders. Then came the tribes: the Astacans with their stick-legs and ability to negotiate steep, rocky ground as easily as the billy goats of Earth; the Awr with their gossamer shots and their scutes—the hard, bony backsides impervious to blades and razors and crystal shot, under which their heads and limbs would retract whenever necessary; and the nineteen other tribes, each with unique weapons, with physical traits that had evolved over generations of adaptation to Boarderland's various terrains.

"Decks at crossings 32-a and 29-d are to converge!" Alyss heard the generals' voices through the speakers on Bibwit's desk. "Converge on the breach!"

But more of the barrier will be left unguarded.

"Chessmen fall back!" the generals shouted. "Tighten the lines around Wondertropolis!"

Alyss conjured a rainfall of orb generators to drop on the Glass Eyes and tribal warriors advancing through the defunct demarcation barrier, then turned her imagination's eye on Dodge for the swiftest of glances. He was standing outside the palace's front gate with his guardsmen, his hand on the hilt of his father's sword, his face stonily alert.

He hates having to wait for The Cat to come to him, hates—

"Alyss!" Bibwit shouted, because her orb generators were, inflicting no harm whatsoever upon the enemy.

Kccrkchsshk! Pfoooghaashhh!

Redd had conjured orbs to collide with Alyss', causing them to detonate uselessly above the heads of the warring soldiers.

"Another breach!" Bibwit reported. "And they've penetrated the Everlasting Forest!"

They were working their way toward the palace, Alyss knew, toward *her.* She reached out for the Heart Crystal, stiffened with the influx of power that coursed through her, but the Boarderland tribes were adept at blending in with their surroundings and she lost sight of them. Where the forest's edge faded into Wondertropolis' outskirts, she imagined finemeshed nets of blade-proof fibers—a mine field of camouflage nets resembling fallen foliage. The Boarderland warriors would have to pass this way in their push to the capital city. They would set foot in the nets, which would fold shut on them like the petal-jaws of a Venus flytrap.

Alyss redirected her imagination to the border battles. She sensed something: Redd watching her. With her scepter, Alyss tried to shoo away her aunt's sight, to block it—once, twice, she tried, but Redd remained there, in her imagination's eye, staring.

"One of the forest bases has been hit!" Bibwit called. "Our Snark Mountain post is outnumbered!"

Alyss began to exert herself with greater effort, moving her scepter left, right, up and down, conducting an orchestra of defensive cocoons, automatic cannons, low-drifting energy clouds that exploded with Glass Eye-piercing lightning, and every form of weaponry she'd ever seen in Wonderland and on Earth . . .

Clashing with Onu and Scabbler warriors in a quadrant of the Chessboard Desert, the white knight and his pawns were nearly surrounded, losing bodies and ammo fast, when an energy cloud unexpectedly dropped in front of them. Lightning bolts flashed out of it, struck dead enough warriors to create an opening, and as the knight and pawns fought their way to relative safety, unmanned bayonets formed in the air to aid their escape . . .

At a forest military base, Maldoids and Gnobi were driving the white rook and a hand of card soldiers into a dry-goods storehouse. The Maldoids' kill-quills lodged into the storehouse's front wall, the warriors yanked hard on the coils extending from the quills' butt ends, and down came the wall. The Wonderlanders let loose with all the firepower they had, but the Gnobi rolled a death-ball into the storehouse. The rook and card soldiers had no defense against the melon-sized weapon. If they moved, it would sense them, and the holes on every gwormmy-length of its surface would spray out crystal buckshot with such speed and force that they'd be killed. Too bad then that a Three Card breathed a little too heavily. The death-ball fired off its rounds. The rook closed his eyes, expecting death, but the projectiles altered course, flying toward the Maldoids and Gnobi as if preferring the heat and breath of Boarderland bodies . . .

Haze was emanating from the Heart Crystal, fogging Alyss' vision. She tried to fan it away. Then she sniffed and realized: smoke. The blue caterpillar was at her side, toking on his hookah and basking in the crystal's glow as if to tan himself.

"Extraordinary," Bibwit gasped. "Unprecedented. A caterpillar showing itself *now*?"

"You will lose unless you court loss," Blue said to Alyss. "Courting loss, though you still will not win, you may prevent victory."

"What?!"

But Blue said no more, swallowed by a thick puff of hookah smoke. Projected on the smoke as on a screen, she saw Hatter unspooling luminescent thread for King Arch, who was sewing a web that held herself, Genevieve, and Theodora—three generations of Heart queens struggling fruitlessly to free themselves. Then Arch dissolved and Hatter was sewing the web, except that his intricate maneuverings of needle and thread produced *holes*, gaps that enabled Alyss, her mother, and grandmother to step clear of their bonds, morph into white butterflies, and flit away.

"What's it mean?" Bibwit asked when the images were gone, the hookah smoke drifting loosely toward the ceiling.

If he doesn't know, how am I supposed to—

Voices screeched from the speakers on the control desk and Bibwit consulted its viewing screens. "She's set the doggerels loose," he said

But Alyss' attention had been drawn to the palace gate where Dodge, impatient to engage The Cat, was leaving his men, venturing out alone into Wondertropolis toward the demarcation barrier.

No, Dodge, no.

The doggerels were galloping into the densest part of the Everlasting Forest, disappearing from view.

"They'll soon be gnashing at the guardsmen around the palace."

Which just proves that even a tutor as learned as Bibwit could, at the worst possible times, not have a clue.

~

The Glass Eyes had been programmed and were massed on the Boarderland side of the demarcation barrier, their ranks extending nearly the length of Outerwilderbeastia, when Redd came trundling up, riding high in her three-wheeled vehicle. Arch, Vollrath, and The Cat were onboard, seated beneath her. Alistaire and Siren marched behind with the tribes.

"Alistaire, Siren, divide the tribes between you and spread out behind the cannons," Redd said. "Wait for my signal."

The Cat hissed.

Amused, Redd asked, "You want to risk the one life you have left in battle?"

The feline assassin hissed again.

"I approve your lack of caution, Cat," Redd petted, then

spun toward Vollrath. "And how about you, Mr. Tutor? Don't you want to bloody yourself in combat?"

"My weapon is my intellect, Your Imperial Viciousness, the library my front line."

"How convenient for you." She turned her attention back to The Cat, Alistaire, and Siren. "Each of you take seven tribes."

The assassins hustled off to confer with the tribal leaders and Vollrath excused himself to oversee the loading of orb cannons. Redd, watching the preparations of her army from the vantage of her three-wheeler, took hold of Arch's arm in the manner of a lady enjoying the sights during a carriage ride with her beau.

"Cheer up, Archy. After I'm again looking dainty in my crown, life will be as it used to be—you, me, the entire queendom as our playground. Put on a happy face or else. Things *could* be worse for you. You could be dead."

"Things could be worse for me," Arch repeated, his happy face looking a lot like his glum face.

Vollrath returned to the three-wheeler. "All is ready, Your Imperial Viciousness."

"Then let's not dillydally." Redd hoisted her scepter aloft, its heart raised toward the heavens. She held it there a moment before, in a single, swift motion, she swung it down and—

The Glass Eyes charged, stampeding toward the barrier as if to sacrifice themselves in its deadly sound waves, to let their inert bodies act as shields for the rest to get through. But just before they reached the barrier, Redd conjured gobs of thick putty in the pylon vents that maintained the impassable energy mesh. The demarcation barrier went offline. With blades drawn, with crystal shooters and AD52s firing, Glass Eyes stormed into Queen Alyss' domain, overwhelming decks of card soldiers.

Redd again lifted her scepter to the sky. She brought it down fast and sure, and hundreds of cannons burst into action. Orb generators blazed out over the front line to explode deeper within Wonderland, killing the support decks lying in wait.

On Redd's third signal, the Boarderland tribes attacked. Her Imperial Viciousness, still on her three-wheeler with Arch, followed behind her advancing forces with a caravan of attendants that she'd poached from Boarderland's former king. What pleasure to see The Cat raking claws across the chests of Seven and Eight Cards! To see her favorite feline beast swat dead two pairs of soldiers with a single blow! What delight to watch Siren force enemy platoons to their knees with her screams, Alistaire going around to the soldiers, beginning autopsies on each but finishing none!

Feeling supreme, Redd focused her imagination on her niece, laughing aloud when Alyss tried to push off her sight, to cloak it in darkness.

"Bring me a pack of doggerels," she said.

Arch winced. "Redd, can't you leave me something to lord myself over?"

"But Archy, I've always liked watching your little pets exercise."

Doggerels of war were half the size of spirit-danes but twice as fast, canine in aspect but with claws and teeth rivaling The Cat's. Redd heard them before she saw them, their usual chant whenever they sensed adventure: "To kill and to maim, that is our aim. Doggerels of war are we, best not to be our enemy."

A keeper approached with twenty of the creatures on a common leash, reining them in before Redd's three-wheeler. They raised their snouts to take in the scent of their new mistress.

"You are to travel through Wonderland's Pool of Tears," Her Imperial Viciousness told them. "Whichever of you lands in London, England, is to sniff out Sacrenoir at the Crystal Palace." She projected images of Sacrenoir and the Crystal Palace on a smoke-screen that issued from her scepter. "Tell him war has begun and that I want him to bring all recruits. Alyss' forces *will* be defeated. Do you understand?"

"Into the Pool o' Tears we'll go," the doggerels chanted, "which of us to find Sacrenoir who can know? But of war begun we'll inform, that he and recruits must come, the enemy to storm."

"Unleash them!"

The doggerels' collars snapped open, and as Redd watched the animals race into Wonderland, leaping over the dead and dying, she thought sneeringly that if they happened to kill or maim any of the piddling, incompetent enemy en route to the pool, so much the better.

CHAPTER 44

THEY HAD reached the outskirts of the Doomsine camp without incident, had recovered Hatter's top hat and coat and backpack from their buried hiding place without trouble. But to enter Wonderland, they would have to join the thousands clashing just over the border.

"We'll fight the rest of the way to Talon's Point," Hatter said.

The Point offered the best chance of safety for Weaver and Molly. Hatter's plan was to ensconce them there, then return to the war and Queen Alyss' aid. He didn't doubt that all-out war had begun. Seeing Glass Eyes and Boarderland tribes fighting together, he assumed Redd Heart was the likely cause, though from his present position he could see only her troops, no sign of the mistress herself.

He slipped his backpack from his shoulders and handed it to Weaver. She put it on and shrugged; daggers and corkscrews poked out, ready for use. Molly flicked open and closed the wrist-blades she was still wearing, made sure the quiver of mind riders was easily accessible. She nodded, and they started out from the shelter of dead trees in which they'd been concealed. Before them: the hindmost of Redd's advancing army. No use putting off the inevitable, Hatter figured, so—

With an underhand snap of the wrist, he sent his top hat blades spinning into a thicket of Gnobi and Awr warriors. The blades sliced through four of the warriors as Hatter launched himself over the rest in a straight-bodied somersault. His wrist-blades coptering, he struck two Awr while in midair, landed, and caught his top hat as it boomeranged back to him, using its blades as a shield against the crystal shot and razor-cards and swords that came at him.

With Hatter attracting most of the enemies' attention, Molly steadily and accurately flung mind riders at the Gnobi, Awr, Scabbler, Maldoids, and Doomsines, so that more and more of them turned on one another—darts protruding from their heads, angst serum pumping through their brains.

"Molly!"

In all the clank and clatter and air-searing gunfire, the girl hadn't noticed the Gnobi death-ball rolling to a stop not a spirit-dane's length away from her. Weaver leaped in front of her as the weapon burst, releasing a supernova of crystal buckshot.

Tet-tet-tet-tet-tet-tet-tet-tet-tet-tet-tet-tet-tet-tet-tet-tet-tet!

The death-ball spent itself and Weaver dropped limp to the ground. Unharmed, Molly lowered to one knee and bent over her mother, snapping shut her wrist-blades and leaving herself vulnerable, open to enemy fire.

"Mom! MOM!"

But the life had already drained out of Weaver's body. A short distance away, Hatter had fallen still in the midst of fighting three Shifog, his eyes on his unmoving beloved, his blades held in front of him as if he hardly cared for their protection.

Molly's bottom lip trembled, and—

"Aaaaagh!"

She ran straight at the nearest warrior, her wrist-blades hacking and slicing. She ran straight at Astacans and Glebog and Scabbler, the Milliner weaponry she wore never put to more efficient use while, with her free hand, she stabbed mind riders into any bodies fool enough to come within reach.

No cry of anguish escaped Hatter. His top hat blades ricocheting among the warriors, he activated his belt sabers and spun, cutting through Boarderlanders as if through a field of winglefruit, maintaining the silence of a master assassin, his expression as steely as his blades. What was left of the tribesmen quickly escaped into Wonderland—probably, Hatter thought, to connect with Redd's other soldiers for a march on the capital city. Hatter folded closed his weapons, stepped over to Weaver's body and lifted it in his arms.

"We need a crystal communicator," he said.

Molly removed the keypad and ammo belts from a dead Four Card, father and daughter not yet daring to say more than was necessary, nor to look directly at each other, lest any word, any direct glance, let loose a grief neither felt strong enough to survive.

~

The wind carried the sound of explosions and hoarse cries—the military outpost on the second-highest peak in the Snark Mountains was raging with bloody battle. But in the cave near the top of Talon's Point, all was solemn, quiet. Hatter laid Weaver's body on the ground and cracked open a fire crystal for warmth. Molly covered her mother with blankets left from earlier days, and she and Hatter sat for a time, each absorbed in silent thought, gazing at Weaver's stilled chest as if in hope of seeing it rise and fall again.

"It's my fault," Molly said. "Everything that's happened. I was given a chance no halfer ever gets—to be the queen's bodyguard—and . . ." she glanced at her mother's body, " . . . I did this."

"Arch did it," Hatter said. "And Redd. Not you."

The usual toughness, the defiant jaw-clench, were absent from Molly's expression. "Dad," she said, crying, for the first time not trying to prove herself an adult in need of no one.

Hatter went to her and held her close. "I didn't know," he said. He lifted her face to his: the watery eyes in which he saw so much of Weaver. "Your mother never wanted to leave you." There was so much to explain, to try and make up for. But they didn't have time. "Please stay here, Molly, and keep watch over your mom," he said.

"Where are you going?"

"Up." He was donning the Four Card's keypad and the ammo belts whose inner circuitry comprised the crystal communicator. "I won't be gone long." He folded his top hat into a stack of blades and sealed them in the inner pocket of his coat. He removed two crowbar-shaped weapons from his backpack, which he left next to Weaver, and stepped out of the cave.

Thinking back on his last time here, he remembered nothing suspicious, nothing that hinted at why Arch and Ripkins had come to Talon's Point the day they found Weaver. But there was still one part of the mountain that Hatter hadn't considered before. Arch had wanted him to climb the tallest spire of Heart Palace; and Arch had been *here*, at the highest elevation in Wonderland. Why? Hatter stared up at the icy rock that narrowed to a point somewhere above the clouds. He slammed the short, chisel-like ends of his crowbars into the ice and rock and began to climb, placing his feet in crags and outcroppings for support whenever possible. Higher and higher he climbed, entering the cloud layer in which he couldn't see even an arm's length above him. But still he slammed the weapons into the rock, still he climbed.

At last, he pushed his head above the clouds. The summit was within view, but not until he nearly reached it did he sight what was beyond belief: a gigantic web made of different colored caterpillar thread stretching as far as he could see toward Wondertropolis. A yellowish thread had been wound around the point, its other end obviously secured to some other high spot in the land, just as the orange and green and red threads that crossed it must have been secured to the tops of volcanoes and skyscrapers.

Hatter pressed the dispatch button on his communicator's keypad. "This is Hatter Madigan!" he shouted into the raw, whipping wind. "I must speak to Queen Alyss immediately!"

The generals' voices came back at him through the crystal communicator, small in the vast space around him. "Hatter Madigan!"

They were unsure of his motives—he had disobeyed the queen, defected—and were inclined to deny his request, but Bibwit, sitting at his control desk in the crystal chamber, overheard the exchange and dialed in to Hatter's frequency.

"Hatter," the tutor said, "what are you—"

Alyss stepped to the control desk. "Hatter?"

"I'm not a traitor, Your Majesty."

"I know that."

"When the fighting is over, if I'm still alive, I will welcome whatever disciplinary action you command for my disobedience. But right now, I need to show you this." With another press of a button, he transmitted a visual of the immense web extending through the sky.

"Wha—?" Bibwit gasped.

"I have reason to believe this net extends over Heart

Palace," Hatter said, explaining how Arch had ordered him to return to the palace with a supply of green caterpillar thread, how he'd been instructed to scale the palace's tallest spire and weave the thread onto the Weapon of Inconceivable Loss and Massive Annihilation in a certain pattern.

With her imagination, Alyss scanned the sky above the palace. Yes, it was there: the web, not attached to the spire but within reach, its mesh finer over Wondertropolis than over the queendom's outer regions.

"Arch couldn't have managed it alone," she said. "Does Redd know?"

"I can't say, Your Majesty."

"We have to cut it down, Alyss," Bibwit said. "Whatever it does—and I don't think we want to find out—we must cut it down."

But Alyss was remembering the images Blue had shown her: King Arch sewing a web that ensnared her; Hatter sewing one that gave her freedom.

"No," she said. "Hatter, you are to sew the green thread where you are, exactly as it appears in the diagram Arch gave you. Contact me when you have finished all except the last thread."

"Yes, Your Majesty," the Milliner said and signed off.

Alyss thought she had begun to make sense of Blue's mysterious message, even though she could only guess at its meaning and hope that her guess was right. Or at least not disastrously wrong.

CHAPTER 45

ON A suburban street where Wonderland children frequently played, outnumbered and outgunned card soldiers were saved from a bombardment of razor-cards by a shield that repelled the projectiles back upon the Glass Eyes who fired them . . .

In an Outerwilderbeastia safari park where families often vacationed, a platoon of pawns was able to defend itself against several Boarderland tribes with the help of orb cannons that automatically reloaded and launched generators . . .

Along hiking trails in the Everlasting Forest, Fel Creel warriors on the verge of routing two full hands of card soldiers suddenly found themselves being routed by the ground upon which they stood, as it crumbled beneath their feet and sucked them down into unknown depths . . .

Supporting her troops from the crystal chamber, Alyss had been able to hold Redd's forces in their current positions for more than a quarter of a lunar hour. But she could feel fatigue overtaking her, even with the Heart Crystal so close. Redd's invasion of Wondertropolis seemed as inevitable as the seasons.

Can't keep this up. Can't be at all places at once.

"The Pool of Tears, Alyss!" Bibwit shouted.

She turned her imaginative gaze upon the pool: Two and three at a time, figures were splashing from its surface.

Are those . . . skeletons?

They were. Innumerable skeletons swimming to shore along with Master Sacrenoir and others of flesh and no good intent. They scrabbled onto dry land and attacked any card soldiers and chessmen within sight: yet another battle, an ambush upon Alyss' senses and strength.

Pointing her scepter at the Heart Crystal, she surrounded the Earth mercenaries with a barrier exactly like the one that had so recently separated the queendom from Boarderland—the pylons, the sound waves that could fry a trespasser's internal organs. But as she did, the scorpspitters that had cornered Catabrac warriors in a dark quadrant of the Chessboard Desert disintegrated into nonexistence. The warriors blasted their way through a spread of Five Cards and advanced toward the capital city.

Redd, informed of Sacrenoir's arrival and rolling toward Wondertropolis in her three-wheeled vehicle, guffawed when she remote-viewed the barrier meant to contain Sacrenoir and the others. The closer she got to the Heart Crystal, the more she felt her powers increase. She stopped up the barrier's pylon vents; the sound waves flickered and went out. Alyss conjured another barrier, but Redd stopped up its vents just as quickly. Alyss conjured a third barrier, but this time, sensing Alyss' gaze upon her and wanting a distraction, Her Imperial Viciousness said aloud, "Let's see how my guardsman friend is doing." She then directed her energies to a particular Wonderland farm, where Dodge, having commandeered a spirit-dane, was speeding through a gobbygrape arbor to the Everlasting Forest, it having been reported to him that The Cat was last seen there, decimating card soldiers with tremendous swings of his paws.

Since the fighting began, Alyss had taken comfort in the fact that Dodge and The Cat were nowhere near each other. But Redd's ploy worked. Alyss let herself be distracted, focused her imaginative sight on Dodge, who had climbed off his spirit-dane and was unsheathing his father's sword, stalking toward—

"Bibwit," Alyss yelled, "tell Dodge The Cat he sees isn't real! It's a construct!"

The tutor repeated the message several times into his desk's audio intake, but Dodge didn't respond. If The Cat were a construct, he would find out for himself. The Cat grinned and stood his ground as Dodge ran toward him with a sword aimed at his throat and—

Bonk!

A pail flew up and hit the guardsman in the shoulder, and before he could recover, another came at him from his opposite side. *Clonk!* Off balance, he swung his sword to defend himself against a hoe that had been thrown at him by some unseen hand.

Redd.

Alyss conjured pails and farming tools of her own to smash against her aunt's. But more than a few of Redd's conjurings made it through, hitting Dodge in the head, arms, legs and stomach, frustrating him, angering him, all while The Cat stood untouched and laughed. And in trying to protect Dodge, Alyss lost sight of what she'd been doing, imaginationwise, on other fronts. Sacrenoir and the rest of Redd's Earth army passed between her barrier's gobbed-up pylons with ease. Elsewhere throughout the queendom, Redd's hordes punished Alyss' forces and closed in on Wondertropolis.

Alyss realized her mistake. But it was then, as she was beginning to think Redd unstoppable, that she truly understood Blue's message.

Court loss or lose. Invite loss.

She stood before the Heart Crystal, her scepter held loosely in her hand, doing nothing.

"Alyss!" Bibwit shouted. "A-lyss!"

I must invite loss to prevent Redd's victory.

Above her, above the city center, the web of caterpillar

thread was more intricate. She rushed to the control desk, sent a dispatch to the generals.

"Let Redd advance," she ordered. "But be sure the soldiers make a show of resistance. If they don't, she'll be suspicious."

"Let Redd advance?" General Doppel's voice croaked.

"All due respect, Your Majesty," said General Gänger, "but that's crazy talk!"

"Just do it!"

With Bibwit fidgeting at her side, and still defending Dodge—who had yet to land a blow on The Cat construct—against Redd's bruisings, she watched the control desk's viewing screens. On the outer streets of Wondertropolis, the first of her retreating card soldiers appeared, fighting weakly and rushing for cover whenever it presented itself. Redd's army came from every direction at once. Redd herself followed along behind the warriors who'd fought their way through the Everlasting Forest, riding tall in her three-wheeler with Arch and her tutor as companions.

Beep, beep beep beep. Hatter's voice pumped through the control desk's speakers: "Queen Alyss, I've woven the green thread, as you requested. The pattern is all but complete."

"Hold, Hatter, and wait until I give the order to complete it."

Redd's forces were quickly surrounding the palace, smashing shop windows, exploding transports, scarring building fronts with crystal shot and razor-cards.

"Are you sure this is wise, Alyss Heart?" Bibwit said, but

he seemed to be talking to himself and Alyss didn't answer.

"Closer," she was murmuring as Redd advanced. "Closer."

Another few blocks and the palace itself would be overrun. Redd's army was already storming down Heart Boulevard toward the palace gate. But still Alyss waited. Redd appeared on the boulevard. Three blocks away, two blocks, one block—

"Now, Hatter!"

On Talon's Point, the Milliner tied the last segment of loose caterpillar thread in place according to the diagram Arch had given him, and—

WUUUUUUUUUUUUUUUUUUMMMMMP!!!

WUUUUUUUUUUUUUUUMMMMMP!!!

WUUUUUUUUUUUMMMMMP!!!

WUUUUUUUUMMMP!!!

WUUUMP!!!

It didn't matter who or what they were—queen, tutor, guardsman, general, evil ex-princess, conniving former king, chessman, soldier, mercenary, or civilian. To WILMA, all were equal, all equally vulnerable to the upside-down mushroom cloud of energy she'd birthed, and for a time, the length of which would be forever unknown in the annals of Wonderland, it was as if life in the capital city had been wiped out.

S HE WAS beautiful. She was powerful. WILMA was everything a despot could want in a weapon. If, in terms of destruction and body count, the annihilation she caused was not as massive as it might have been, the loss could still prove inconceivable . . .

Redd was among the first to revive. She found her scepter, which had been knocked loose from her grip, and stared groggily about. Her three-wheeler was nowhere to be seen. Her army—her niece's too—lay scattered before her in various attitudes of unconsciousness.

A quarter of a block away, Arch and The Cat were gradually waking. Arch recognized the effects of WILMA but did not understand what had happened. The effects were not as drastic as they would have been if Hatter had activated

WILMA per *his* instructions. Still, the weapon could not have failed to operate upon the imaginatively gifted. Wasn't Redd's three-wheeler gone? Every one of her conjurings would have vanished. But precisely to what extent Redd had been affected, and for how long she would remain so, Arch didn't know. He would have to bide his time, to watch and learn. He hadn't become Boarderland's king by being reckless. He would not ruin his chances to be king again by acting too hastily.

Approaching Redd, he said, "Alyss must have harnessed more power from the crystal."

Redd snorted, dismissive. But a power that could flatten entire armies in one go? She sought Alyss in her imagination's eye, but it was as if she'd been blinded and she saw only darkness. She *had* been feeling somewhat less tingly since she'd awakened . . .

She tried to conjure a transport, unable to summon so much as a wheel into existence. She tried for something smaller, simpler: a rose vine. No vine formed. She tried to conjure what even a talented child would have considered child's play: a tarty tart. Again, she met with failure.

She was powerless. She had *no imagination.*

How could she face her niece without imagination? She would kill Alyss for doing this to her. A slow death. A torturous death. But not now. No, she first had to regain her former strength, again suffuse herself with power, and then . . .

Arch was watching her. She grimaced to hide her panic.

"Bring the doggerels!"

From her caravan of attendants, the dazed doggerel-keeper shuffled up with three packs of the dazed creatures.

"Heads ache, not quite awake," the animals chanted, "let us alone and give us bones."

"Shut up!" Redd said. "You are to sniff out Vollrath, Sacrenoir, Alistaire, Siren, and whoever is still alive among the tribal leaders. Tell them we're returning to Boarderland. They are to consider today a practice run for the genuine attack we'll soon make on this, my queendom. Now get."

Their collars clicked open and the sixty doggerels trotted lazily off in various directions. Redd stomped over to a spirit-dane struggling to its feet. Not yet recovered from WILMA's impact, the beast nearly buckled when Redd climbed onto its back.

The Cat transformed himself into a kitten and jumped up to sit in his mistress' lap.

"Arch!" Redd aimed her scepter at him as if to strike a blow with her imagination.

Amused, Arch said, "Coming, Your Imperial Viciousness," and hopped into the saddle behind her.

Spurred on, the spirit-dane loped toward Boarderland, carrying Redd and Arch into a future that could never accommodate both of them.

CHAPTER 47

THE REPORTS were identical to the ones received after the Crystal Continuum had been rendered useless. Conjurers were unable to conjure, writers unable to write, inventors unable to invent, musicians unable to play their instruments or compose. The sole difference between WILMA and Arch's prototype lay in degree, scope. WILMA had left imaginationists throughout Wonderland without their abilities.

"If I myself hadn't seen the Heart Crystal as dim as a volcanic rock," Bibwit said, "I wouldn't have thought it possible. Whatever else has happened, the universal imagination has been scrambled, and I pray this is merely a temporary problem, as it was in the continuum crisis. But I do grow paler than usual when I consider what might have occurred if Hatter had done Arch's bidding and sewn the caterpillar thread over the city's center."

They were in Heart Palace's war room—Bibwit, Alyss, General Doppelgänger, and Dodge. Waking from WILMA's shock in the gobbygrape arbor, Dodge had found no evidence of The Cat. With Redd's forces retreating, and with coaxing from Alyss, he had reluctantly come back to the palace.

"We're lucky Redd thinks you still have imagination," Bibwit said.

"Does she?" Alyss asked, watching Dodge.

"There's no other reason for her to retreat."

The general cleared his throat. "How long are Hatter Madigan and Homburg Molly to remain at Talon's Point?"

"Long enough to grieve," said Bibwit.

The force of WILMA had knocked Hatter off the mountain's peak, but he had slowed his fall to the mouth of the cave by raking his crowbars down the rock. Inside the cave, he'd found Molly woozy but uninjured. He had climbed back to the summit and cut as many of the caterpillar threads as he could reach. The loose ends flapped and furled and the entire web had crackled into dust and been carried every which way by the wind. Weaver would be given a proper funeral. Hatter would mourn her death a second time, but at least now he would do it with his daughter.

In the war room, General Doppelgänger said, "Hatter has always exemplified devoted service, but Queen Alyss, he *did* disobey you. I can't help wondering if he should not be subjected to the same tribunal that a Two Card would be."

"Hatter expects punishment," Alyss said. "He welcomes it. But the fact is, General, that if he hadn't gone to Boarderland when I told him not to, Redd might at this moment be wearing Wonderland's crown."

The general bowed his head, satisfied, and consulted his crystal communicator. "Redd's army isn't retreating quietly," he announced. "We're still receiving reports of intermittent skirmishes. The good news is that we've captured enough Boarderland tribespeople to fill a smail-transport."

Alyss nodded. She wanted to be alone with Dodge, to whisper in his ear, *How strangely free I feel without my imagination.* She'd been left with the chance to explore who she might be, unburdened by such a great gift. *I want you to feel what I feel, Dodge. The Freedom.*

Perhaps later they would discuss it. Yes, she'd confide in him as she would for the rest of her days. But right now, as if she still had the power of remote viewing, she looked off in the direction of Boarderland, to where she knew Redd was already plotting another attack, and she longed for a single, unified imagination, neither Black nor White.